A MONSTER Like Me

WENDY S. SWORE

SHADOW
MOUNTAIN

Library of Congress Cataloging-in-Publication Data

Names: Swore, Wendy S., author.
Title: A monster like me / Wendy S. Swore.
Description: Salt Lake City, Utah : Shadow Mountain, [2019] | Summary: Convinced that if she looks like a monster on the outside (a blood tumor covers half of her face), she must be a monster on the inside as well, Sophie tries to find a cure before her mother finds out the truth.
Identifiers: LCCN 2018047099 | ISBN 9781629725550 (hardbound : alk. paper)
Subjects: | CYAC: Disfigured persons—Fiction. | Friendship—Fiction. | Mothers and daughters—Fiction. | Tumors—Fiction. | Hemangiomas—Fiction. | Monsters—Fiction. | LCGFT: Fiction.
Classification: LCC PZ7.1.S98 Mo 2019 | DDC [Fic]—dc23
LC record available at https://lccn.loc.gov/2018047099

Printed in the United States of America
Lake Book Manufacturing, Inc., Melrose Park, IL

10 9 8 7 6 5 4 3 2

This book is dedicated to my parents for loving me, my family for believing in me, and my writing group for dreaming with me.

Most of all, this book is dedicated to every child who ever felt different, alone, or unwanted. You are magnificent just the way you are.

AN INTRODUCTION

Beware all who enter here, for things once seen cannot be unseen. There are monsters among us. They are crafty and sly, patient and wise.

But wait, you say. If such things exist, why do we not see them? Prove to us such things are real.

It's your human sight, dear friends, that hinders you.

You may have seen centaurs and minotaurs but thought them only horses and cattle. Magic can cloud the minds and memories of men. Few have seen a dragon and lived, and fewer still have wept at the sight of a unicorn and remembered. The pages to come are filled with secrets no human was ever meant to know, a list—albeit incomplete—of magical creatures great and small.

You must understand, dear reader, the only beings who truly know what is hidden are those who are in hiding themselves.

ONE

Book of Monsters

*Y*ou'd think monsters would have their own grocery store, but they don't. They walk around with a cart the same as regular people and keep the monster part hidden inside where no one can see it. Mom's grocery cart squeaks with every step like an elf getting squished, but Mom's not a monster—not that I can tell anyway.

She grabs a box of granola cereal and sets it in the cart beside all our other stuff. "Pick something, Sophie. Then all we need is milk."

Bright boxes of all colors crowd the shelves. A silly dragon peers out from behind a bowl on one box, but I bet real dragons don't look that stupid—after they shed their human skin, I mean. I skim past the marshmallow cereals and snag a box of Honey O's before cracking open my book and waiting for Mom's cart to move on. The raised lettering on the cover fits nicely against my hand, and I know what it says without looking: *The Big Book of Monsters*. The page corners curl a little from the thousand times I've turned them, but mostly I'm careful.

Shuffling behind Mom as we near the dairy aisle, I peek over the edge of my book, trying to read and watch the other shoppers at the same time.

A woman shushes a screaming kid, giving her a doll and shoving a pacifier in her fat little mouth. As we pass, the red-eyed girl turns her tear-streaked face to me, and I squirm under her stare. She raises both hands and shoves the doll behind her head while sucking on the pacifier so hard, I expect the whole thing to pop into her mouth and disappear.

With a shudder, I speed up so Mom's between me and the little creature; I'm sure I've seen something like it before. Pages whisper as I flip through the book until I see the futakuchi-onna. In the picture, a woman feeds two mouths—one on her face, and the other on the back of her head, hidden in her hair.

If not fed properly, the mouths
screech obscenely and demand food.

I peek around Mom as the kid drops her pacifier and cries harder, her little eyes scrunched into angry slits like she knows I figured out her secret. If I were braver, I'd go right up there and look in her hair for that other mouth . . . but I'm not.

My arms ache from carrying the book all the time, and my steps lag behind Mom's. Someone should install those moving sidewalks they have at airports in grocery stores. It'd be like riding a scaly basilisk through the aisles, and we could grab stuff we wanted as the shelves whizzed by, and if we missed it the first time around, we could just go for another ride. I bet my idea would get a million dollars, and all the little old ladies would love it—unless they fell off. Then maybe not so much.

"Do you want string cheese for your lunch tomorrow? Maybe a special treat for your first day?" Mom hovers by the cheese, and I nod.

"Yeah, and fruit snacks." We moved from Beaverton to Portland, Oregon, last month. And we're renting, not buying. I'm pretty sure Mom didn't have a choice about coming here, but she pretends it's all a great adventure. New house, new school, new doctors. None of that is a good thing, but Mom did get a teaching job here, so at least there's one bright spot in the middle of all this.

"You got it." She grabs a package of white cheese sticks and moves on. Her black tennis shoes barely make a sound—not that we could hear anything over the wheels—but it's nice to be near her. She's graceful and pretty. I think her eyes might be bad though, because she still smiles when she looks at me.

My last school was not so nice. That's where I first saw my book in the library, and lucky I did or it would have been a lot harder to find out about monsters. The whole school was full of them—mean ones who learned my secret until I couldn't stay there anymore. Mom says this new school is a new start, a clean slate. I don't think I've ever seen a slate, dirty or clean, but if it's better than the old place, I'm willing to try.

I pick out some fruit snacks and line up with Mom at the checkout.

A bunch of kids in front of us load the conveyor belt with junk food as their mom reads a magazine behind the cart. The littlest kid, a boy with black hair and a gold chain necklace, scopes out the candy bars. I wonder if he might be a troll since his nose flares and he likes shiny things, but he scowls when he sees me looking. I should have hidden my face then, but I didn't. Sometimes I forget.

Most of the time, grown-ups look away when they notice me—like it's more polite for me to be invisible than different. Most of the time, I believe them.

He tugs on his mom's pink sweatpants until she puts the gossip magazine down and turns her bleached-blonde head. "What?"

The cashier scans the last bottle of pop and presses a button. "That'll be thirty-seven dollars even."

The blonde lady follows the kid's pointing finger and stares at me, her eyebrows arching up into her poofy hair, which is okay, but then she opens her mouth, which is not. "Hey, look, kids! That girl doesn't even need a costume for Halloween! She's already got one."

Four heads peek around their mother like a five-headed hy-dra to stare and stare and then laugh. They point their fingers and giggle like it's the funniest joke in the world, but it's not funny. And I'm not laughing.

Mom's mouth drops open as the hydra family walks away, and I bury my face in my book. The echoing laughter hurts my ears. It grates and stings, and I press my face against the pages so I'll never have to see anyone ever again. My eyes burn, but I blink fast and hold the tears inside. I don't want Mom to see me cry, and besides, I don't want to wreck my book.

"Sorry about that," the clerk says over the sound of our gro-ceries beeping across the scanner.

I peek over the book to see if he's making fun, but he really does look sorry.

Mom's face is red, her lips mashed tight in a thin line. The rest of the shoppers around us are quiet too, and I duck back into my book, hoping that Mom doesn't understand what the hydra lady was talking about. She knows part of the truth about me, but not all. And she never will if I can help it.

The checkout machine prints the receipt, and I hear the cashier rip it off. Mom's gentle touch pries my hand from the book and presses it against the cart's handle. I wait till we're out of the store to close my book, but even then, I keep my head down, my hair falling over my face like a curtain.

"You can open the fruit snacks now, if you want," says Mom.

I pretend I don't hear and run the last few steps to the car.

Lights flash as she pops the trunk with her key button. "We have one more place we need to go today after we drop off the groceries, then we can do something fun. Maybe plan for your birthday next week?" She winks and flashes ten fingers plus one.

"Place? Like an appointment?" My stomach churns like I ate a pile of worms, and I slip into the back seat, my hands gripping the edges of the book till my knuckles turn white. When she starts the engine, I close my eyes as the car vibrates and rumbles around me.

"Don't worry, honey. It's just a quick physical for the school this time." Mom uses big words like *hemangioma* and *blood tumor* when she talks about my face to the doctors who poke and prod, and I die inside, wishing to be anywhere but there. I keep quiet and let them think what they want.

"Sophie? You okay?" Mom checks my reflection in the rearview mirror.

I know what she sees: a spiderweb of blood-filled lumps

bubbling up from inside the skin between my right ear and my eye. The mark is puffy and swollen and scary to look at because it keeps reaching for more of me, the purple-red bumps spreading out from the main body to stretch from my cheekbone up to my temple.

I know she worries about it—the loads of doctors' visits prove that—but she doesn't know how frightening it really is because she believes them when they say it all fits in a medical book. She doesn't feel the hidden part pulsing inside, always one heartbeat away from pushing through my skin.

"I'm fine," I mumble.

As long as Mom never finds out the truth, it'll be okay. She'll still love me, and I can stay at home. Until then, I have to do what every other kid—who's not really a kid—does and hide my true nature from her. Only I can know.

I really am a monster.

GUARDIANS OF THE UNDERWORLD

Count yourself lucky, dear reader, if the only monsters you encounter are small and human-sized, for many can grow so tall in their true form that their heads touch the sky. Such are the scorpion men. Spawned by the goddess Tiamat of ancient Babylon, the aqrabuamelu (pronounced AWK-raboo-AMA-loo) guard the entrance to Kurnugi, the underworld. Each morning, the scorpion men open the gates for the Sun God, Shamash, to start his journey across the heavens, and again for his return each night. Though they have power to see over the horizon and warn of danger, few travelers dare seek their help because a single glance from an aqrabuamelu can kill.

TWO

No Picture Days Allowed

Today should be my first day of school, but it won't be. Mom let it slip that today is picture day and unfortunately, I'm sick.

As soon as I find out when retakes are, I'll be sick that day, too.

Once I totally screwed up and actually went to school on picture day. Big mistake. Ten steps inside the door and I saw the huge white umbrella and backdrop that filled half the hallway. My stomach flipped like a mermaid's tail whacking against dry land.

The photographer reached deep inside a bag and slid out a venomous black camera, drawing the weapon out as an aqrabuamelu scorpion man unrolls his stinger. He probably thought no one would notice he'd slipped away from his job guarding the underworld, but I did. A single glance from an aqrabuamelu could mean death. Even if I didn't actually die, having a photo taken of me would make me wish I had.

There was only one thing I could do—I turned and ran straight out the door.

Mom was already pulling out of the parking lot, but I cut across the corner of the ball field where the sprinklers were shooting everywhere. Freezing water hit the back of my head while another squirt went right up my nose. Gasping, I ran even faster. I probably should have walked, but it was *picture day*, with a scorpion cameraman besides. No measly bunch of sprinklers was gonna make me miss my ride home.

I burst onto the street, and tires screeched to a stop. Hand over her heart, Mom rolled the window down on our Buick. "Sophie, what on earth are you doing?"

Shivering, almost crying from the thought of facing that camera, I held onto the doorframe and bowed my head. Right. She needed a reason. Something with no fancy doctors. "My stomach's upset. I think I'm going to throw up." Thinking of going back inside made me queasy for sure.

"Oh, honey, you're white as a sheet." She peered at me through the window. "My gosh, you're trembling. Get in." Mom popped open the door.

Success!

Since then, I've avoided picture days like werewolves avoid silver. And this time, I've got a plan.

I blink a drop of sweat out of my eye and pray that twenty minutes of hiding under the electric blanket is enough to do the job. With the heated fabric draped over my head, I sit on the floor, dying to breathe fresh air.

"Sophie?"

At Mom's call, I rip off the electric blanket and jump into bed. The cool sheets raise goose bumps against my superheated skin, and I shiver.

The door opens. "Honey, you need to get up, it's—oh! Are you sick?"

A thin white streak from her temple contrasts against her pretty auburn hair, which is twisted up professional-like, except for a few harried strands that never seem to behave. She sits at the edge of my bed and touches the good side of my face. "You're burning up. No school for you today."

I nod sadly. I can't quite squeeze out a tear, but I've got sweat running into my eyeball, so that's pretty close. My monster mark is always warm, but the extra heat makes it throb.

"Should I stay home? I could call a substitute." Mom slips her phone out of her pocket, but I shake my head.

"No, I'm okay." Mastering the pathetic "let me stay home cause I'm sick" look without tipping into the "take me to the doctor cause I'm dying" look is tricky, but I manage. I've had lots of practice.

She hesitates and glances at her watch.

"I'll be fine. I swear."

"Okay, call me if you need me. Oh, a neighbor brought by a plate of cinnamon rolls as a housewarming gift. They're on the counter if you get feeling better. I'll pick up chicken noodle soup on the way home." Bending over me, she smooths my sweaty hair away from my forehead. Her kiss is soft and light, a beat of a butterfly's wings. Then she slips out the door.

I wait patiently, faking sleep just to be safe while she bonks around the house. After forever—ten minutes at least—the front door opens and closes, her car starts up, and she drives away. *Finally!* I fling off the covers and peek out the window as our car disappears down the street.

The wooden stairs creak under my bare feet, and I pause at the bottom where sunbeams toast the carpet. My toes sink into the warm shag, and I close my eyes and listen to the empty spaces of the house. A clock ticks in the entryway. The refrigerator hums in the kitchen. The fan inside Mom's computer buzzes quietly from her bedroom. The air in my lungs moves in and out, and I'm sure I'm the only monster here. With the human away, this monster will play.

With my arms spread wide, I spin in the middle of the living room, my head back and eyes closed to soak it all in—one last stolen day of safety before I start my new school and everything changes. Wobbling a little, I stop, lean against the counter, and squint to read the fancy writing on a note attached to the plate of cinnamon rolls.

> *Welcome to the neighborhood. I look forward to getting to know you and your wee lass.*
> *Best,*
> *Mrs. Barrett*

Perfect. A cinnamon roll will make a great breakfast, but first, I've got an audience to please. I grab a bag of unshelled peanuts and slip out the back door.

Dozens of yellow finches flit from Mom's feeder to the nearby tree, but I ignore them. Squinting, I scan the branches higher up.

"Prrp." I trill my special call, and seconds later, several bushy tails flick into view.

I started out with one squirrel the day we moved here—I

named him Bob—but now a half dozen come when I call. To the average person, they look like normal squirrels, but for monsters like me, they're the best magic-show audience I could ever hope for.

Zipping along the top of the fence, the five newcomers follow Bob to the perch I made for them. The old board hangs like a bridge from the fence to the pear tree, making it the best seats in the house.

I crack open a couple of peanut shells and give each one of them half a nut as a bonus for showing up. Like always, Bob grabs his and stuffs it in his cheek quick just in case I'm going to give him more, but when I don't, he settles down to eat it. Most of the others take their nut more slowly, and the last one is still scared of me. I put hers on the board beside her.

When they finish eating, their little ears stand up, and they watch with shiny black eyes.

It's showtime.

I start by rolling a peanut across my knuckles. Flip, flip, flip—the peanut walks end over end from my thumb to my pinkie, back and forth. Easy peasy, my hands come together, and the peanut marches from one hand to the other and back.

The squirrels watch so hard, their tiny heads moving back and forth, following each movement.

"Keep watching, guys." I roll my hands and suddenly both peanuts are gone.

The squirrels chatter anxiously, and Bob clicks his teeth. He thinks anything that makes peanuts disappear is stressful.

I show him my hands. Nothing in this hand, or that one.

His tiny claw reaches for my finger, just in case a peanut might be hiding inside.

Grinning, I twirl my fingers, and peanuts appear between my knuckles on both hands.

"Ta-da!" I smile, and the crowd goes wild! At least, I pretend they do. Really, the squirrels just snatch the peanuts and stuff them inside their faces so their cheeks bulge like they've tried to swallow a boomerang. While they work the shells off their treats, they watch as I roll a quarter across my knuckles, making it disappear and reappear.

I keep hoping I'll manifest magical powers to go along with my monster-ness, but so far all I can do is regular human-style magic tricks. The squirrels like my sleight of hand stuff, but card tricks? Not so much. Whenever I have Bob pick a card, he chomps down on it and runs off. I bet his nest is full of cards by now.

"You've been a good crowd." I drop six more peanuts on the board by the tree.

Bob holds his cool for about two seconds before cramming three peanuts into his cheeks. He reaches for a fourth, but by then, the other squirrels have claimed the rest.

"Thanks for watching," I whisper. I'd take a bow, but my audience is already halfway up a tree, chasing each other like a bunch of furry pixies doing a war dance.

I slip a deck of cards from my pocket and fan them open and closed, rippling them back and forth like a paper wave cresting between my fingers. One card flips from the pack, and I catch it by balancing it on one finger. I blow, and the card spins on the tip of my finger like a pinwheel.

Laughter echoes from somewhere nearby, and I snatch the card, listening for which direction the voice might be coming from.

Somewhere overhead, squirrels scold each other.

Again, a girl laughs, light and airy like fairies playing on the wind. She's at least a couple yards over. Part of me wants to follow the sound, but I don't know what I'd do if I actually found her. Making friends is definitely *not* one of my monster powers.

I spin the card again, but Bob and the others couldn't care less about my card tricks. If there aren't nuts involved, they don't even come down to look.

Maybe Bob would be more impressed if I had a top hat and wand and all the things that real magicians have, like the stuff in the Magician's Apprentice Ultimate Magic Kit. It costs gobs of money, and Mom can't afford it, so I don't ask. But I want it. Gosh, I want it. Of course, I'd like to put on a show for somebody other than my squirrels too. But then I'd have to stand in front of people. So maybe not.

My card slips a bit, and I snatch it before it falls. Things would be different if I had a friend. I wouldn't be picky, either. It's been so long since anyone wanted to be my friend, I've almost forgotten what it feels like. I'd be friends with any old monster that wanted to—as long as they didn't want to eat me or steal my mom or anything. There's loads of nice magical creatures out there—unicorns, sprites, fairies, and brownies—but they'd probably run from me. I'm pretty sure they keep to their own kind, and monsters aren't invited.

"Autumn!" a lady calls from somewhere nearby. "You're going to be late for school."

"Coming, Nana!" The girl's peal of laughter rings out again.

Suddenly, even with my squirrels playing overhead, our yard seems too empty.

Sliding the cards back into the box, I head inside the house and try not to think of who Nana and Autumn might be, because it's crazy to want what I can't have. I'm better off alone, and I know it. It's dumb to let loneliness ruin my special day. I tried to make friends at my old school, but once kids know you're a freak, it follows you forever. Schoolkids are just monsters with sharp teeth and sharper words. If I could get away with faking sick every day, I would, but there's no escaping tomorrow.

Don't think about it. Only think of today. Today *will* be awesome. First off, no school! I could stop there, but there's ice cream in the fridge, a bubble bath for later, and a TV with my name on it. Best of all, there's no one to see me. Not a single soul.

With a stretch, I crack my knuckles, grab the video game controller, and push the power button on the console.

The screen lights up. "Multiplayer or One Player?"

What a stupid question. Who wants screen-sharing anyway? Someone else hogging the whole thing? Ridiculous.

The flashing light toggles over the "One Player" option.

"Okay, Mario Kart, let's do this!"

WEATHER CONTROL

Anyone enjoying a mild, summer day should thank their lucky stars for the absence of the inkanyamba. These migratory sky eels from the Zulu nation of South Africa take the form of tornadoes and create violent storms in order to ride through the sky in their annual search for a mate. Often compared to a winged serpent, the inkanyamba are said to have an eel's body, winged fore flippers, finned manes, and a fanged, horse-like head. They rest in the basin of the legendary Howick Falls, and the Zulu are careful to leave them alone, for inkanyamba are easily offended and destroy all who trespass against them.

THREE

Koschei the Deathless

A pile of fruit-shaped gummies glow in my hand, lit by sunbeams streaming through the car window. I watch them bounce and jiggle as our car rolls down the road. Satisfied, I pop one in my mouth and chew. Fruit snacks make everything better. Almost as good as ice cream, only less messy. I smush a fake bunch of grapes between my fingers and pull apart the grapey-purplely-goo of deliciousness. My head bobs against the back seat with each bump in the road as Mom winds through town.

I lucked out with no school today—second day in a row!— because there's some appointment that Mom's had scheduled forever. Sometimes we drive a lot for her errands, but I don't mind because it's nice spending time with her.

Inside the car is all warm and cozy, but outside, the wind howls and throws bits of leaves at us. My sunbeam disappears when gray, fast-moving clouds gobble up the sky, and I curl my hand against my chest, missing the warmth.

Popping the whole pile of snacks into my mouth at once, I flip the next page of my book and stroke the paper, my fingers pausing right below the Kabandha, a Hindu demon with one big fiery eye on its chest and a wide mouth on its belly—no head at all above its shoulders. I think I might have seen one at the pool one time, but it was hard to tell with all the inner tubes, masks, and snorkels clogging the water.

A few minutes later, a big gust of wind knocks the car sideways, and Mom steers us back into the middle of the lane. "Goodness! Where did this storm come from?"

I frown at the blackening sky just as lightning sizzles, leaping hop-frog from cloud to cloud with flashes of light sparking like a million-billion lightning bugs all going crazy. A boom of thunder vibrates inside my chest at the same time, and Mom's steady grip on the steering wheel tightens.

"Your Grandma Barr used to say that thunder was actually giants playing with great bowling balls in the sky." She laughs. "I imagine it'd take some pretty massive pins to make that sound."

"That's silly." I roll my eyes to the sky and study the low-hanging clouds, searching for any signs of black fins or tails hidden in the mist. Giants have nothing to do with it. Everyone knows that the South African inkanyamba eels bring storms when they fly through the sky with their serpentine bodies.

"It is silly, I suppose, but the world always seemed a little more magical with Grandma Barr beside us." She flips the blinker and changes lanes to pass a semi as a spattering of raindrops flick across the window and then stop, as if the inkanyamba can't decide if they want to rain on us or not. For just an instant, I think I see the quick swish of a tail dip out of the clouds, but it's gone so fast I can't be sure.

I wish Grandma Barr was still here so we could talk about magical things. If she believed in magic, maybe she knew about monsters. And if she liked giants in the sky, maybe she wouldn't mind little monsters who didn't mean to be monsters.

Mom goes quiet, like she often does when she talks about Grandma Barr, and I know she misses her, too.

The dome light in the car goes on and we slow down all at once.

Mom gasps and steers us over the rumbley-bumpity line to the side of the road. "What on earth?"

"Is it a flat tire?" I peer out the window at reeds bending almost in half—the whole field bowing to invisible deities.

"No, honey, we lost power. I don't know why." She turns the key. "C'mon, c'mon! Start!" Ten tries later, she sighs and looks out the window. Sometimes she seems lost. I'm not sure if it's because her mom is gone, or if Dad took something from her when he went away.

Or maybe it's one of my powers doing it, except I don't know how it's happening, so I can't stop it. Kind of like how werewolves trick people into seeing normal dogs instead of giant beasts when they run through town. They don't cloud people's minds on purpose. It just happens. I turn another page, trying to think of a monster that confuses people even when it doesn't mean to.

"Well. The car won't fix itself, and since the car fairy hasn't stopped by, I suppose it's up to me." Mom takes a deep breath and pops the hood before stepping out into the howling wind. Her hair flies all around her head, whipping her cheeks.

I smirk. *Car fairy?* Seriously, I've showed her my book a thousand times, but she still comes up with the most ridiculous ideas about monsters.

She props up the hood and disappears behind it. I scoot closer to the door and press my cheek to the glass, but I still can't see.

Another, closer rumble shakes the car, but not from thunder. A man on a shiny motorcycle pulls over behind us, his arms spread wide across handlebars with leather tassels that flutter like tentacles. My heart hiccups at his skeleton face, but then he pulls off the helmet and removes the skull bandana from his mouth. A few dirty blond hairs flap away from his ponytail, and I shrink back from the scars covering one side of his face as he stalks past my window—toward my mom.

I've seen someone like him before. In my book. Cold marbles roll inside my stomach.

I shove the door open a bit, but the wind catches it, swinging it wide, bouncing the car as the hinge stops it. The frigid air steals my breath, but I scramble out anyway. I have to get to my mom. Gravel squirms out from under my shoes like beetles, and I stumble forward against the car as the wind shoves me one way and then another.

"Mom!" I gasp, clawing my way forward till I can see under the hood to where they are both hunched over the engine.

The man's hair flails around his head, and the skull grins from the cloth underneath his chin. He cocks his head, listening because Mom's mouth is moving, but the wind carries her voice away, and I can't hear the words. His temple next to his eye has a hole, as if someone scooped his flesh like Play-Doh and then dragged it in a jagged line down his cheek toward his mouth.

Globs of pink mar his stubbled cheek, and one bit even hangs at the corner of his mouth, a shiny slug curled beneath the side of his lip. A splatter of tiny pockmarks surround the awful scar, and I can almost imagine his skeletal teeth showing through when the wound was fresh. He turns his head and smiles at me.

I shudder. I don't mean to, because I know what it's like to have people look at you differently, but I can't help thinking that something awful hides behind the hideous mask.

A spiderweb of veins bulge on his muscled forearms like a colony of worms trapped beneath his skin as he prods first one part of the engine, and then another. After a few minutes, he takes off his shirt and wraps it around his hand before thrusting his arm deep into the engine and twisting something.

I stare at the scars that cover his shoulder like a giant connect-the-dots paper with all the marks and none of the lines. Tattooed letters peek out from beneath his sleeveless undershirt and sprawl across his body like some kind of rune or spell inked onto his skin.

He says something to Mom, and she runs to the car and cranks the key. The engine roars to life, and they both smile.

Bracing myself against the wind, I stumble to the back seat and climb inside, but the wind is too strong for me to close the door.

The man slams the hood and walks around to Mom's window, leaning in to talk to her. The right side of his face isn't so bad. If I hadn't already seen what he really looks like, I might even think he looks nice—for a grown-up—but I have seen, and I know he's something inhuman. They talk with their heads way too close together, and Mom laughs—as if any of this is funny.

Finally, he goes away (good riddance), and Mom twists in her seat, yelling, "Sophie, can you close the door?"

"I'm trying!" I brace my feet and pull, but it's stuck in the wind like tar from an ogre's bog.

A grimy hand grasps mine, and I jerk away with a shriek. The man grins like it's the funniest thing in the world, then slams the door and strides to his motorcycle.

"Thank heavens for Good Samaritans!" Mom brushes her wild hair out of her eyes, tucking the white stripe behind her ear, and checks the mirrors as the car purrs beneath us. "If he hadn't stopped, I don't know what I'd have done. A loose fuel filter! I can't believe it."

The motorcycle rumbles past us, and we pull into traffic as I open *The Big Book of Monsters* on my lap. The pages flutter while I search for the right page. Djinn, kraken—no and no. Gnome, hippogryph—no. Aha! A wild man riding a white steed, his ratty hair flying behind in a whirlwind of his own making.

> Koschei the Deathless, a powerful shape-shifter known for riding naked across the wild Russian mountains on his magical horse.

The scarred man rode off on his mechanical steed with just an undershirt, didn't he?

> When searching for maidens, Koschei turns himself into a whirlwind to whisk his victims away.

So *he* controls the weather. I glance outside and shiver as I remember the way his fierce winds tossed me against the car. I bet he thought that was all sorts of funny. I can imagine his glee:

"Watch me make the little monster girl flap around in the wind like some kinda chicken while I schmooze all nicey-nice with her mom." Bleh.

I stare at the disfigured face of the man on the page for a long moment before reading more.

> Nearly impossible to kill, he hides his death inside the eye of a needle, which is then hidden inside an egg, inside a hare, inside a duck, etc., so if any of his hiding places are ever discovered, each form is capable of escaping danger.

A rabbit inside a duck? My lip curls as I imagine the bulging belly of a duck too fat to flap with a big ol' rabbit jumping around inside it. Eww.

> Once a maiden is targeted, Koschei transforms into a whirlwind and surrounds the woman, carrying her off with his powerful winds to his domain.

Another gust shakes the car, and I glance at Mom again, just to be sure she's still there. I mean, the car's still going, so she has to be there, but I feel better double-checking. Her fingers tap a rhythm on the wheel, and she's humming along with the radio as she exits the freeway and meanders through side streets. Koschei can howl and blow all he wants—till his cheeks fall off from puffing so much—just as long as he's far, far away from my mom.

She's all I've got.

I close my eyes and sigh, glad we don't have to worry about

him anymore. That huge motorcycle is probably long gone, whipping up wind around someone else's mom.

Mom spins the wheel, and we turn into a driveway. A huge "Kelsi's Shop" sign hangs over the blue garage—and a giant black motorcycle sits by the door, leaning on its kickstand.

I suck a breath and grip the edges of my book.

Koschei the Deathless waits beside his ride, grinning his skeletal smile as he watches us pull in.

THE FAIR FOLK

Fools assume fae to be small, winged things, petite lovers of flowers, givers of gifts. But, dear reader, beware! Be not fooled by beauty and grace, for hidden behind the gentle masks are fangs and claws. Trolls, banshees, gremlins, elves, dryads, selkies, gnomes, changelings, goblins, and elementals are but few of the thousands who draw their power from the earth, air, fire, and water. Most hide in nature, but some masquerade as men. Dangerous when bored, many are as mischievous as they are devious, eager to drive a man mad if only for something to do. They give gifts or curses, may lead wanderers to safety or devour children whole. For every creature of light, there is another of darkness—and sometimes both are one and the same.

FOUR

Kelsi's Shop

op. Pop. Pop. Yellow popcorn bubbles up, spills out of a hanging metal pan, and falls into the glass cube of awesomeness that holds it all. I stand with my nose almost touching the glass, but I'm not looking at the popcorn—I'm looking through it at my mom and Koschei in the garage. The demon *knows* how to woo women, that's for sure. So far, he's pulled out a tall stool for her to sit on, guided her by the hand around a slimy puddle of oil—probably demon slime—and even pulled a bottle of pop out of a little brown fridge for her. He offered me one too, but one of us has to keep our brains on alert, and it sure isn't gonna be Mom; she's Silly Putty in his hands.

Mom laughs again and rocks back, her feet kicking a little before settling on her stool. She's all pink-cheeked and flustered like she just won a whole year of Popsicles. He touches her shoulder, and I wish that I could shoot laser beams out of my eyeballs because I'd fry his greasy hands right off. I narrow my eyes and concentrate—just in case I really do have laser-beam eyes—but nothing happens.

Except then he looks up from the car engine, spies me through the glass, and winks!

My mouth plunks open, and I duck fast. How'd he even know I was here? He controls the wind, so maybe the air told him? I lick a finger and hold it up, but there's no breeze at all in here. Maybe he's got other powers I don't know about yet, like mind reading. Then he'd know everything I could ever think of before I could even do it. With that depressing thought, I flop onto the waiting room couch with *The Big Book of Monsters.*

I thought a demon's lair would have more torture things, or maybe spears, but Koschei disguised the whole shop with boring junk—stuff from cars and motorcycles and parts and gears and oil and whatever else is on the shelves. Even the magazines are boring. I fan the stack like it's a deck of cards to see the pictures. Motorcycles, semitrucks, a lady in a way-too-small bikini lying on the hood of a shiny car—which doesn't look comfortable at all, even if she is smiling. There are some campers, a barbecue with fire spitting out the sides, a bearded guy holding a big gun next to a dead deer with its tongue hanging out . . . and a frog sitting in the cupped hands of a princess.

I shove the whole pile to the floor and snatch the last book into my lap. *The Princess and the Frog.* I've heard the story before, but the pictures are really good in this one, so I read the whole thing again.

Basically, this prince was minding his own business when a mean ol' witch came and turned him into a frog. He lives that way for years with big warts and slime all over, hopping around and eating bugs and worms, all the time waiting for someone to save him from the curse. When the princess comes, she kisses him right on his slimy frog-lips to break the spell. And they live happily ever after, I suppose, but I stop reading on the page where the princess is kissing that nasty frog with the giant warts.

My hand slides up the side of my face and touches the thing growing there. I can see the purple-red mass out of the corner of my eye, even when I try not to. It's blobby, and hard underneath, but soft on top, and really warm, almost hot. I wonder if that's what the frog's warts felt like.

Except *he* got rid of his warts, and now he's fine and normal and everybody in the whole gosh-dang kingdom loves him to bits, and he doesn't have to be an ugly frog anymore.

Slamming the book shut, I fling it back on the table and smash my eyes shut tight so no stupid tears come out.

Stupid story with its stupid, beautiful princess and stupid, perfect, human prince. I never liked it, even when I was little, but now it's worse somehow. Now that I have to see all these doctors. Now that there are goblins at school.

I sniff and glare at the window where I know Koschei's making googly eyes at my mom. I can't explain demons to her without telling her monsters are real, and if she knows monsters are real . . . It's only one more step till she knows my secret. That's too much to risk.

Everything would be easier without the monster part of me. But no, that miracle is wasted on the prince. What did the dumb prince ever do to deserve a cure? Just because some princess likes kissing slimy things, *he* gets to be a normal human while regular monsters have to keep living the same way forever and ever? How can that possibly be fair?

Except *he* didn't start out as a monster. He started out as a boy. So he could break the spell because he never really was a monster. He was always just a boy stuck in a frog's body, waiting for the right person to break the spell.

My heart speeds up, and I stare at the cover of the book again. Maybe *I* was born a regular girl and some witch cast a spell on me when I was being naughty to teach me a lesson—or maybe the witch was just mean, and I cried at the wrong time or barfed on her shoe. Maybe underneath the curse, I am just a girl.

A normal girl.

And all I need is something to break the spell.

The idea swells up inside my chest till I can hardly breathe. I want it to be true so bad.

A spell.

I snag my *Big Book of Monsters* and try to find where the best spot is to find a witch, but they seem to live in gingerbread houses in forests, and I can't see anyone keeping a gingerbread house up with all of the rain we get in Oregon. We do have loads of trees though, so maybe if I try hard enough, I can find a witch who *doesn't* live in a gingerbread house. Then I'd just need to make her break the spell . . . without getting turned into something worse—like a frog, or a bat.

I can't see my mom kissing any frogs or bats good night. Nope. I'd lose her for sure then, if that sneaking demon doesn't steal her first. I turn back to the page with "Koschei the Deathless" scrawled across the top.

Bare-chested and thin as a jump rope, the ugly old man grins from the pages. His horse's tail and mane whip in the whirlwind, and a woman kneels before him, crying. A frown yanks on my lip, and I wonder if any of those poor ladies ever got away. I flip a few pages and read "Methods for Warding Off Demons and Evil Fae."

I sit bolt upright. Here we go! There's a whole list of useful things like wind chimes, rowan trees, cinnamon sticks, and salt.

I set aside the book on the leather couch with a thump and stand to look around the room.

There is a glass salt shaker by the popcorn machine, and—I double-check—the demon is still working away with his head under the hood. My shoes squeak when I walk to the counter, but the fancy salt shaker is smooth and heavy in my hand, and my smile explodes out of my face like something fierce and sharp. Maybe my fangs are coming in now that I know about the curse.

Creeping to the doorway, I sprinkle enough salt to make a solid line across the floor. Gingerly I reach my toe out to see if I can cross the line, and I can. If *I* can cross the line, then maybe he can, too. My excitement dampens, but then another idea grabs me. Even if he can cross it, maybe it makes him sick to be around it all the time. Like a bad rash from poison ivy, except made by salt that he'd have to dig out of all his clothes and shoes.

The hood of the car slams shut, and Mom claps her hands as the demon pats the car. "Well, I think that should do it," he says.

My time is almost up!

I sprinkle salt *everywhere*. On the floor, on the couch, across the counters, over the file papers. I spill a bunch on the keyboard so it'll burn his demon fingers off.

Their footsteps are coming closer, and I still have half the shaker left, so I wrench the lid off and start flinging the white stuff all over the place, a blizzard of microscopic crunchy snow coating his chairs, his desk, even his jacket hanging on the peg.

The door handle turns, and I race to the popcorn machine, drop the empty shaker and lid on the counter, and throw myself back onto the couch. Bits of salt bounce off the cushions and rain down over me and my book. But Mom and the demon don't see, 'cause they're busy laughing and making goo-goo eyes at each other. They don't even notice the salt shaker spinning to a stop on the counter.

I hold my breath as my mom walks in, but Koschei steps over the salt line just fine. I bite my lip and let my head fall forward so the hair covers my face. Maybe the salt takes longer to work on demons. It might be tomorrow before he bursts into flames.

"Thanks again, Kelsi," Mom purrs, and then laughs.

I want to barf.

"It was my pleasure. Truly." He holds her coat up so she can slide her arms into it, and then he pats her shoulders like he already owns her. It's enough to make me grab my book, jump off the couch, and take her by the hand to pull her out the door.

Mom stumbles following me because she keeps looking back at him, but I don't let go till we're both by the car. I make sure that *I* am the one who opens and closes the door for her, not him. I open and close my own door, too.

I don't relax until we're on the road and far away from Kelsi's Shop. Maybe he'll sit on all that salt and think twice about coming after us. I don't really think so, but I let a part of myself believe it, just so I don't have to worry so much.

Cars whiz by, and we wind through traffic and slip over freeway bridges that hang over the Columbia River like cement rainbows. I try not to think about how high up we are and how a little wall is all that separates us from taking a dive right into the water. I'm not positive, but I suspect my monster powers do not include breathing under water.

"Well, that was an adventure." Mom sighs, dreamy-like. "What luck to have him find us."

Said the mouse about the cat. Gag. The sooner we can forget about him, the better. A thought pops in my head. "Mom, what did I look like when I was born?"

"Ten fingers, ten toes, beautiful blue eyes." I can hear the smile in her voice, even from the back seat. "Tiny as could be. You were perfect."

We sit quiet for a minute, but I *have* to know. Was I born a monster? I clear my throat, but my words still come out as a whisper. "Nothing else?"

"Nothing else like what, honey? You were healthy and beautiful and—" She catches her breath, and I know she remembers what I look like. She forgets most of the time, and I shouldn't have reminded her. What if she figures out what it means?

Panic surges inside me, and my chest squeezes tight. My head hurts. Never mind, never mind, nevermindnevermindnevermind . . .

"Love, your birthmark came a couple months later. I think you were two months old when a red dot appeared by your eyebrow. Nothing one day, and then *poof!* It was there."

Like magic.

"We're lucky, really. Sometimes they appear on eyelids, or lips, or noses. Yours is more out of the way, around your eye, but not infringing on your vision. But don't worry, honey, the doctors said—"

"Mom!" Too much. It's too much. I blurt the first thing I can think of, "Where are we going?"

"Well, your appointment . . ." Mom checks the time, and then looks again. "Shoot. We've missed it. I'll have to call tomorrow to reschedule."

"So this was a specialist appointment, and I missed it?"

"Right. Sorry, hon."

Well, what do you know? Something good came out of that whole demon disaster. I gaze out the window and wonder if he's noticed the salt yet, sticking to his shoes, crunch, crunching, or maybe it'll make his feet slip and slide like trying to walk on a whole bunch of tiny marbles.

I smile a little, but hold it in so Mom won't see.

Even if salt doesn't burn him, maybe it will be enough to let him know my mom is off-limits to demons. He can't have her. I won't let any monster or demon take her away from me. Not ever.

Like I said, she's all I've got.

A POEM OF WARNING

A curse upon your houses
    follows families for years.
A plague on kids and spouses
    can feed upon your fears.
A tricky jinx of dreadful luck
    lies in wait for the naive.
The evil eye can run amok
    with envy and pure greed.
Some magicked items bring success,
    while others bring true misery.
A deadly hex with no defense,
    the darkest kind of witchery.
Beware gods, men, fae, and spirit.
    Let tombs and sacred places lie.
Shy from magic, learn to fear it,
    else destruction lingers nigh.

FIVE

The Witch's House

There are always puddles here. The clouds leak all the time, more out of habit than anything. Dewdrops hang from fern leaves that curl up like green millipedes stretching up out of the ground. And the slugs!

I haven't found a slug monster in my book, but if there is such a thing, her babies are running loose all over Portland. Slugs longer than my foot leave slimy trails all over the sidewalk, and we can't walk barefoot—ever. My first week here, I went outside to grab the paper and the slimiest, grossest, giant snot-glob squished right between my toes—*all* my toes, all at the *same time*. It was like having the biggest booger on the planet barfed up between every toe. The wet, squelch sound was horrible.

I'm not a screamer, but I almost made an exception. I shuddered and dragged my foot all over the grass, trying to wipe off the slime. It didn't work. I had to use soap. I think I'm still traumatized.

So, shoes. I don't forget them anymore.

When I ride my bike, I wear a helmet and ski goggles. The helmet is my mom's rule, and the ski goggles are mine. They are beautiful with a silver, shiny lens that acts like a one-way mirror. Between the side strap and the big lens frame, they cover every bit of my monster mark, even the part that goes from my temple onto my cheek below my right eye. They're kind of like my own super force field where I can see everyone else, but no one can see me.

Exactly how I like it.

This evening, the puddles are bigger than normal after all that wind and rain. My bike tires catch the water and rocket it out in giant circles like fireworks on both sides of me. Drops speckle my face and goggles, but I'm invisible behind my disguise, and it's wonderful.

A squirrel darts across the road, and I turn my handles to not hit it—except a boy runs right out in front of me, a BB gun raised over his head like a club.

"Look out!" I scream, and squeeze my brake handles hard. I can't stop, and he doesn't try. We smash into each other. The front tire catches his knee and knocks him down, and I go flying. The world does a flip, and I fall, cracking the back of my head and rolling into a pile of scraped-up knees and elbows. My hands skid across the cement and sting like fire when I finally stop.

Beside me, the boy rises up out of the puddle, water streaming down his hair and face like a swamp monster. He grits his teeth, and his nose bunches up in a snarl. "You let it get away!"

Gravel sticks to my arms and knees, and little trails of blood leak from a bunch of scrapes. A heartbeat later, the pain hits, each cut and scrape plucking individual nerves till my whole body zings with shock. I open my mouth to answer him, but my throat closes off too tight. My goggles are cracked right down the middle, and my head throbs with every heartbeat.

He snatches the gun out of the puddle. "My BB gun is soaked! You probably did it on purpose."

I didn't mean to, and I try to say so, but I can't think—can't make the words.

"Oh, my. Are you dears all right?" An old woman hurries out of the house beside us. "Taggart, what in heaven's name happened? Is this your friend?"

"She's not my friend!" He crosses his arms and scowls at me. "She ran me over."

"It looked to me like *you* are the one who ran into *her*. Didja bother to look at all before you ran into the street like a reckless fool?" Soft hands touch my chin, and then piercing blue, sea-glass eyes stare into mine. "Oh, honey, a bit scraped up, are ye?"

She removes the helmet and lifts my goggles, and suddenly I can move again. I clutch the goggles back to my eyes, but it's too late.

"What's wrong with your face?" Taggart leans in close and reaches with long, goblin-pale fingers. His pointer finger has a black nail, and scabs cover his knuckles. "Gross! It's like hamburger. Did that just happen?"

I shake my head, and cross my arms over my face. My head is bowed, but the curtain of hair isn't enough because it's wet and clumpy and I'm too vulnerable. Visible. I wish the puddle would rise up and swallow me whole, but it doesn't, and I'm wet. Wet and hurting.

"That's enough," the woman barks, and the goblin boy backs away, his feet splashing in the puddle. Her warm hand pulls my arm until I'm standing on wobbly legs. I shiver in the street. "Come, dear, let's get you warm and dry. Taggart, grab her bike and bring it to the house."

"But my squirrel! She let it get away."

"Then the lass has done the world a service."

"What about my gun?"

"Do as I say, or your mother will hear of it."

I shuffle beside her black pointed shoes. She is wearing striped socks, which is all I can see since I won't lift my head. My shoes splash-splash through the puddles on the sidewalk to her house. A million colored pebbles, shiny like wet gumdrops, line her walkway, and I sneak a look at the brown cottage-style house frosted with white trim. I know I shouldn't talk to strangers, but I can hear the goblin grumbling behind me, and my knees sting too much to think right.

"That's it, lad, lean the bike against the flowerpot, and run along." The old woman pulls me past a thick-bristled broom standing upright against the corner of the porch, and that's when I know the paper-soft fingers holding me tight belong to a witch.

I know I should pull away—run, even—because everyone knows you never go into a witch's house. But she pulls me so quick, I barely have time to remember the lore before I'm tugged inside a warm room with rag rugs and the smell of cinnamon rolls filling my nose. Doilies stretch across the armrests of a cushy, mint-green chair that squeaks a little when I sit.

The witch's apron is hemmed with gingerbread men, all holding hands with wide chocolate-chip smiles; I wonder if they used to be kids that wandered into the wrong house one day. I stare at them while she cleans my scrapes with a white towel and puts some smelly stuff from a brown glass vial on the wounds before covering them with bandages.

"Now then, I do believe introductions are in order. My name is Mrs. May Barrett. Aren't you the wee lamb who moved in to the Foster's old house up the road?"

I nod.

"And do you have a name?" The witch smiles gently with wrinkled lips, but her teeth aren't sharp or iron like the Russian witch Baba Yaga.

It takes a couple tries, but I manage a muffled, "Sophie."

"Lovely. If memory serves, your mother's name is Marlene?"

I sit very still. Do her witch powers let her read minds?

"Don't fret, lass. I met her the other day when I brought a plate of cinnamon rolls by. Do you know her number?"

I nod again, and she hands me the phone to dial. When it starts to ring, she takes it and walks out of the room, talking to my mom. Or at least pretending to. Witches can be sneaky.

Bundles of dried flowers and plants hang in the windows, and pretty jars of every shape and color line a shelf against the far wall. None of them seem to have eyeballs or toads in them, but they might be in disguise. On a coffee table beside me, light flickers through a lampshade covered with a zillion tiny crystals hanging like icicles that never melt. Rainbows of light speckle my arms, drift across the doilies, and rest on a statue of a frog sitting on a log on the floor.

The witch laughs in the other room. It's not a cackle, so

maybe she's not super wicked. I study the stone frog. His eyes are fixed on something in the distance, webbed fingers reaching toward whatever he's looking at, like he's begging the princess to come and kiss him. I hope this isn't the real prince, frozen like that forever. His sad eyes shine. Probably he feels lonely and wants to be human more than anything in the whole world. Just a normal boy. Not a frog.

Not a monster.

I peek around the chair toward the kitchen where the witch's voice drifts up and down in soothing tones. She's giving Mom the address, and it sounds legit, so I won't be here long. Nothing to do but wait.

I sit up straight and stare at the frog again—unless I can find a cure.

Witches have spell books; everyone knows that. Talismans, too. All I've gotta do is find the right book or amulet and I can break the spell myself.

The floorboards creak under my shoes as I circle the edges of the room, searching. Some of the plants hanging in the window smell like pickles, and some like soap. But mostly I smell cinnamon rolls.

"Your mother will be here in a jiffy," the witch calls from the kitchen, and I hear glasses clinking together. "Care for a roll and cocoa?"

"Yes, please," I answer before I can stop myself. Is it safe to eat food from a witch? Or is that how the prince got cursed in the first place?

A bunch of books have pictures of plants and titles referring to some guy's gardens. I'm not sure who Herb is but he must like plants a lot because his name is all over the place. None of these look like spell books, except for a little leather one tucked in the corner.

A tiny dust cloud poofs up when I slip it out of place, and I wait a breath to see if anything else might happen—a booby trap or something magical—but nothing does. The cover is smooth and soft in my hands, and when I crack it open, a dried flower falls out, its mummified petals shattering against the floor and settling like broken moth wings. I gather the pieces as carefully as I can, but they don't quite fit in the flower-shaped depression on the page when I stuff it back inside.

Pencil scribbles run all over the paper. Tiny, loopy cursive and sketches of plants and measurements squirm up the side and into the margins like they want to spill out onto a bigger page, but can't. Or maybe it *was* a bigger book, a whole spell book, and she shrunk it down to hide it better.

"Ah, I see you've found my wee book."

I jump and flinch away from the doorway where the witch watches me. I curl inside, waiting for the spell that will turn me into a frog to match her other one.

"Bring it to the table, and I'll show ye." She steps back inside the kitchen, and I can breathe again, though my heart is pretty sure I almost died and bounces around inside my chest like a will-o'-the-wisp.

The kitchen is bright and has a nook surrounded by windows that poke out the back of her house and into the garden. Vines hug the edges of the glass, and a hummingbird feeder hangs just outside with a bunch of tiny specks darting there and gone almost faster than I can see.

A chair creaks when she sits and slides up to the table, her wrinkly hand patting the lace tablecloth. "Come sit."

Gently, I lay the book on her side of the table and hobble gingerly into a chair opposite her. The plate between us holds a pile of cinnamon rolls with butter and frosting dripping down the sides.

I swallow hard, drool pooling inside my mouth.

"Now, look here." She opens to a page in the middle and points to a drawing. "See how the tall swirl on the stalk looks like those just under the window?"

I glance between the tall, pale-green curls outside and the black-and-white version on the page. "Yes."

"That's garlic. It'll be curing all sorts of ailments. Good for the liver, heart disease—it'll even cure the common cold."

I stare at the pale-green swirl. "Will it cure other things, too?" *Like curses?*

"Sure t'will. In fact, this book o' mine is filled with things the good Lord and Mother Nature gave us for healing." Pages whisper as she flips, pausing to point to different plants. "Horseradish lowers blood pressure and aids in weight loss. Peppermint settles the stomach and keeps ants away. Chamomile helps you sleep and eases stress. And basil will heal cuts and scrapes—we dabbed a bit on your wounds when we cleaned you up." She leans closer and whispers, "It cuts back on the gas, too, if you be in dire need."

She closes the book tenderly before selecting a cinnamon roll off the top of the pile and taking a big bite. Frosting drips onto her plate. I can already taste the deliciousness just by breathing. I lick my lips. If she was planning on poisoning me, she wouldn't eat it herself, would she? That'd be crazy. She must be a nice witch, like the good one on *The Wizard of Oz*. With my mind made up, I grab a warm roll and bite.

If heaven had a flavor, it would taste like Witch Barrett's rolls. I lick my fingers, my eyes almost rolling back in my head from the gooey perfection.

"Mmm," I moan, and she smiles, but it disappears when she looks at something outside.

"Oh, dear. Poor wee thing, barely escaped with his life this time." She taps the window, and Bob stares back at us from under the feeder, his fluffy tail motionless, a single ear erect—a bloody stump where the other ear should be.

"Oh, no!" I touch the glass, but Bob just stands there and shakes, his little chest heaving a million miles an hour. "Do you have a peanut?"

"A peanut?" Witch Barrett asks.

Seriously, you'd think grown-ups could keep up, and magical grown-ups twice as fast. I rush to the door and step onto the back deck. "Bob? Bob, are you okay? Let me see you."

Shaking, panting, he stands still till the very last second and then bolts off the windowsill, across the yard, and up a tree.

"A friend of yours, is he?" The witch slips a handful of roasted peanuts to me and closes my fingers around them. "Don't take it personally. He's been through a scary ordeal and is hurting. It may take him a while to feel like himself again."

A giant rock sits square in the center of my throat, and it hurts when I swallow around it.

"That boy should spend half a day as a squirrel and see how he likes being shot at, or whatever he does. Maybe I *should* talk to his mother, teach him a lesson. He's turning into a monstrous beast these days. Come back inside, lass."

I consider her idea as we walk, but I think he's more goblin than beast. Anyway, pulling the Mom Card seems like a good enough place to start, unless his mom is a goblin too, then talking to her would be useless and probably scary.

Settled at the table again, the witch takes another bite of her roll. I wonder what spell she'd use to turn Taggart into a squirrel. I can't say I'd miss him much, especially since a squirrel wouldn't make my bike crash. Maybe she'd change him and never turn him back. Or maybe she'd undo the spell at the end of the day after his lesson was learned.

My eyes drift back to her little leather book. It holds cures, she said. Could it really cure me? Was it even possible? If I could be normal again, I wouldn't have to wear my goggles, and a hundred Taggarts wouldn't bother me one bit. Without my mark, no one would say anything, there'd be nothing to tease me about, and everything would be perfect with my mom.

I take a deep breath. "Could I, maybe, borrow your book?"

"If you promise to be very, very careful, yes, you may." Her chair creaks as she sits back. "I'll even show you where the plants from the book are in the garden if ye like."

My mouth is too full to talk, but I nod in earnest until I can swallow. "You mean like an apprentice?" Do witches even have apprentices? Or is that sorcerers? She did have a wooden broom on her porch, and another tucked in a corner of the kitchen, but I didn't see any suspicious water buckets.

She winks. "If ye want to call it that, I suppose it doesn't hurt anything. Just be sure to come back and see me often. I enjoy the company."

Her soft gray hair curls around the edges of her face like wispy feathers, and deep wrinkles decorate her eyes, a map to all the smiles she's ever had. Somehow I know that during all this time we've been talking, she hasn't bothered to look at my monster mark even once. She's not scared, or nervous, or grossed out.

She looks at me, and I know she likes me just the way I am. A tingly warmth fills my chest, and I smile back at her. A real smile. To a real friend—even if she is a witch.

"I'll come back," I promise.

"Wonderful." She claps her hands, and I can almost see the magic sparking around them as sunlight reflects off her rings. "Now, let me get that cocoa."

WITCHES

Witch lore across the globe transcends culture and time. Some witches delight in destroying the innocent or meddling in the affairs of kings and nations. But don't despair! Despite what Hansel and Gretel might tell you, not all witches are evil.

While many magical creatures are spawned with their nature predetermined, witches are unique in their power to choose. If blood, pain, suffering, or death fuels their magic, they become black witches most vile. Yet if they vow to do no harm to any creature and rely on nature and love for their spells, they become white witches—wise women who aid those in need.

Like witches, humans have the power to choose. Would you help someone in need? Or laugh when an enemy falls? Remember, the way you treat others defines who you are. Is your heart black or white?

But just to be safe, dear reader, it's best to let gingerbread houses lie.

Witches through the ages, at a glance:

- Circe, the Fates, and Morgan le Fay faced heroes of old.
- Baba Yaga's house walked on chicken legs.
- Jenny Greenteeth delighted in drowning the weak.
- Grimhildr encircled herself with fire.
- Hecate ruled as Goddess of Witches.
- The Witch of Endor summoned a spirit and brought down a king.

SIX

Spaghetti Is Good for Monsters

Spaghetti with meatballs is the best food for monsters. The ones with no teeth can slurp it up same as they'd do with worms and such, and the ones with fangs can stab the meatballs like marshmallows on a stick and save them for snacks later. Mom likes it, too, which is a good thing for me.

"Sophie?" Mom peeks at me from the look-through in the kitchen. "Will you put out some hot pads?"

"Sure." My monster book rattles the glasses a little when I thump it on the table, but I'm way more careful with Mrs. Barrett's spell book when I put it on top. I open the drawer, push the lacy snowflake napkins aside, and grab the thick hot-pads from underneath before placing them in the middle of our round table. Mom showed me once how the table has a "leaf" that makes it bigger—more like an oval—but we've never used it that I can remember.

Photos of Grandma Barr and Mom hang on the wall, and

there's a big one of Mom and me walking away from the camera, holding hands. There's another of me when I was little with Mom cradling my face, looking at me like I'm the most special person in the world. I know things are hard for her because of me, but I think she does pretty good.

Mom sets the spaghetti and sauce on the table, right between our two yellow ceramic plates, alongside two clear glasses, two sets of silverware, two napkins, and two mugs of hot chocolate. Mine has marshmallows, but hers doesn't. Once in a while, we get out all the other plates and cups in the cupboard and wash them to get rid of the dust. I think we should just box up the dishes we don't use so we don't have to worry about them, but Mom thinks two dishes on the shelf would look lonely all by themselves.

It's Mom's turn to pray, and I bow my head, but my eyes keep popping open to stare at the spell book.

We say amen, but not before I add a quick, "And please bless Bob that his ear won't hurt too much."

Mom gives me a funny look, but I barely notice because *spaghetti*! Inside my head, a tiny monster chants, "Eat *all* the spaghetti," and I'm eating until I'm almost ready to pop! It's so good.

"I'm glad to see you've got your appetite back. You've got school in the morning. I remember when I was little, my first day at school was always so exciting! It's a chance to meet new people and make friends." She sighs. "Maybe things will be different this time?"

All the flavor leaks right out of my mouth till I could swear I was chewing the tassel off a rug instead of my favorite food. The lump of pasta sits in my cheek for five minutes as my mom goes on about her new job at another school. I mean, I'm happy she likes her job, but this is *school* we're talking about.

The glob in my cheek seems bigger by the second, and I consider my options:

Option A. Risk death by spaghetti while trying to swallow the goopy mass. Of course, this would be a lot easier if I were a Hindu snake goddess like Nāga and could open my throat up to swallow prey whole. Unfortunately, I'm positive I'm not a snake. (My skin won't shed.)

Option B. Spit the glob onto the plate and suffer the wrath of Mom.

Option C. Run to the bathroom and let the toilet have my dinner.

I'd go with option C, except Mom is already wise to my sudden need to pee during dinner and gets her feelings hurt whenever I try that one. I give my plate one last pained look and go with A. I don't choke to death when I swallow, but it's a near thing.

With a gulp of water, I wash it down and push the plate away. "I'm full. But that was really, really yummy." The fake smile on my face fools nobody, so I change the subject. "So, that neighbor lady let me borrow a book today."

"Oh?" Mom stabs a meatball and swirls it in the sauce, but stops. "Wait, you're reading a book that's not your monster book?"

Gingerly, I open the leather spell book for her and point to a scrawling drawing. "See? That's dill. It smells like pickles and is good for warding off evil spirits."

"You don't say?"

"I do say—I mean, this book says so." The brittle page crinkles under my fingers.

"Are you planning on running into any evil spirits anytime soon?"

"Hopefully not, but you never know. I got some just in case."

"What if the book is wrong, and it attracts evil spirits instead of warding them away?" She winks, but the thought fills me with dread.

That could happen. Mrs. Barrett is a witch, after all. What if I do a warding spell wrong, and I make things even worse? Maybe the demons and evil things will come running when I wave the dill around. I can't remember ever looking around while eating pickles. I wouldn't know if they backed off or not.

Mom reaches across the table and taps my hand. "Honey, don't look so serious. I was just teasing. I'm actually very impressed that you're reading another book."

"I'm just borrowing it." Without thinking, I touch the spine of my monster book as if part of me is afraid it will disappear if I set it aside to read another.

Nope. Still as solid as ever.

A clatter on the back porch rattles the window, and a sharp chattering rises and breaks off.

"What on earth?" Mom's on my heels as we rush to the sliding glass door and peer out.

A writhing mass of brown fur hangs from the feeder, its tail bristling, legs scrambling to climb up the side of the smooth, seed-filled container. Below, a water dish makes one last spin and then falls flat beside the broken flowerpots, which the squirrel must've knocked off when he jumped for the food. As the feeder rotates, Bob hangs on for dear life, his one good ear twitching.

My mouth pops clean open. "Oh! It's him!" I stare at Bob's wounded ear. Does it hurt a lot? Will his sisters make fun of him now that he's different?

"Is this the little guy you were telling me about?"

"Uh-huh."

His hind legs slip off, and he dangles from his front claws, though his back feet spin like he's running on a treadmill.

"Can we give him some easier food to eat?" If I was any closer to the window, my nose would be smashed against it.

"What about an apple?" Mom grabs one out of the basket and passes it to me.

Carefully, slowly, I inch the sliding door open just far enough to roll the apple onto the deck and then I shut the door.

Seconds later, Bob loses his grip on the feeder and falls, arms out wide as if he wants to hug the whole earth at once.

Instantly back on his feet, he stands on his hind legs, tail twitching as he spies the apple, dashes forward, and snatches it in both hands. Except it's too big for him to carry. He tries to bite the apple and drag it, but he can't quite manage that either. He shakes his head quickly and kicks at his wounded ear with his hind foot. Then he hugs the apple and tries to carry it again, but the most he manages is a slight lurch. Chittering in frustration, Bob rolls and claws, dragging the apple backwards toward the edge of the deck.

"He sure wanted that apple." Mom laughs at the angry chatter and walks to the kitchen, but I stay and watch. It's probably a good thing that I don't speak squirrel, because I'm pretty sure Bob's swearing like crazy.

As soon as he disappears, I grab my books from the kitchen table and sit on the couch in the living room. I slide the spell book onto my lap and turn the pages. What I need is a sign that says "Use This Spell to Break the Curse," but the closest thing I can see is a note on how lavender can heal burns.

I carefully close the book and hug it to my chest. Maybe I need to make up my own spell—something strong enough to undo a curse. Except—what if my spell doesn't work like I want? What if it makes it worse? If the witch who cursed me was sneaky, she might have built a booby trap into the curse that makes my mark grow all over if someone messes with it. One second, you think the mark is shrinking, and then *bam*, your whole body is covered with bumpy, blobby, red growths.

With a shudder, I slide my fingers from my temple to my cheek to be sure the monster mark hasn't started crawling across my whole face on its own.

A magical cure is risky. Plain and simple.

But is it worth it?

I open the book again, and the scrawls on the page seem to warp from wispy drawings to wicked vines, their cruel thorns embedded in the paper.

Every day I hide what I am. I cover my face, pretend everything is normal when I know it's not. It's not perfect, but it's working so far. I'm good at hiding.

I glance at Mom, humming in the kitchen.

But could I hide if the cure backfired and the monster part of me spread all over?

Mom steps around the corner and smiles down at me. "Would you like to invite someone over for your birthday party? We could do whatever you want. Go to the park, or roller skating, or maybe—" Then her smile melts a little. "Or you and I could stay home. Maybe play a card game?"

I can't quite make myself smile back. If I was normal, I'd have friends. If I was normal, if I didn't have to hide, we wouldn't have moved or changed schools. We'd go out like other people. Maybe I'd be in dance, or tumbling, or a million other things.

"Thanks." I mumble. I look around the room at the photos on the wall. The one of Mom smiling beside Grandma Barr. The one of me, walking away. The one of Mom smiling at me, her hand covering the monster side of my face.

I swivel in my seat and look at photos on a bookshelf by the table.

Me, wearing a Halloween mask.

Me, with goggles and a helmet on my bike.

Me, on the couch with a blanket pulled up over half my face.

Me, running toward the ocean and away from the camera.

Me, peeking out from behind my monster book.

Me, alone on a swing, not swinging, my head bowed so my hair covers every part of my face.

I'm hiding so well, I barely exist.

I stroke the cover of the spell book and lift my chin. I *need* this cure. It might make things worse, but for my mom, for me, it's worth the risk.

EARTHEN CREATURES

Goblins are known to be vicious, greedy, savage, and cruel. Some say there are as many as ten subspecies of goblins.

Goblins are cousins to orcs, descended from Orcus the God of Death during the time of Beowulf. They are kin to the ogre, which isn't far from the troll. With powerful glamour and a craving for human flesh, which rivals their obsession for gold, these cave-dwelling creatures should be avoided at all costs.

Nasty redcaps earned their name by dipping their hats in the blood of their victims. Whereas mischievous hobgoblins of England (like Shakespeare's shape-shifting Puck) are usually kind to humans. But, reader beware, if mistreated or abused, hobgoblins will transform into boggarts—nasty creatures who torment families, and who can cause milk to sour and dogs to limp.

If your family accidentally acquires a boggart, make an intense effort to be polite, helpful, gracious, and kind. (It also helps to leave gifts of milk and honey.) Love in the home will melt a boggart's frozen heart and bring peace to all therein.

SEVEN

Goblins and Swamp Monsters

What about my goggles?" I trudge up the stone stairway, following my mom into the brick school whose doors loom over us like a steel-toothed maw ready to gobble us up.

"You can't wear goggles to school." Mom sidesteps a line of girls with pigtails, all holding hands and squealing with laughter. Most of them have silver and gold bracelets on their wrists. I eye their glittery arms and hair things, and the way the littlest girl trails behind no matter where the rest lead—their hands stuck fast like superglue. The first girl turns and charges toward us, her mouth wide and flapping with laughter. If she wasn't in hiding, she'd probably be spouting fire instead of laughter. Chinese dragons are all sparkle like that.

"But I might ride my bike home. And I'll need my goggles." Stopping just out of arm's reach, I look back at the parking lot and spy our car. It's not that far away. I could run back.

"Sophie." Mom uses that "listen to me or else" voice, so I *have* to look at her. "Honey, I know it's hard. But you'll make new friends here. The reviews all said this was a really nice school. Just give them a chance. Besides, your bike is at home; I'm picking you up after school today."

I don't answer because I spy the goblin boy running ahead of us and darting through the door. I pat my pocket to see if my baggie of dill is still there—a present from my witch friend—and it is, but I don't know how well it will hold up against goblins. One hand on my pocket, I follow Mom in silence. I consider faking a stomachache for a quick getaway, but I already did that this morning, and she didn't buy it.

As we walk, my book bump-bumps against me from inside my backpack, its heavy weight reassuring me like a pat from a friend.

The principal ogles behind giant magnifying glasses that make her eyeballs dart around like baby squid stuck inside the frames while she spouts gushy, suck-upy things to Mom. Her lips smack before she smiles, and she pats my head, though I'm not a dog. "I'll make sure she gets to class. Don't worry about a thing."

Mom pries her hand free of mine even though I'm squeezing as hard as I can. "I'll see you in a few hours. Love you." She kisses my forehead.

When Principal Marsh wraps her moist, cold fingers around mine, I wonder if her frilly collar is really hiding gills. Her fingers don't seem to be webbed, but maybe the webbing is invisible. Her many necklaces sway like seaweed as we walk. "This is Mrs. Joy's classroom where you'll—" She bends closer to me, sniffs, shudders, and wrinkles her nose. "Do you smell pickles?"

"Um . . ." *It's to protect me against monsters like you.* I'm equal parts thrilled and terrified that my dill apparently works great as a swamp monster deterrent—or at least irritant.

Her ink-spot eyes scurry to focus on me, and her mouth thins in distaste.

"You must be Sophie!" A warm voice calls from inside the classroom, and we both turn as a plump lady bustles out the door. "How exciting to meet you!" She holds out her hand, and I'm so glad to let go of Principal Marsh's swampy claw that I almost leap forward to shake it. Principal Marsh's footsteps recede down the hallway, and Mrs. Joy's smile warms me like sunlight glowing from the inside out.

"Hello." A half smile squirms its way onto my face.

"Let's find your desk and get you settled before the bell rings." She stops and sniffs the air. "Is that pickles?"

"It's dill." I fish out my packet and show her the little cloth bundle.

Her dark lashes close while she takes a big whiff and smiles. "I love the smell of dill, don't you?"

I nod, listening as she tells me all about her classroom, which has paper daisies and tulips on the walls. My desk is two seats back on the far left side by her big desk and furthest from the door. The desktop is smooth except for a heart and a rough *Janiel + Jerry* scratched into the bottom corner. My backpack goes right under my chair, and I measure the cubby under the desktop with my hands to see if my monster book will fit. I frown at the narrow space. Probably not.

I pull my backpack upright beside my chair and leave the zipper open so I can grab my monster book fast if I need to.

The bell rings, and a zillion feet stampede through the halls and pound the linoleum floor until kids spill into the room like ping-pong balls in their rush to take their seats.

With my head ducked, I double-check that my hair is covering my mark since that little bit of shelter is all I've got between the whole class and me. If Principal Marsh had assigned seats, I'd say she put me on the wrong side of the classroom on purpose, but the way Mrs. Joy beams at me, I'm pretty sure she doesn't know what it means for me to have my right side facing everybody all the time.

Trying not to panic about it, I slide a finger along the edge of the desk again. Maybe Mrs. Joy would let me prop a few folders up as a mini-wall.

I watch the students out of the corner of my eye. Most of them ignore me, but a petite girl in pink flits into the room, sees me, and skips to the chair beside me. "Hi! I'm Autumn! What's your name? Are you new? I was new last year, but now I'm old—well, not old, but I've been here for a year."

She pauses like I'm supposed to talk now, but I'm not sure what the question is. I'm too busy trying to listen to her voice. Is this the Autumn I heard laughing the other day?

"Are you shy? I'm not shy. I have friends who are shy sometimes, and we can be friends too, so that's okay. Is that okay with you?"

A friend? With me? I offer a tentative smile. "Okay."

"Okay!" Her grin lights up her whole face like we've both just won free movie tickets plus popcorn and drinks—the huge kind that barely fits inside the cupholders.

"Class, have a seat and let's get started. We have a new student today, so everyone be extra nice to Sophie and make her feel welcome." With a wink at me, Mrs. Joy starts the lesson, and I relax into my chair, glad to have the introductions over.

At recess, with my book snug under my arm, I watch Autumn bounce because she really doesn't walk. She skips, hops, dashes, and even slides—light as a butterfly—but no walking. It's almost like she keeps forgetting that feet are supposed to be on the ground. Her long, blonde pigtails stream behind her like little wings with bright petal-like bows binding them on either side of her head.

My heart skips a little along with her because I'm so excited to have made my very first fairy friend. She's *way* talkative, but definitely friendly. She doesn't mind my quiet answers because she has so very much to say. I think she might have had a pipe clogged inside her brain, and now that it's unstopped, a whole year's worth of talking is rushing out all at once. Her words wash over me, surround me, and lift me up till I'm floating on a bubble of belonging. It's like we were best friends before we ever knew each other existed.

She taps the spine of my book as she skips ahead of me. "I bet your arms are strong from carrying that book all over the place. Have you tried carrying rocks? I bet they'd work just as good. Or maybe really big bricks. I could look behind my nana's house for some if you want."

"Ah, no thanks. I'll keep my book." Only a fairy would think a rock was as cool as a book. She probably likes shiny things too.

"Are there pictures? What's it about?" She gasps. "Oh! Is it an assignment? I've never had that much homework before.

Your old teacher must've been really, really mad at you. Mrs. Joy is way nicer. What did you do anyway?"

"Um." My brain can't decide which question to answer first. "It's not an assignment. I—"

"Hey, Autumn, have you had a *fall* lately?" A group of boys walks up beside us, jostling and snickering.

Autumn's happy skips stutter until her feet stick to the ground like everyone else.

It's the goblin again, long fingers pointing, cruel mouth twisted and sneering. "In autumn, what do trees say to each other? *Leaf* me alone! Ha ha, get it? Autumn leaves?"

I fold my arms around my book, fingers brushing over the bandages that still cover the wounds on my elbows. My knees are bandaged too, but my pants cover those. For once, I'm not the one being pointed at and hated, but it's worse seeing it happen to my friend.

"Ignore them." Autumn slips her arm through mine. "They act worse than a pack of orcs—and their manners are just as bad, but some of them aren't so bad when they're alone. It's mostly Taggart. I hear his mom dropped him on his head as a baby."

"Orcs?" Goblin boy sucks in a breath like a toad and lifts his chin. "I bet you think that joke about my mom is funny, don't you? I'm gonna count to three, then we're gonna get you."

Autumn backs up a step, her glance darting to me and then the boys. "Get me?"

"Don't leaf, Autumn!" They laugh. "Watch out, Autumn, you might fall!"

"You already said that." Her pretty face is pinched, and red splotches bloom across her fair skin. "And it wasn't funny the first time, you giant idiots!"

"You heard her, we're orcs—giants even!" The goblin points his long finger. "Get her!"

She flies away, zipping through the playground, and I clutch my book as the pack of orcs knock me aside in their mad dash after her.

They try to corner her, but she's too fast, too smart, and too wonderful for them. She can climb better, jump farther, and turn quicker than any of them, but she's only one fairy against so many.

I see the mistake before Autumn does as she climbs to the top of a ladder archway. Two orcs head up either side, with her sandwiched between them at the top while the rest wait below for her to jump or fall. She could fly away, of course, but then everyone would know her secret.

Someone should help her. I glance around, my fingers tight around my book, but no one seems to care that the most extraordinary person I've ever met is in real trouble.

No one, except me.

My stone feet stumble as I run to the teacher on duty, a lady with curly hair and lots of scarves. Hefting my book in the crook of one arm, I gasp and point with the other, my words tumbling over each other. "Monsters. Those boys, picking on my friend. She's trapped."

When we arrive at the playground, Autumn's face is stoplight red, and she's scolding a boy below her who is taunting her with her shoe in his hand while the other boys laugh and pull on her pant legs. She might be mad enough to turn them into mushrooms or something, but she settles for yelling.

"Boys!" The teacher's stern voice swings everyone's heads around. "That's enough. Give Autumn back her shoe and then go stand by the door. You've lost recess privileges for the day."

"Man! We were just playing," one of them whines.

"Yeah, it was all in fun," says another.

"Do you think it was fun?" the teacher asks Autumn.

She shakes her head. "Not at all. They're beasts. All of them."

"Orcs? Beasts? Make up your mind," the goblin mutters. Slowly, the group walks past us toward the school, but this time *I* am the focus of their dark looks.

"Thanks a lot," one of them mutters.

"Yeah, new kid. No thanks at all," another one says.

But goblin boy stops and peers closer, recognition oozing through him with a laugh. "It's hamburger girl! Guys! This is the freaky, monster-chick I was telling you about. Seriously, come see this!"

He reaches for my hair, and I cringe, burying my face in my book.

"Taggart!" the teacher calls. "That's enough! Go to the wall this instant." Bending to retrieve Autumn's shoe, she brushes it off and passes it to my friend aloft.

The goblin hesitates, then he leans down and whispers, "And you call *me* a monster? Seriously, do you even own a mirror? Who are you trying to fool with that thing on your face?"

"Taggart!" the teacher shrills.

"Going, I'm going. Geez." With a glance at the ladder arch, he says to me, "I've seen what you are. Catch you later, monster freak." He jogs away.

He knows.

A whole box of chains hangs round my neck, pulling me down and down, and I wish I had never come here. My dill! I pat my pocket, thinking maybe it had fallen out, but no. The dill is still there, and it doesn't seem to work on goblins. I'll look in my spell book again. Maybe I can find something else to use. Except then what if I run into another monster and it doesn't work on that one either? I bite my lip. Will Autumn believe them if they tell her what I am? Will she want to still be friends with me? My fingers brush over the warm lump on my face and I shudder. I can't hide like the goblin, can't blend in without a mask.

"Don't worry about those boys. They're idiots." Autumn is beside me, her words already bubbling out like a drinking fountain. "That was fast thinking, getting the teacher. Thanks for that. He was going to tie my shoelaces in knots."

We bump along, her arm sometimes through mine, and sometimes not, while she skips and bobs, her mouth never closing for long.

Her touches are light and easy, gentle and trusting. And her laughter fills me up till the chains let me go, carried away by a magic hydrogen balloon of smiles. I wonder at the strange miracle. She wants to be *my* friend.

I can't decide if she really doesn't know, or if she knows but doesn't care. Even with my hair parted and covering one whole side of my face, it still isn't enough to hide what I am from someone who knows where to look. Being with Autumn is thrilling, and a little scary, because I'm afraid I'll blink and find she's just a daydream.

I drop the packet of dill into the garbage as we pass. Whatever it does, it didn't affect me or the goblin at all, and it's sure not a cure. That's what I need to focus on. I'll try any spell, wear any amulet, do *anything* I must to make this happen. I only need to think of one monster to keep away forever: the monster inside of me.

OLD ONES

There are creatures who moved from star to star across galaxies for eons, their awesome power growing until they did not live, but could not die. The first of these Old Ones to inhabit the earth was Cthulhu. With an octopus-like face, dragon's wings and claws, and a humanoid form, he stood as tall as the sky and wrought destruction wherever he went. Chaos was his only love. His worshipers claim he still lies beneath the sea—not dead, but sleeping, waiting for the day when the planets align again for him to rise.

Pray, dear reader, that such a day never comes.

For all their devotion, Cthulhu's followers can never find happiness while wishing for chaos and destruction. This is the secret they do not understand: what you give to the world comes back to you. Anger brings hatred and resentment. And kindness brings love and peace.

EIGHT

Strange Doctors and Fiery Grills

ophie!" Mom's arms are outstretched and waiting for me when my class files down the stone steps of the school. "How was your first day? Did you make any friends?"

I snuggle into her embrace, a temporary shield of love and softness. "Mm-hmm."

"You did?" She hugs me tighter and kisses the top of my head. "Oh, honey. That's wonderful!"

Light footsteps skip up behind us. "Is this your mom? She's pretty! Hi, I'm Autumn. Sophie's my friend. I think we're best friends, but I didn't ask her yet, and she doesn't say very much but she listens really well—she's maybe the best listener in the whole world—but I think best friends is probably what we are."

"Nice to meet you, Autumn." Mom lets me go, and I grin at my friend, my very *first* best friend in the whole world.

"Can Sophie come play with me? I mean sometime soon,

when you—Oh! My dad is here. Daddy!" She zigzags through the crowd and leaps into the arms of a man with a mustache. He's huge—a giant. I never would have guessed that he could be the father of a fairy. Maybe some subspecies of mountain troll-fairy or something?

"My Autumn!" His happy bellow rolls across the parking lot. He whisks her against him for a swift hug then twirls her around, and her ringing peals of laughter make me grin because I know *that* dad loves his little girl with all his heart.

Something inside me twinges, like a string snapping on a toy guitar, because I'm pretty sure I've never been lifted and spun around like that. I think I would like it.

I'm still watching them when he sets her down and takes her hand, swishing it back and forth, and I barely notice when Mom tugs my hand, leading me away and into the back seat of our car. What would it be like to have a dad? Would his mustache tickle when he hugged, or would it poke and prick like a bristle-brush? I try to remember if my dad had a mustache. I don't think he did. But if he did have one, I wouldn't have minded—even if it was poky.

Mom holds the door while I scooch my book of monsters over, settle in, and put on my seat belt. But when the door shuts, something feels different—or at least smells different. Mom slides into the driver's seat, and I open my book. "Mom, why does it smell like oil in—"

Two faces smile back at me from the front seat: Mom and Koschei the Deathless.

I suck all the air out of the car and jerk against my seat, like I could magically melt right through it and hide in the trunk. But once again, my power to walk through solid things refuses to work, and I'm stuck. I touch the door handle, but if I leave, then *he'll* be alone with Mom, and what's to stop him from driving off with her and never coming back?

My eyes bounce back and forth between them, trying to make sense of this madness. "What . . ." I'm not sure what my question should be. Why is *he* here? Are you crazy? How'd he get in here? I must've been really distracted outside because I didn't even notice any wind.

"Sophie, you remember Kelsi—the nice man who helped us with our car problem the other day?" Her eyes are ridiculously tender when she looks at him, and I know I've lost ground in this battle somewhere. "Well, we've been texting, and I thought it would be nice to take him for an early dinner with us as a thank you for his help."

"If you don't mind, that is." He turns his Cheshire grin on me, but I'm not buying it, and his smile fades after a second or two.

"I do." I don't know how he got Mom's number, but texting her is *not* okay, and him being in the car with us is ten times worse.

At my mom's dark look, I try a different tactic. "I mean, we rescheduled my appointment for today so we can't go to dinner because we'd miss the appointment *again*, and that would be bad." Whew! I lift my chin and stare back defiantly. Take that, you mom-stealer.

They both shift and face the road while Mom puts the car in gear and turns the wheel. "Oh, don't worry. I told him we had to make a stop first, and he doesn't mind. We'll go eat *after* your appointment."

Great. Just great. I flip my book open and reread the pages

about Koschei the Deathless again, and then the pages about demon wards and things.

> Salt tossed over the shoulder as a gesture to ward off evil was often used while turning in place three times and spitting. Horseshoes were known to keep witches and demonic spirits out of a dwelling, and special candles burned in a home would keep evil creatures away as long as the flames remained lit.

Salt tossed *over* the shoulder—not just sprinkled around. Gotcha. I chew on this new information and drag my book with me when we get to the doctor's office. I'd rather not have to talk or look at any of the doctors anyway.

My plan of ignoring the appointment completely works pretty well until Dr. Steven lifts my chin up and stares right at my face. Gloves hide his hands, and I can't help but stare at the goatee framing his mouth, the whiskers trimmed so neat and tidy it looks almost fake. With one hand on my chin, holding me fast, he pokes and prods with the other at the thing on my face.

A stethoscope hangs around his neck, one end dangling like a big metal eye stuck wide open, the other ends in pincers with earbuds. I think Steven might be his first name, and he's kind of strange. He must be human, though, because if he has any powers, he's not wasting them on me. He mostly sticks with poking and staring, like I'm some bug pinned to a board.

It's worse because Mom is sitting behind him, and I wish she wasn't, but it's better than leaving her with Koschei. He waited in the car, probably to make sure we can't leave without him.

"Excellent." Dr. S lets go of my chin and presses against my temple with fingers from both hands. "See how the hemangioma has deflated? The blood flow has diminished substantially."

"Which means?" Mom prompts.

Dr. S removes his rubber gloves with a *snap* before chucking them in the garbage and folding his arms. "As far as hemangiomas go, it's fairly straightforward. I believe that if you wish to do reconstructive surgery to remove the largest mass of the growth, it would be safe to proceed this summer. We can do laser treatments on the rest to help them fade. With that timeline, the scars would be mostly faded before the next school year started up again."

"This summer?" Mom sits up straighter. "What would we need to do?"

I gulp. Having my monster mark gone would be great. Really great! Dream-come-true great! But having someone actually cut it out . . . What if they cut too far? Or I didn't wake up from the surgery? Or worse, what if the monster part of me is rooted so deep, they *can't* cut it out? It might be a never-ending bubbling cauldron of monster-ness. I could end up being poked and stared at forever.

"I can refer you to our specialists at the children's hospital. If we send blood work along with her records, you should be able to meet with them and put together a feasible timeline relatively soon."

They talk some more, but I stopped listening at the mention of blood work. That's just a fancy name for when someone stabs you in the arm with a needle and steals your blood in tiny glass tubes. Who even knows what they actually do with the blood? There could be a vampire waiting around the corner to suck it all down, and Mom would never know.

When Dr. S leaves and the bloodsucker nurse comes in, I stare at my book with all my might. I've tried fighting before, but nurses have reinforcements, and it makes Mom cry when I do, so I don't anymore.

The nurse taps my arm. "Ooh, that's a good one. Look at that nice vein."

If *she* isn't a vampire, she is at least best friends with one. Who says things like that? Nice vein. Sort of like, nice eyeball, or nice—*Ow!* I grit my teeth but don't make a sound. Once the prick is done, and I know my blood is dribbling into her little vials, I feel a little sick, and a little cold, like maybe some of the monster side of me is leaking out of my arm. I peek, but look away again. It looks like normal red blood, but you never know. If the vampires don't get it first, maybe real doctors with microscopes will see monster blood mixed inside and know the truth.

I don't look again until a cotton ball is stuffed in my elbow and the pink wrap is so tight it's hard to bend my arm. Mom offers to carry my monster book, but I hug it with my good arm and shake my head. Usually, leaving the doctor's office is a good thing, but today, with Koschei leaning against the hood, I almost wish they had kept me there all day.

Almost.

"How'd it go?" His grease-stained hand holds the door for Mom, but I open and close my own door.

"Better than expected." Mom starts the car and waits for

him to get in. "He's referring us to a specialist at the children's hospital."

Blah, blah. I tune them out and read my book until we get to the restaurant, but it's not Aunt Bonnie's Café like I was hoping for. It's some kind of Japanese restaurant.

"You'll want to leave the book in the car." Koschei opens his door and mine before I can unbuckle. "The hibachi grill might splatter on your pages."

I hug the book tighter, ignoring him, and slide out awkwardly, my pink bandage pinching each time I move.

"Oh, we'll sit at a booth, not the grill," Mom says. "We usually try to find a private table."

We walk to the glass doors, and Koschei pulls on the bamboo-shaped handle. "You mean to tell me you've never sat at the grill?"

"No. Booth for three, please," Mom says to the waitress.

The waitress grabs our menus and walks us to the far back of the restaurant.

The room is dark like miso soup and teases us with whiffs of teriyaki, fried rice, and sizzling fish. Shiny spatulas and knives flash and clank in quick rhythms, sometimes flying through the air at the hands of talented chefs. As we pass, fire billows up from a grill where customers gasp and clap, seated in a crescent moon while they ooh and aah over the show. Firelight flickers over their faces. Every table in the restaurant has tiny candles, but their glow can't compete with the grill's ginormous blaze. Everyone can see everyone there, and there's no place to hide. Overhead, paper lanterns line the ceiling like delicate, trailing stars against a night sky.

With each step, I slip further into a dreamlike land of shadow and fire.

A paper lantern drifts to the floor in front of me, its bright colors and trailing tassels splayed like a beached jellyfish.

I stop without meaning to, trying to decide how to pick up the lantern without dropping my book, but before I can act, silverware scatters across the floor in a chaotic jumble, and a girl at the grill jumps off her barstool, smashing the lantern flat with both feet. At the crackling of the fragile lantern frame, she laughs and twists, shredding the delicate paper to bits.

My breath catches at the destruction, and I step back, but her dark eyes follow my movement. She peers at me intently.

Brushing dozens of tiny braids back from her shoulders, she raises both hands to her face, her mouth forming an O as she stares at my monster mark and grins.

She knows!

A laugh gurgles out of her throat, and she wriggles her fingers, each one a blobby tentacle, fanning out like seaweed. Another tentacle that passes for her tongue lolls out of her mouth, all wet and slimy.

It's hard to think, or even move, and my heart beats a million miles a minute.

She steps closer to me, and I raise my book to cover my face. Once out of her sight, my mind clears, and I know where I've seen this monster before—though I didn't know Cthulhu could transform into such a small vessel. I know if she wants to, her infinite tentacles could slip around the book and grab me anyway. My arm hurts, and I've lost track of where the waitress and Mom have gone. But I don't dare move because just looking at Cthulhu can make a person go mad.

Cthulhu gurgles her laugh again, and I shut my eyes, pressing my forehead against the leather-bound cover.

A shadow blocks the light from the grill, and Koschei is there, pulling me forward, matching my steps, his hand lightly steering my shoulder. "The booth is just around the corner."

I shudder at his touch, but I don't pull away until I see my mom, then I run to our booth and wedge myself between her and the wall. No one is sitting in this area but us, and the emptiness helps me relax. Cthulhu doesn't follow; she's probably off to destroy some other part of the city.

The seat squeaks as Koschei slides into the bench opposite us.

I sneak a glance at him and flinch. He's watching me thoughtfully—both me and my book. There's no reason to hide my mark from him, because what could a demon care if the woman he steals is a mother to a very small monster? So I square my shoulders and open my book, hiding the pages while I read about ways to get rid of Koschei the Deathless forever.

After the orders are taken, Mom excuses herself—probably for the bathroom—and Koschei wanders across the room to look at some lobsters crawling in a tank with bright bands on their claws. Now's my chance! I snatch the little candles from our table, and all the tables beside us, and I line them up between his side of the table and ours, a mini wall of flames to block the evil from our lives.

The book said to turn around three times and spit, but I can't see any way to spit in a restaurant. Mom would have a fit, so I pretend instead, turning around and puckering, but not spitting. And, oh, I can't forget to toss the salt *over* my shoulder this time.

I reach for the shaker, but a wide, oil-stained hand grabs it first and snatches it away. "How about *I* hold on to the salt this time."

GLAMOUR

It may seem impossible that monsters can exist and yet remain invisible to the world of men, but glamour is a powerful thing. Glamour works in two parts. First, the magic conceals a creature's true form from human eyes. Glamour can hide something as large as a troll and make it appear human, though imperfect. That's where the second part of glamour comes into play: the human mind's desire for normalcy. Admitting that there is magic in the world is a step that most people cannot take.

If you, dear reader, are brave enough to want to look beyond the safety of average sight, there are some things you can do to see beyond the glamour.

- Soak a ring of rowan wood in salt water and rosemary then peer through the circle to see true.
- Carry a mirror and watch your surroundings in the reflection. A reflected image can reveal many things that are hidden, including a creature's true face.
- If something odd is seen at a glance, yet all appears normal when you look at it straight on, watch the place or person out of the corner of your eye. Oftentimes a direct look will only show what is meant to be seen, but from the side, the truth is revealed.
- The sense of smell is harder to fool than the eye. Creatures smell of their homes in nature. Thus, the ocean breeze follows a selkie in disguise, and a faun will ever smell of sweet pines.

NINE

Date with a Demon

Koschei's eyebrows lift at my wall of candles.

We settle into the booth warily, the demon and the monster, waiting in silence for my mom to return. I chew my lip. Nothing seems to affect him. What's it gonna take to get rid of this demon? Maybe my witch friend would know.

"Are you trying to get rid of me?" he asks.

My whole body stills. Did he just read my mind? If he knows my plan, will he skip the part where he woos the woman and whisk her away in a whirlwind right now?

"I won't hurt you, or your mom. I don't bite . . . much." He winks.

So he does bite, then. I don't remember reading that part. And as for the "I won't hurt you" part, demons never admit to wanting to hurt anyone. They're all about sneaky words and lies.

"This"—he gestures to his ruined face—"might be intimidating, but you don't have to fear me. Inside, we're the same."

The idea punches me in the chest. Me? A demon like him? It can't be. I might be a monster, but I would know if I was evil, wouldn't I? I shake my head. "I'm not."

He waits like a spider, watching to see if a fly tangles in a sticky new thread of web. But this fly isn't stupid. I know a trap when I hear it.

Mom and the waiter arrive at the same time, and I'm happy to have Koschei's attention go somewhere else. The food is amazing and pretty, too, with tiny shrimp and green onions glazed with teriyaki over my noodles.

Without having to ask, Mom tucks a few crab rolls on my plate, and I swirl a big forkful of noodles to drop onto hers. Sharing makes more tastes for everyone—except I don't share with Koschei. In fact, I try not to look at him at all. The melted scars wriggle across his cheek whenever he takes a bite, and I can't help but think of worms dropping from his mouth to the plate.

"Is that the same book you had when you came to my shop?" Koschei asks.

When I don't answer, Mom elbows me. "Sophie. Be polite."

Reluctantly, I nod in answer.

Mom's chopsticks click when she snatches at a sushi roll and misses. "She takes it everywhere. It's been her favorite book since kindergarten."

"What's it about?" He reaches across the table to tilt it up, and I snatch it back, but not before he mouths, "*The Big Book of Monsters*." His eyes slide to me like I've done something very interesting.

"That's a pretty big book to carry around. I used to carry

around comic books." He mimes weighing something in the air and winks. "Way lighter."

"I've always loved books." Mom says. "English was my favorite subject."

Koschei's chopstick jabs the air. "Mine was recess."

"Recess, too." Mom laughs and starts to look all sappy-eyed again.

"But really," he asks me, "don't you want to try a different book? Isn't it boring always reading the same thing, over and over?"

I wilt under Koschei's gaze. He probably just doesn't like that I'm reading about ways to get rid of him. Why would I ever read anything else when I run into these creatures every day? How can I know what they are, how to fight them, without my book? I've read it a hundred times, but I still can't figure out which of the monsters is like *me*. I *need* to know. He already knows what he is, so he wouldn't understand.

With a hesitant laugh to cover the silence, Mom explains. "She's shy. You know, with the . . . Well, you know."

"I know what it's like to want to hide your face, but you can't let it hold you back." He dribbles soy sauce into a little dish beside his plate. A demon would probably prefer to sprinkle blood on everything, but soy sauce is all we have.

"Yes." Mom raises a finger. "But you didn't seek out people who mocked you, right? You found your way and avoided cruelty when you could."

He sits back and studies me again. "The army isn't known for its kindness, but, yes, I found my way. What will you do when she hits high school? Will that book go with her there, too?"

"I hope not." Mom waves off his question. "She's got a lot to deal with. We've got time."

He wipes his mouth on a napkin. "Sure. Sure. But sometimes a person needs to face things head-on. Trust me on this, I know."

They talked between every bite for most of the meal, so eating took for-ev-er—half an hour at least. Once I had to kick his foot for wandering too close to my mom's leg.

It's so weird to see Mom batting her eyes at a demon. I suppose it's nice that she doesn't mind the deformities. I mean, she doesn't mind me either, most of the time. But that's probably because she thinks the scars are only skin deep. If she knew what lay beneath the ruined skin—the fire and ash that make up a demon—surely, she wouldn't want to be near him, would she?

I push my plate away. What if she knew and liked him anyway? Would that mean she'd like the real me too? Monster and all?

Mom laughs, blushing, and I shake my head. Of course she doesn't know. She might be polite to a demon, but blush because of one? No way. To her, there are no monsters or demons at this table. Just him and just me, flawed as we are.

Obviously, she likes us both. I narrow my eyes at the demon. But *I* had her first.

Finally, Mom says, "I think we best get going."

"Thank you for the wonderful afternoon. It's been a long time since I've enjoyed a meal this much." Koschei and Mom sit there and stare with stupid grins on their faces until I clear my throat. Really loud. That gets them moving. Barely.

Ten minutes later, we're finally pulling into our street, and Mom smacks the steering wheel. "Oh, darn it. I forgot."

"What?" I try to peek over the seat to see if her purse is there. "What'd you forget?"

"I promised Mrs. Barrett we'd stop by for a visit."

"Mrs. Who?" Koschei asks.

"Sophie made a friend the other day when she crashed on her bike. I promised her a visit today."

Oh, my witch friend. I'm not sure she'd want us to bring a demon to her door, but she probably has wards for that sort of thing.

Even before we knock on the door, a powerful whiff of vanilla fills my nose all the way up to my eyeballs.

Witch Barrett's smile dances in her eyes when she opens the door and spies me. "Well, hello! Hello! Come in, my dears. And who, pray tell, is this strapping young man ye brought?"

"Ma'am," Kelsi drawls and offers a hand, like he's some kinda pretend cowboy. "I'm Kelsi. Marlene tells me you pulled Sophie out of scrape this week."

"T'wasn't any trouble." She steps aside, and I slide past with my mom into the house, but I keep my eye on Koschei the Deathless to see if a witch's wards are strong enough to hold him.

He hesitates on the doorstep when Mom slips inside, and a jolt of hope runs straight through to my toes. *He can't get in!* Ha! Take that, you old mom-stealer!

"Oh, don't be shy, come on in." The witch sweeps him inside with a wave of her hand, and my hope pops faster than soap bubbles. She *invited* him in. Any old demon or vampire can go anywhere if they're invited. Maybe my witch doesn't understand what he is, or maybe she knows and isn't scared. Maybe she's either too old or too powerful to worry about a demon whisking her away.

The door shuts behind us, making the rainbows dance all around the room from the crystal lamp.

"Oh, Mrs. Barrett," Mom says. "It smells lovely in here. What are you cooking up in the kitchen?"

I step onto the linoleum floor of the kitchen and blink. There, standing on a stool beside a bubbling pot of something delicious-smelling, is Autumn.

She gasps. "Sophie! What are you doing here?"

"So you've met my wee granddaughter, have ye?" Witch Barrett wraps her arm around Autumn's shoulder and squeezes her in a quick hug. "She's one in a million, this one."

Autumn pulls a ladle covered with tapioca pudding from the pot and sets it aside before jumping off the stool and rushing to me. "Oh, Nana! This is the girl I told you about. She saved me from those boys who chased me and made the teacher come and send them away and it was wonderful. My shoelaces would have been in a giant knot or maybe up a tree if it weren't for her."

"I'm not surprised," Witch Barrett says, smiling. "Sophie and I became fast friends just the other day, and I knew right away that she was a good one."

Friends? A tingly warmth hums inside my chest. I have a witch friend and a fairy friend. That's two more than I ever had before.

"Now, Autumn, dear, both of you run outside to bring me back a few sprigs of chocolate mint, and I'll make some cocoa to have with our tapioca."

"Yes, Nana! We'll be right back. I know just where to look."

She grabs my hand, and we're running, stumbling toward the door. "Once you get to know the herbs, it's really easy. We use them all the time for all sorts of things. They smell so nice, it's like magic!"

She jumps from one clump of greens to another until she finds one with purplish stems and pointed, dark green leaves growing at the base of a tree. With a few quick snaps, she presses a small pile of leaves into my hands. "Here, I'll pick them, and you hold them."

"What can these do?" The minty smell is strong. I wonder if it tastes as good as it smells.

"Oh, all sorts of things. Nana says it cures a sour stomach and helps you breathe and makes you remember things better and makes your skin glow. It wakes you up!"

More tiny purple stems snap off under her quick fingers. Snap. Snap. Snap!

"My nana can fix anything with herbs. Colds, rashes—you name it. Momma says Nana is a miracle worker."

If I was ever gonna be brave enough to tell her, this was the time. "That's good. Because I need one."

"A mint?" She holds up a sprig. "Take all you want."

"No. A miracle." I hold my breath.

A little O forms on her lips. "A miracle? For what? Are you sick? Is it your mom? Nana can fix loads of things—"

"I need to break a spell."

My words sort of gum up inside my mouth, and my fairy friend sits quietly, waiting for me to go on.

"See, I wasn't born like this." My fingers touch my cheek, and I slide my hair behind my ear. She might as well see how big a curse I'm under if she's gonna help me find a cure. But pulling my hair back makes me feel naked, and I let the curtain fall back into place. "I think I must've done something that made a witch mad, because when I was a baby I was normal. Totally human, but I got cursed and turned into"—I swallow, and my voice box almost stops working—"something else."

"And you can't change back?" Eyes wide, she leans in, peering under my curtain of hair at my monster mark.

"I don't know. Maybe? I need to break the spell." My chest feels as though it's filled with frothy bubbles, light, exciting, and scary. I whisper, "I never thought I'd tell anyone my secret."

With a quick flick of her wrist, she zips two fingers across her mouth and throws away the key. "I'll never tell. Cross my heart and hope to die." She bites her lip. "What do you mean when you said you turned into something else?"

"I'm not sure yet what kind I am. I keep looking in my book, and I think I'm not dangerous, but I can't really figure it out."

"You don't know what kind you are?" She takes the mint from me and stands, carefully cradling the leaves in her cupped hands. "What do you want to be?"

Maybe fairies don't mind being different. I know I wouldn't mind being a fairy. "I want to be a human."

Some of the leaves fall from her hands to the ground, and she stills.

Does she think that's impossible? I rush on, "I mean, I wouldn't mind being a fairy, like you, or something else. But it's hard being a monster. What if I accidentally hurt somebody? What if my mom finds out?"

"You think I'm a fairy?" Her eyebrows wrinkle, and a familiar panic seeps into my heart.

I talk faster, trying to head it off. "And you're beautiful. I know it's a lot to hope for—changing who I am. But I already lost my dad. And I can't lose my mom. I just can't." A sniffle creeps into my voice, and breathing gets harder. "I mean . . . it's just the two of us, and I can't . . . I don't want to be alone."

Two small hands hold mine, and Autumn is there in front of me, looking right in my eyes. "Don't cry. It's okay. I'm here. I'm still your friend. Do you really think I'm a fairy? I always liked fairies."

Throat too tight to speak, I nod, my vision blurry. Stupid tears. Why can't I be a monster without tear ducts? You'd never see a kraken crying, but me? Open up a tiny bit to a fairy, and here comes the waterfall.

"My nana will know what to do. We can ask."

My feet drag as she pulls me into the house. Mom is nowhere in sight—and neither is Koschei. "Mom?"

"Oh, don't mind your mum," Witch Barrett says. "She'll be back soon enough. That nice young man whisked her away for a spell."

He used a *spell* to take my mom?

A ringing sound echoes inside my ears, and I drop Autumn's hand in my flight for the door. "Mom? Mom!"

The door bangs against the wall, and I'm outside, running to the street, but it's empty. Right or left? Right or—? I take a step toward my house. All that talk at dinner with him pretending to be nice. I was only in the garden for a few minutes, and he took her. I left her alone. Alone! So stupid, stupid! My fingers dig into my sides, and I stumble forward. "Don't be gone. Please . . ."

"Sophie! Lass! What on earth? They'll be back." Witch Barrett hobbles down her walk, but Autumn reaches me first.

"Stop, don't go." She laces her fingers through mine and tugs me back to the sidewalk.

"I give you my word. They will come back," Witch Barrett says. "The two of you were bonding so we didn'a want to disturb ye. They've just gone to the picture show, but, lands, if I'd known you'd take it so hard—"

"You promise?" I grasp for the small hope she offers. If a witch says they'll come back, they have to. It's binding. A demon wouldn't have any choice, right?

"My word is as good as gold. Autumn, dear, what were the two of you talking about in the garden? Thick as thieves, you were. Anything important?"

Autumn nods. "It is. Nana, Sophie needs something special. A charm or something to break a curse. A spell, maybe? Do you know anything we can use?"

"A spell?" Witch Barrett's frail hand guides me inside the door and closes it behind us. "I certainly won't be placing a spell on anyone today."

"What about tomorrow? Or maybe you could just tell us what to do?" Autumn pats my hand. "Look how sad she is, Nana. Can't we help?"

"Ach, dears, I haven't the power to do any sort of spell, but if we sit a bit and have some pudding, I daresay we'll pass the time soon enough. It'd be a wee bit of magic of our own."

She serves bowls of steamy, delicious yumminess, and I manage to eat a few bites, but all I can think of is the fact that Mom is alone. Whisked away, even.

And there's nothing I can do to get her back.

DRAGONS

Few creatures capture the imagination like dragons do. Exquisite in grace, full of power, and often cruel, these creatures were born to rule. While most fly, some claim the sea, and others slither through endless, deep caverns. Besides teeth and claw, they have lethal breath. Each dragon's breath is unique, but always fatal. Fire, ice, acid, and poison are only a few of the vicious substances known to be spewed from dragon mouths. Their telepathy can render most humans helpless.

But, you may ask, if they are so powerful, why don't they rule the earth now? It is because of their fatal flaw: greed.

Dragons spend most of their time slumbering upon a hoard of gold with every trinket and coin counted more carefully than a mother counts her children. And therein lies the rub. They are tied to their hoards, unwilling to leave, unite, or conquer for fear of losing their wealth.

Thus the greatest of creatures is conquered by their own choices.

Take care, dear reader, that you never let wealth or material things become more important than the people around you. A dragon may be content with its self-made cage, but humans were never meant to live alone.

TEN

Droid Bodyguards

I wonder if it hurts to be whisked away in a whirlwind. There must be a lot of pressure from all that air pulling you this way and that. And what about hair pulling? Mom's hair isn't that long, but even shoulder-length hair would hurt if you had some big wind yanking on it so hard that it lifts you up into the sky. Would your ears pop?

A demon who rides the whirlwinds naked on a stallion must live in a hot place, or else he'd freeze to death. Maybe Mom could pretend she was on a tropical island instead of trapped inside a demon's lair.

"Sophie?" Autumn pats my hand, and I look across Witch Barrett's kitchen table, past our pile of mint leaves, to where my fairy friend sits with her own bowl of tapioca pudding. I try to eat mine, but with my brain full of worries, the pudding might as well be a bowl full of fish eggs for all I care.

"Give her a few minutes, love. She'll be right as rain soon

enough," Witch Barrett says. She balances two delicate teacups on saucers in her hands and then eases them onto the table in front of us. A tendril of steam rises from rich hot chocolate piled high with marshmallows. The aroma is so delicious, I can almost taste the perfection already. "I've got just the thing for a lonesome heart—especially for a heart that aches for a mother. I think you both could use a dose."

Delicate flowers wind down the handle of each teacup and support an image on the side of a woman playing a harp. Draped in a toga, the woman doesn't seem to mind the ocean spray from waves crashing all around her, blowing her hair, and soaking her clothes.

"That is Ériu, the Goddess of Ireland and sovereignty—a protector, of sorts, for independence and freedom. I suppose she was a fitting companion for a young lass striking out on her own."

"Did she give you powers?" I wonder aloud.

Her rich chuckle soothes me. "Ach, no. You see, my dears, these teacups were part of a beautiful china set that once belonged to my great-grandmother in Ireland. When my mother heard I was to be crossing the sea to find my new life here, she gave them to me to remember her. Even now, with my mother long passed, I think of her every time I use them, and I know that, somewhere, my mother is thinking of me, too. When you take a sip from these cups, you're not only warming your belly with cocoa, you're warming your heart with all the love a mother could give. Therein lies the power of the cups."

Autumn and I take furtive sips and watch each other to see if either of us bursts into some sort of supernova of love. While neither one of us starts glowing, I could swear a tiny part of my heart burns with a new warmth. With a contented sigh, I take another sip.

In a peaceful trance, we sit together until the cocoa is gone, watching the occasional hummingbird dart to and from a feeder hanging in the eaves outside the window. The power of the cups was exactly the kind of magic I needed.

"Dears, we probably have time to run up to the hospital for a quick visit. What say ye?" Mrs. Barrett whisks two empty bowls and my mostly full one back to the kitchen, then returns and gently takes the empty teacups.

"Can we?" Autumn lights up like she's channeling pure sunlight.

"Hospital?" I shake my head. Are these people crazy? I spend my time running away from doctors, not toward them! "No doctors."

"Not for an appointment, silly." Autumn rolls her eyes. "It's to see William. You'll like him."

I think, "Who is William, and why should I care?" But what I say is, "What about Mom? What if she comes back and I'm not here?"

"I'll ring Marlene and let her know, but I do believe we'll beat them back."

I shuffle behind Autumn, who skips and fairy-flits down the hallway.

Twice as long as a normal car, the witch's golden Cadillac Seville peers back at us with chrome-rimmed eyes. Shadows shroud a hoard of mysterious boxes in its lair, and I walk softly, careful not to wake it up.

Autumn opens the back door, and leather squeaks as we slide across the seats and into the belly of the beast. Part of my brain is sure it's going to come after us and turn us all into crispy critters, but with our witch behind the wheel, it roars to life and obediently slips out of the garage. Easy peasy.

We glide through the streets of downtown Portland on a ride so smooth, I imagine Mrs. Barrett is only pretending to drive while our metal dragon soars in and out of traffic, flying on its own. We circle the hospital as if searching for treasure and ease into a parking space between two golden lines.

Once inside the hospital, Autumn wiggles even more than normal, grasping my hand, then letting go, pushing the elevator button, then pushing it again. I can almost hear her wings humming in nervous little starts and stops. She clings to my arm and whispers into my ear, "Don't be scared, okay, but William has some tubes and things in him. It keeps him alive. Oh, and beeping. There's always lots of beeping things in his room."

Beeping tubes? Is this kid some kind of cyborg?

"Just remember," Autumn says, stopping me and looking me straight in the eye, "underneath all that, he's just my little brother, William. You'll like him, I think. He's smart, and cute, and he follows me everywhere—I mean, he used to." She sighs. "I didn't mind."

Mrs. Barrett is talking to the nurses at the counter, so Autumn pulls me down the hall and into a room. A curtain hangs from the ceiling, blocking most of the room from view, but Autumn zips right around it and disappears. On the other side, a woman says, "Honey? What are you doing here?"

"Momma, Nana said we could visit," Autumn says. "And I brought a friend. You'll like her, William. She's taller than me, but still kind of short, and she's nice and—Hey! Sophie? Where'd you go?"

Before I can gather the courage to step forward, Autumn reappears from around the curtain, snatches my hand, and tugs me inside.

"See? I do have a friend. Told you so!"

Orange-tinted rays of sunset spill into the room through the far wall, which is basically one gigantic window, so it takes a minute for my eyeballs to adjust. A weird bed with plastic rails and a raised head takes up the middle of the room. Tall machines on wheels beep and flash, and tubes run around the head of the bed and into the middle where a little boy curls on his side, a little fairy prince surrounded by his droid honor guard. His eyes are open, but ringed with shadow, and he hugs a stuffed puppy. A three-headed dog like Cerberus would probably protect him better than these droids. I mean, if Cerberus can guard all of Hades, how hard could it be to guard one little kid?

A woman sitting in the corner pulls herself up from the chair like a dryad coming out of a tree. Bits of blonde hair fly about her face where they've escaped her messy bun. Something about her face seems hollow, the cheeks not quite full enough, the eyes a little too sunken.

Autumn hugs the lady. "Momma, I made a friend at school, and she's really nice, but she's kind of quiet so I have to talk enough for both of us sometimes. I wanted you to meet because a phone call wouldn't work if you were the only one talking— can you imagine? It'd be like talking to nobody at all—so this is a better way to meet, don't you think? Her name is Sophie."

Autumn's mom musters a tired smile. "Hello, Sophie, I'm Christa."

"Hi." I smile even though I know my hair hides most of it.

"Did Nana bring you?"

"Yep! She's right outside. I think she's at the nurses' station again. I'll show you." Hand in hand, the two of them slip out of the room, leaving me alone with the silent boy in the middle of the noisy droids.

His eyes are so dark, I can't tell if they're brown or green. A splatter of freckles stands out against his ghost-white skin, and I lean in to see better. It seems he's got no hair at all!

He looks at me and scowls, then pulls his dog up to cover his face.

I blink. William is hiding his face from me? I must've been staring too hard, but I've only ever seen bald old people and bald babies before. I've been stared at way too many times to not try to make things better, so I snatch a Lego off his table and show it to him, holding it between my thumb and pointer finger.

Just like it was a peanut, I let it roll and flip over my knuckles one by one like a Slinky walking down stairs.

"Now watch this." A quick flick and the Lego disappears.

He lowers the puppy and darts a look at my other hand, searching.

"I think your puppy has it." I take a step forward and reach an empty hand out to his dog's ear where suddenly the Lego appears again.

His gasp of surprise is a billion times better than any chittering squirrel, and I grin as I take my bow.

"You can do magic!" Autumn says from behind me.

I whirl around and drop the Lego. No one ever has seen my tricks—at least no one old enough to talk.

"You can do magic, but you can't magic yourself into a human?" she asks me in a quiet voice.

Nodding, I stoop to pick up the brick. "Not by myself. That's why I need a cure."

Before Autumn can ask anything else, Witch Barrett and Autumn's mom walk back in and the rest of the visit is full of doctor talk and school reports and stuff, and eventually, they announce it's time to go.

Following Witch Barrett, we shuffle down the hallway much slower this time because the spring in Autumn's steps seems to be broken.

"So, what's wrong with him? Your brother?" I ask her.

"Mom says it's aplastic anemia." Autumn sighs like the next words are too heavy to lift out of her mouth. She reaches for my hand and squeezes it before answering. "That means he has to have a bone marrow transplant or he's gonna die."

"Will he get one?"

She shrugs. "Maybe. Mom prays for it all the time. So does Nana. All of us pray for his cure. He's on this list, but it doesn't seem to ever get any shorter. We wait and wait, and we're still waiting."

I stop dead. "A bone marrow transplant is a cure? Can anyone have one?"

"No, silly. It's only for people like him." She offers me a sly glance. "But if you want to find a cure or whatever for you, I'll help."

"Really?"

"Yep. I can't do anything to get William his cure, but maybe I can help you get yours."

"It's a deal!"

GHOSTLY ENCOUNTERS

The opportunity not taken, the kindness not shown, the loved one ignored—such are the regrets that cause spirits the greatest grief and unrest. Tell those around you that you love them, and live each day with joy. Let no unfinished business fill your own spirit with regret.

A partial list of ghost varieties:

- Spirit orb. Most commonly caught on camera and can appear as a floating white or blue ball of energy. Believed to be formed by the soul of someone who has died.
- Repeaters. Oftentimes these ghosts continue on their daily routine as if nothing were wrong. They may simply ride the subway with you on their way to work. After many years, they fade and disappear on their own.
    - Not to be confused with a death echo, which is created when the manner of death is so traumatizing that the ghost relives that moment over and over until it either comes to terms with the event or it fades into nothing.
- Poltergeists. These may be mischievous but more often are filled with anger. They are powerful enough to move physical objects.
- Phantoms. Usually more independent of thought and are a mix of ghost and malevolent spirit.

ELEVEN

Messages Are for Losers

The witch was true to her word, and we beat Mom back from the movies with enough time to search her bookshelves. Since Herb's plants didn't change me, I traded the leather spell book for a new book, and a new master plan.

When Mom and Koschei show up, I hug her real tight and bury my face in her side, inhaling the scent of her to be sure she's the real deal and not some demon-made fake. Sure enough, she smells like my mom, and even sounds like her. Best I can tell, she's okay, but I sit in the front seat and hold her hand to be sure.

When we leave Witch Barrett's house, Koschei slides into the back seat without complaint, but he sits on the edge and talks with his arms folded over the seat so it's almost like all three of us are in the front seat.

I slide closer to Mom.

That ol' demon hangs around like he can't believe the visit is over. I bet he'd had Mom halfway to his lair when suddenly, he had to turn around and come back because my witch's promise *made* him bring her back. Koschei promises to call, and Mom does that whole blushy-sappy thing again. And me? I almost barf.

Mom watches all wistful-like from our front room as Koschei's taillights disappear down the street, though we can hear the Harley rumbling for a minute or two after he's gone. Like thunder rolling along after the storm has past.

Best to distract her while I've got the chance.

"So, Mom. It's my birthday next week."

"Mm-hmm."

"And you asked what I wanted for my birthday, right?"

"Mm-hmm."

This isn't working. I walk around the chair, grab her hand, and pull her away from the window and whatever demon spell has her glued to that spot.

"Mom!"

"I'm listening." Her bright hazel eyes shine with a happiness I don't quite trust. And her smile muscles are broken, stuck on some kind of goofy setting. My mom, who usually smiles once in a while just for me, smiles, clears her face, smiles again, and again. It's like her face forgot how *not* to smile. She laughs. "Sorry, honey, I'm listening. I promise. It's all been sort of a whirlwind, hasn't it? And it's been so long since I've felt . . ." She hesitates. "I just, well—I had a really nice time tonight."

"Where'd he take you?" Would she even remember? How does a person's brain process being swept up in a whirlwind?

"Oh, we did this and that."

My eyebrows lift, and I give her *the look*. The one Mom uses to say things like "I'm not putting up with any of your baloney," or "You better fess up before I make you."

"We saw a movie and had donuts."

I touch her cheek, and her eyes focus on me. "Donuts are for morning. Are you sure?" *Can't you remember what really happened?*

She laughs. "I'm sure. There's this darling little place downtown called Voodoo Donuts with the most amazing treats. They have this whole witch-doctor theme going on, and donuts shaped like monsters and bones and things. There was a huge line, but we talked the whole time. Kelsi is really funny if you give him the chance."

"Riiiight." Voodoo, seriously? How much of a red flag do you need? Earth to Mom! You've been brainwashed! "Anyway, Mom, about my birthday."

Her eyes wander back toward the window, and rage boils up inside me. His claws are in her so deep that he's got her even when he isn't here!

"*Mom!* Focus. Autumn's parents are busy with her brother, and instead of having a party or something, I want to *do* stuff with her and you. By ourselves." I stare her straight in the eye so there's no misunderstanding. "Without anybody else."

"What about cake?" She blinks and rolls her shoulders like she's just waking up. Probably that demon's spell is wearing off.

"I don't need cake, or anything. I just want to do stuff with you."

"With me."

I nod.

"And Autumn."

Double nod.

"What do you have in mind?"

I pull out the latest book my witch friend lent me: *Off the Beaten Path: A Guide to Unusual Places around Portland.* "I've marked some pages. See the sticky notes?"

Eyebrows raised, she flips through the book, which bristles with tiny yellow papers like a porcupine born in an office instead of the woods. "Witch's House, Shanghai Tunnels, Wildwood Trail, Portland Zoo, Japanese Gardens, Haystack Rock, Multnomah Falls—" She closes the book. "Honey, some of these aren't even *in* Portland."

"We could go to the stuff that's farther away on the weekend and do the closer stuff after school." *And for a whole week, you'll be too busy for that demon to catch us! Ha! Take that Mr. Deathless.*

"You sure this is what you want? You don't want a party here?"

"Does it count as a party if nobody comes?" I don't mean to say it, but it pops out anyway.

She blinks like I slapped her. "I would be here. And Mrs. Barrett. And Autumn." I can tell she wants to add Koschei to the list, but she sees my look and lets the names stop there.

"Grown-ups don't count. Besides, this is what I want." I tap the book. "Please?"

"Okay. I'll look this over and see what we can do."

I wait till she's gone to her room before I do a fist pump. *Yes!* While Mom is looking at the sights and stuff, Autumn and I will be looking for a cure! To celebrate my victory, I slip a card deck from under the couch cushion and splay the cards into a fan. Smooth as the wheels on Koschei's steed, the deck expands into a spiral, and then shrinks with a flick of my fingers.

The bathroom door shuts, and water runs as Mom takes her nightly shower.

I stand and repeat the move behind my back, easy as a minotaur running a maze, but the cards fight me and slip when I try to spin. If I had the Magician's Apprentice Ultimate Magic Kit, I'd have loads more tricks to do besides cards. Heck, someday I'll be able to do all the tricks as easy as breathing, and then . . . Well, I won't show anyone because I'd have to be in front of people to do it. So I guess I'll do it just for me and my squirrels—unless I can get one of those masks like the Phantom of the Opera wears. His whole side of his head was mangled, and he still rocked the theater. Maybe he was a monster like me?

Outside, trees block out most of the light, but stars still peek from between the dark leaves. I crack the door open and slide a few peanuts onto the deck in case Bob stops by for a midnight snack.

On the counter, Mom's phone lights up with a new text, and my happiness sours as I stare at the name above the message: Kelsi.

> *Hey, Marlene, long time no see.* ☺ *Haha. I had a really nice time tonight. I think you did too. I hope I can whisk you away again soon. What do you say? Have a nice night. See you soon.*

If I had laser eyes, the screen would be a puddle of plastic goo dripping off the counter already. Whisk my mom away? Never.

"Leave. My. Mom. Alone," I say.

Never has deleting a text felt so amazing.

THE REALM OF THE FAE

Few places in lore hold as much wonder as Underhill, the fairy realm. It exists on a different plane, a dimension tied to our world by anchors in nature, though separate and only accessible through special doors. Humans who accidentally wander inside Underhill rarely find their way out, and if they do, a hundred years or more may have passed since the time they went in. There are oceans, forests, deserts, palaces, mountains, and meadows inside. But Underhill is more than a place; she is a creature all her own. Please Underhill, and she may mischievously give you a peek inside her domain. Offend her, and you may never find your way home again.

When traveling over unfamiliar territory, it's safest to treat such roads with respect. Leave nothing behind, and take nothing without permission.

TWELVE

Fairy Kingdom

I n video games, characters get to "level up" when they find treasures. They start to glow or get extra strength or become straight-up invincible. Well, that's how I feel every time Autumn smiles at me. Kids look at me weird and I try to hide best I can, but then Autumn is there, smiling, and suddenly everyone else fades into the background. Today she brought me bundles of sage, chives, thyme, and basil to try to ward off the goblin boy, and I slipped them into my cubby, but every one of them was a big giant *fail*.

When I get back from recess, all of Herb's plants are shoved to the side, and my lunch money is gone. Nobody fesses up, but I know it was Taggart and his bunch of orcs because they all grin at me with their nasty toothy smiles while they eat extra peanut-butter crisps from the cafeteria. I try to tell the lunch lady, but I'm pretty sure she's a goblin queen in disguise. Everybody knows that goblins love money, and everyone in the whole school gives her money every day. I've even seen Principal Marsh and Mrs. Joy pay the lunch lady. Goblins stink. That's all there is to it.

After school, I go home with Autumn because my mom has to work late, but I don't mind because as long as Mom is at work or with me, she's not with Koschei the Deathless.

Witch Barrett makes us another cup of cocoa, and I slurp it right down since it tastes about a million, billion times better than the stale peanut butter sandwiches the school gives to kids who have no lunch money. With a satisfied sigh, I place the cup gently on the saucer. "That was de-lish."

"Sure was." Autumn crooks a finger. "Follow me, I've got something to show you."

My *Big Book of Monsters* slides easily into my arms where it belongs, and I follow her out the door and across the yard.

Clumps of wildflowers and tidy rows of Herb's plants line the stone walkways which wind across the yard. We hop from one paving stone to the next, like the ground is lava. It doesn't look like lava, but at a witch's house, you never know. One wrong step might fry your whole foot off.

In the back corner of the yard, a bramble of blackberries perches on the corner of the fence with its long vines sprawled over the last few rows of vegetables, like a giant kraken dipping its tentacles in a pool of water to see if it wants to climb all the way in or slip back into the ocean.

At first I think Autumn wants to show me the blackberries that hang from every vine, dark purple jewels ripe for the picking, but suddenly she darts right into the bush. For a second, I think the kraken ate her. But when I crouch down, I see her feet disappearing into a shadowed hole near the wall.

"Come on!" she calls. "There's space if you crawl."

I peer into the hole where a board leans against the fence, creating a barrier to keep the brambles at bay. It's hard with my book, but I manage to hobble through the tunnel in a three-legged crawl. Finally slipping through a hole in the fence at the far corner, I emerge into a whole new land and blink at the sudden brightness.

Butterflies flutter through sunbeams, their wings flashing gold as they catch the light. A hidden creek babbles nearby. Birds swoop from one tree to the next, darting into the bushes to feast on berries and lifting off again in a never-ending game of tag. Autumn skips from one side of the path to the next, touching ferns and running her fingers over lush moss that clings to rotted logs and branches.

"It's a fairyland," I whisper in awe, and her answering smile is radiant.

"Do you like it? It's my favorite place in the whole world, and this isn't even the best part yet. Come on!" Like the white stag of myth, she's there and gone so fast I'm left staring at ferns bobbing in places she used to be.

"Wait!" Hugging my book to my side, I stumble after her, catching glimpses of her blonde hair and pink sweater as she disappears behind a tree at the next corner. My heart races and I start to panic; what if I lose her and can't get back? Fairyland would be kind of like Underhill, wouldn't it? It's beautiful, but I'd hate to be lost in here for a hundred years.

Finally, I skid to a stop in a clearing. Autumn stands in the middle, her arms spread wide, a fern frond in each hand as she spins slowly with her face upturned and her eyes closed. With sunbeams striking her shoulders, I can almost see her wings. On either side of her, lines of stones curve through the middle of the clearing and lead to an archway.

My lips form a little "O," but my brain hiccups, and I can't get the words out.

"I found this last year, when William first got sick. It was awful. When Dad explained that he might die, I just started running, you know? I ran and cried—mostly I wanted to scream—but then I looked up and found myself here, and somehow it felt like everything would be okay. It's been my special place ever since. Want to see?"

I nod and follow her through the arch and into her own personal cottage. I always wondered what a fairy house would look like, and now I can say for sure it's a little small, but really cool. Magazine cut-outs of butterflies, ballerinas, and ponies hang from dozens of pins pressed into the rough wood walls. Handmade pillows rest atop tree stumps to make chairs, and a shimmery tablecloth drapes over a large, wooden spool table in the middle of the room. At the rear, more logs form shelves with a wonderful collection of stones, pinecones, and bundles of dried leaves.

"Do you like it?" Shifting from one foot to the next, Autumn tugs on a blonde lock and watches me.

Do I? What kind of question is that? "I love it!"

"I'm so glad! I've never showed this place to anyone. At first, I thought it was kinda spooky, because I never saw anyone out here at all, but then I was thinking that if I was the only person I saw, then it can't be spooky unless *I'm* spooky. And I don't think I'm spooky, so it must not be, don't you think?" She kinda freezes like she broke her brain for a second, but then her mouth kicks back into gear. "Anyway, I just knew that I could show you, because best friends share everything together, right?"

"Right." I'm not sure what other rules come with being best friends, but this seems like a good place to start.

"If we work on it more, we could add a curtain for a door, and maybe another one over the window? Or we could hang pretty streamers from the trees." She prattles on, but I know that if ever there was a time when I could tell her my secret, this was it.

Carefully, I lay my *Big Book of Monsters* on the table and open it to the first page. "This is my most special book in the whole world."

She peers over the book and studies the illustrations but doesn't interrupt.

"I've learned all sorts of things from it, like how to tell when people are really monsters in disguise, and how to tell what kind they are. It's how I knew that you were a fairy."

"So, it's like a secret code-breaker for magical creatures? And it told you about me?"

"Yep, and I know your nana is a witch, but she's one of the good ones so you don't have to worry."

She blinks. "Nana's a witch?"

Proud to be the one to teach her, I turn the page. "A good one for sure. Sometimes it's easy to tell what people are, but other times, it's tricky. Taggart is a goblin, and I think Principal Marsh is some kind of swamp monster."

"Is everybody something? A monster or magical thing, I mean?"

"No, my mom isn't, and Mrs. Joy isn't. Lots of people aren't."

"Are you sure you got cursed as a baby? Maybe your mom

was cursed before you were born?" She turns a page and touches a picture of Medusa, a shadowy woman with a serpent's tail, claw-like hands, and a mane of snakes writhing around on her head.

"Nah, my mom is just a plain old human. My monster mark didn't show up till I was a couple months old."

"Wow. Cursing a baby is seriously messed up. Have you always known? Or did you just find out? Does your mom know?"

I hold up a hand to stop the flood of questions. "My mom can't know. What would a human want with a monster? It'd be like a werewolf pretending to be a poodle. Sooner or later, other poodles will notice something's fishy and run."

"You never know. She might be cool with it. I am." Her hand squeezes mine and we grin again.

"But you're a fairy. It's not the same. I've seen monster shows. Watch any Godzilla movie and you'll see a perfectly normal Gojira monster with everyone running away as fast as they can go. I bet he'd be a lot nicer if they'd quit hurting his feelings."

"So, how can we fix this?" Autumn asks.

I tap the book. "With this. Or maybe we'll find something in one of the places Mom's going to take us. I'm sure there's a way to break the spell somewhere. All we've got to do is find it."

"We can do it! I know we can." Autumn closes the book and hands it to me.

"Autumn! Sophie?" Witch Barrett's voice echoes through the forest.

"My mom must be here!" I'm out the door faster than Pegasus in flight. "Come on, Autumn. Let's go find my cure!"

DJINN AND WISHES

Djinn are powerful spirit creatures who fall somewhere between angels and demons. As legends show, djinn can be bound to an object such as a lamp, and rubbing that object may summon the djinn, though they don't actually live inside. Their immense power to grant wishes is well documented, but the gifts may come at a steep price. As clever as a Sphinx, djinn should never be underestimated. If a human strikes a bargain for a long life, the person may live only a year—for compared to a fly's lifespan, a year is a very long time. What's more, one person's wishes could be undone by the next.

The promise of wealth isn't worth the risk of angering a djinn. An enraged djinn can do more than make a person wish they'd never been born; they can make it so a person never existed. We cannot say how many people this happens to, because those who never exist have no one to remember them.

Oftentimes we fickle humans have fleeting wishes for a life not our own, but such superficial desires lead to discontent and unhappiness. Better to take heed of all the good in your life, and take nothing for granted. Look for the good and you will find it, no magic or wish required.

THIRTEEN

Ghostly Falls

Most of the time, it's bad when things fall. Plates shatter. Bones break. Airplanes crash. Knees scrape. But when water falls, it's a whole different world—more like a portal into an ancient realm. It's Jurassic Park, Oregon style.

From the moment we emerge through the pedestrian tunnel to the falls, the roar of the water calls to me. Chipmunks scurry from one tree to the next, sometimes racing along stone walls and dashing across the wide patio before leaping back into the trees. I squeeze Autumn's hand and we smile our special BFF smile.

"Do you think there's fish in there?" Autumn peers at the stream babbling beside the walkway, runoff from the falls.

"Maybe." I shrug.

"The stream seems so peaceful here but look up there where

the water comes from. It's been bashed to smithereens. I bet if it could talk, it'd be saying, 'Ow, ow, ow, ow!'"

We giggle at that, and I roll my eyes. Everyone knows it's not the water that talks; it's the kappas inside the water. I spy a turtle-shaped shell beneath the water and point it out to Autumn. "I bet that kappa spends all day telling fish to go back, that it's not safe ahead."

At her confused look, I try again. "See that shell thing?"

"The green turtle?"

"It only wants you to think it's a turtle. It's part of its camouflage. It's got scales and a beak, and it carries a little dish of water on its head. It's shaped kinda like a monkey, but with a shell and stuff."

"Can we see it?" Autumn steps closer to the stream, and I yank her arm back.

"No! If you go too close, it'll probably drown you!"

"So, kappas are bad monsters?"

"They can be, but they can also help. He could move this whole stream if he wants, but I've only ever heard of them doing that in Japan." My heart gallops along inside my chest at the thought of Autumn getting in with the kappa. Seriously, I need to teach her everything from my book before she gets eaten on accident.

"Can they grant wishes?"

"You're thinking of a djinn. Kappas make deals sometimes, but then you have to marry them. I'd rather stay a monster than marry one."

We walk toward the lodge, and Autumn waves behind us. "Bye, kappa."

The gift shop is full of beautiful necklaces, stuffed animals, games, and all sorts of wonderful things. It's sort of like a mini-Santa's workshop, except everything costs money.

"What are we looking for?" Autumn runs her fingers over a pretty beaded belt.

"I don't know exactly. Sometimes waterfalls can heal people like in Saut d'Eau, Haiti, where the voodoo goddess Erzulie Dantor blesses them. And sometimes, a water goddess lives inside the waterfalls, like Sága—that's a Norse goddess who tells the future."

"Does a goddess live here?"

"I don't know. But it's the only place anywhere near us that might have healing water."

Mom buys a couple fancy chocolates for both of us, and we skip past a group of tourists to the rock wall by the base of the falls. Normally, I'd be more careful since Mom said I couldn't bring my goggles, but I've got my shades on, the big, shiny black kind that famous people use to hide when they want to go to Walmart or McDonalds. The trees seem deeper green to me behind my shady force fields, but I don't mind. It's pretty anyway.

Stone walls line the paths everywhere to keep people out of the water, so bathing in the waterfall is a no-go. Besides, there's car-sized boulders in the pool that fell from the cliffs up high somewhere, so it's probably not safe to hang out in the waterfall anyway.

"Should we go all the way up? Or just to the bridge?" Mom rubs my shoulder. "It's probably pretty different up there since last time, with the fire and all."

I peer up at the trees. From here at the base, it looks as green as ever, with trees everywhere, even on the cliff face. But on the way here, scorched trees marched over the hills and even skipped down to the Columbia River now and then. With all that devastation, the fire must've been huge. How did this island of green survive?

Autumn dashes to the path, and I hurry to keep up. "Oh, can we go up? I don't know if I've ever been all the way to the top. I mean, everybody goes to the bridge—even old people—but the top is *so* much higher. I bet we could see for miles and miles."

Once we leave the main area by the water basin, more burned trees pop up beside the path. Some browned, but still standing, and some charred. Sort of like the fire was a picky eater and decided to really chew on one tree, but spit the other one out because it tasted bad. At the top of the first path, Autumn rushes right out onto the stone bridge, pointing at the waterfall and bouncing in excitement, but I take my time.

Mist surrounds us and envelopes the old bridge in a kind of fog that makes the pathway slick and coats the stone rails so everything shines. I take a few steps and breathe deep, sucking as much of the spray inside as I can. If I can't get into the waterfall, maybe just breathing the tiny bits of it floating in the air will work.

Mom steps through a puddle on the bridge, but something floats to the surface, and I stoop to pick it up.

A picture of a beautiful Native American girl in a white dress stares back at me from the soggy flier with the headline "Princess of Multnomah Falls." Gently, I turn it over, but the print is dirty and hard to read.

"What did you find?" Mom peeks over my shoulder. "Oh, the legend of the falls. I always liked that one."

"The paper says something about a princess?" Autumn

points to the faded image. "I didn't even know there was a king here."

"No king," laughs Mom. "She was the Multnomah chieftain's daughter."

With a gasp, Autumn claps her hands. "A princess and a chief? How romantic!"

"You'd think so, but it's actually kind of sad," says Mom. "There was a great sickness that nobody could stop, and people were dying."

Autumn grasps my arm, and suddenly I'm reluctant to hear the rest of the story.

"At first, it was just the old and the very young, but then even the strong began to fall sick. So, the chief called his council and best warriors to try to find a cure."

A cure? I wait, breathless. This could be the clue I was looking for, and my mom knew about it all along!

Mom continues, "Then an old medicine man told them the only way to save the tribe was to sacrifice a young woman by throwing her off the mountain to appease the Great Spirit."

I step back and peer up the massive cliff face above the roaring water. "Off the cliff by the waterfall? He wanted to throw a girl off that?"

"There was no waterfall, but yes. The maiden had to fall from the cliff overlooking the Columbia River. The chief didn't want to sacrifice any of the girls, but when his daughter's betrothed fell ill, she decided to save him *and* the rest of her tribe."

I watch the water leap off the top and free fall into the open air. My insides quiver as I imagine standing at the top of that cliff, knowing the only way to save my family would be to jump off. A shudder ripples through me. "How'd she know it would work?"

Pursing her lips, Mom watches the waterfall, remembering. "I think she waited for a sign that the Great Spirit would accept her sacrifice and save her people, and when the moon rose over the trees, she knew it was a sign that her sacrifice was accepted."

"So she fell?" Autumn squeaks. "She fell by herself?"

Mom nods. "Yes, and everyone got better, but the chief was sad so he asked for a sign so he could know she was safe in the land of the spirits. And that's when water started flowing over the top of the cliff."

"It was his answer!" Autumn claps.

"Wow," I whisper, eyeing the mist-shrouded pool where roaring water breaks against black, shiny boulders jutting up like giant's teeth.

With a wave, Mom starts walking to the far side of the bridge. "That's the story anyway."

We pass people going up and down the mountain, but I can't shake the story of the princess falling to cure her family. Falling wouldn't do me any good at all. Cure or no cure, if I fell, I'd die. Better to be a monster and alive than a human and dead.

The farther the switchbacks wander from the horseshoe-shaped waterfall basin, the more burned trees line the path. Pinecones lay in scorched piles where they've been swept off the path. I bet the magic that cured the Multnomah tribe protected the trees just like it protected the people all those years ago. A place as powerful as this *must* be magical.

At last we reach the top, and I hurry because we're right next to the stream, which disappears over the top, but Autumn sits on a rock to tie her shoe, Mom waiting beside her. "Don't go too close to the edge, honey."

"I won't." I hold tight to the railing and peer through the bars. From way up here, the people on the stone bridge seem to scurry like ants, and I feel a little sick from the height. Past the lodge, cars buzz back and forth on the freeway that splits either side of the parking lot. I think I can see our car, but then my eyes drift to a tugboat pushing a barge down the wide gray waters of the Columbia. The brown hills on the far side of the river are in Washington, but they're so far away there could be a whole herd of bison over there and I wouldn't be able to tell a bison from a bush.

Someone walks up beside me and thin white gauze brushes my face. I brush it away and scoot over so the lady's dress doesn't blow into me again. Then I freeze as I take in her wispy white dress and long black hair. Her face looks older than it does in the picture, but the ghost of a Native American princess can probably look however she wants to look.

She notices my stare and nods at the view. "I haven't been up here since the fire. I never get tired of the view."

I blink. "You were here during the fire?"

"I was down there." She points with her chin toward the lodge. "We had firefighters from all over the state. We couldn't let the flames take the lodge, so we made a stand."

My breath catches. "You fought it?"

"We did." She gazes over the trees far below. "We battled it all night."

"And saved the lodge."

She nods and I wonder if the firemen knew the spirit of a Native American princess was standing beside them, adding her magic to the fight that night. Maybe she was invisible and they never saw her. I steal a glance back at Autumn and Mom, who crouches beside her, both of them pointing to something in the grass beside the path.

Sunlight flashes off a pendant hanging from the princess's neck and I reach out to touch it, then stop myself.

"Oh, this?" She lifts it so light glints off a large crystal. Gold leaves curl away from the colorful gem nestled in the foliage. "I've had this for years."

"Is it magic?"

"To me it is, because I made it myself." She leans closer, and the wind rising from the falls catches her hair. I smell blackberries and sage. "Sometimes, when you see something special, you just know where it needs to go."

"And then, when you put it all together, the magic works?"

"It did for me." She squeezes my shoulder and a frigid jolt of electricity shoots straight down my arm. I've never been touched by a ghost before!

I watch her leave as Autumn and Mom rush up beside me, Autumn's fingers grasping the bars in wonder. "Wow! Look at the tiny people on the bridge!"

"Did you see her?" I whisper in her ear.

"See who?"

"The princess!" I point down the trail and gasp.

The path is empty.

A FATAL KIND OF LOVE

Much of the lore surrounding magical creatures speaks to how they serve or destroy humans, but what of those who enjoy human company? There are a few who choose to keep humans as servants or pets, but most self-respecting monsters would never admit to such a thing. Why else do you think monsters so often demand maiden sacrifices? Granted, there are some who devour the poor maidens, but others use this trope as a way of gathering companions or servants.

Think how difficult it would be for dragons of immense size to keep their lairs tidy. Certainly, dragons have better things to do, like dream of gold. It's far better to employ a team of maidens to clean and cook. As a bonus, if one of the maidens gets uppity or looks at the hoard too closely, the dragon can have a midnight snack. However, if a creature falls in love with a human, the results—as shown by King Kong—are often fatal for the monster.

FOURTEEN

Back Seats Should Have Tissues

It's up to me to save my mom from herself. Last night, I saw a new name and number scribbled on the whiteboard by the refrigerator.

Kelsi.

That demon just doesn't give up! I wiped off the new entry with my sleeve and peeked at Mom's cell phone. Sure enough, he'd left another text.

Grrrr.

I deleted that one too.

Problem solved, right?

Wrong.

This morning, my mom said that we can't go to the Japanese Gardens until tomorrow because she's got to go out with—you guessed it—Koschei the Deathless.

"No! You can't go with him!" I stomp into the kitchen and shove a chair into the table.

"Sophie!" Mom catches the chair, straightens it, and grabs my arm so I *have* to look at her. "That's enough! I don't know why you've decided to act monstrous when Kelsi has never been anything but nice to us."

Probably because I am one, and so is he! I twist in her grasp. "You don't know him. You only think you do! And this was supposed to be *my* week."

"And we *are* celebrating your week. You, me, and Autumn. Kelsi knows this is just a quick trip, but he wants to see me sometime other than at lunch."

My mind stills at the words.

Other than at lunch.

"You've been seeing him at lunch too?" All my defenses seem like a joke now. Koschei can get Mom any day he wants—while I'm at school—and there's nothing I can do about it. Knees suddenly weak, I slump into the chair, head down. "Mom. You can't. You just can't go with him."

"Give me a reason, honey. Is there something you haven't told me?"

He's a demon, I want to shout, but then I'd have to tell her the rest of it. Reluctantly, I shake my head.

"You just don't like him." Judgment solidifies in her eyes, and she frowns. "Of all people, Sophie, I thought you would be a little more forgiving about how people look."

The lecture leaves a bitter taste in my mouth, worse than orange peels, but the only way to win this argument is to tell her everything. And then I'd lose her.

"Get your jacket. It's supposed to rain again this afternoon."

Robotically, I rise from the chair, retrieve my hoodie from my room, and stand by the door.

A rumbling shakes the house; Koschei is here.

"Kelsi!" Mom acts like seeing him is the biggest surprise ever, but she knew he was coming, so whatever. I stumble along behind her, slip into the back seat, and drop my hoodie on the floor. I watch through the window as he climbs off his massive bike, which takes up most of the carport.

Koschei jogs over to the car and slides into the front seat as Mom closes my door and gets into the driver's seat. He waves at me. "Your mom told me about the fun things you've got planned this week. Sorry to put a wrench in it."

I bet you are. I don't bother to look at him.

"Sophie . . ." Mom starts, but Koschei interrupts.

"No, it's okay. It's hard having someone blow into your world and change things up."

Now I'm staring at him, wide-eyed. Blow in? He just admitted to the whole thing! *I knew it!*

We pull up to the curb in front of Witch Barrett's house and walk to the door.

"We really appreciate you watching Sophie on such short notice," Mom says as she nudges me past the threshold and into the house.

"Ach, think nothing of it m'dear. Sophie and I'll have a grand time, we will."

"Thank you anyway," Koschei's deep voice sends shivers between my shoulders. "I've been wanting to steal Marlene away since I met her."

That does it. I race to the kitchen where Autumn sits at the table and slide open the door. "You've got to stall them, right now! Koschei just admitted that he's stealing my mom!"

She gasps, but runs to do as I ask.

I skitter through a neglected gate on the side of the house, smashing a few of Herb's plants along the way, and dash to the car. Bent at the waist, I rush to the far side and open the door just wide enough to squeeze inside.

"Wait!" Autumn yells, and I catch a glimpse of Mom and Koschei turning back to the house before I wriggle behind the passenger seat and curl up on the floor.

I drape the hoodie over my head like a brownie camouflaging its lair so Mom and Koschei won't see anything more than a pile of clothes.

Outside, Autumn continues, "Um, I . . . was wondering what time will you be back? You know, so I could tell Sophie. Because she's worried about you, like really, really worried. You could stay here, if you want. We could play games, or I could show you the garden. Nana is really good at growing stuff and I know all about it, and—"

"Another time. That sounds wonderful, but we really do have to go. Sophie knows we won't be gone long, a few hours at most," Mom answers.

I hear Koschei beside the door and stiffen. "Huh, I thought she closed this already. I'll have to check the hinges and make sure everything's good."

The door slams shut and I'm locked inside. The seat in front of me bows with Koschei's weight as he settles into the car, and I breathe as quietly as possible. Mom hops in the driver's seat, and within minutes the car purrs along the freeway.

Huddled on the vibrating floor, each bump jostles me like I'm riding a weird magic carpet.

He murmurs something, and she laughs.

I almost catch her reply, but with my head down against

the door, it's hard to hear anything over the hum of the road. After another laugh, I can't stand it. I sit up, careful not to press against the seat, until the road noise fades and I can hear better.

"Take a left here," Koschei says. "I can't believe you've never been to the food carts."

"I've been busy with Sophie, you know? We don't go out much."

"You both need to get out more, explore this great city. You'll need to be in the right lane."

My stomach drops as the car whooshes into a new lane.

"Sophie has some . . . " Mom hesitates, and I strain to hear. "Challenges. People stare, and it makes her uncomfortable. We try to avoid crowds when we can."

"What about all the things kids do, like dance, or gymnastics, or swimming? How can she possibly hide when participating in—"

"She doesn't. We don't do those things. If it weren't for her problem, if she looked different, then maybe. I mean, who doesn't dream of their daughter doing those things? Other people's daughters dream about being ballerinas or something, but mine obsesses over a book—a *monster* book no less."

"Not everyone wants to be a ballerina. She might have other talents that she could—"

"Like what?" Mom sighs. "How to hide behind the curtain? Those dreams can't happen. If things were different, if she didn't have the hemangioma, then sure. We'd do all that. But she can't. I won't put her through it."

"Sophie can't handle the way people stare? Or *you* can't?"

"Is there a difference?" Mom's voice bites. "I can't stand it."

My insides turn to sludge—like tar and curdled milk.

The ride is silent for a long while and Mom's words play in my head with every bump and hum in the road.

If she looked different.

If it weren't for the hemangioma.

I can't stand it.

"Pull over here," Koschei says. "Just forget about everything for a moment, and let yourself enjoy this. Right here, right now."

I pull the hoodie down just far enough to see his scarred hand brushing her hair back. "You're about to have the very best fish and chips you've ever had in your life."

"I've been to England," she warns.

"Pfft," he snorts. "What does England have that we don't?"

"Red phone booths. A queen. The Atlantic Ocean."

"The Pacific is bigger."

She laughs softly. "Fine. I give. You win. Where are these fish and chips?"

"The Frying Scotsman. You'll love it."

After they get out of the car, I count to thirty before peeking out the window to watch them.

Her hand in the crook of his arm, they wander over to a camp-trailer booth. The back end has been cut out and propped up to support an awning, and menu items line the windows on either side.

I squint to read:

Mushy peas.

Ew.

Fried Mars Bar.

That one sounds worth a try.

In front of the booth, Mom hugs Koschei's arm and leans

her head against his shoulder. Both of them are laughing about something.

Mom's cell phone rings on the seat in front of me, and I almost have a heart attack. Wrenching my head down, I pull the hoodie over me and wait. Did they see me?

The car door opens, and I hear Mom answer the phone with a smile in her voice. "Hello?"

"Do you want to try haggis?" Koschei calls from farther away.

"What? No. Wait, what do you mean you can't find Sophie? We just dropped her off. But we saw her go in—" Mom's fingers drum on the roof of the car in a nervous, quick rhythm. "She told Autumn what? So, where'd she go?"

"Trouble?" Koschei's voice is soft, but closer now.

"It's fine. It's not your fault. We're coming." The smile's gone from Mom's voice. "I need to get back. Mrs. Barrett can't find Sophie."

"She's gone?" Koschei calls to someone, "Sorry, cancel that order. Family emergency."

"I shouldn't have left her. Why did I think this would be okay?" Mom starts the car, and dust poofs out from under Koschei's seat as he jumps in and slams the door.

I almost fall over as she pulls out into traffic.

Her voice cracks, "Do you know she begged me not to go with you today? Not asked, begged. It's like she's afraid to let me out of her sight."

"It'll be okay," Koschei soothes, and I feel like a jerk for making Mom cry.

"How? How can anything possibly be okay? We don't do things like this. I don't leave her. I don't date. I don't take her to dance, or swimming, or whatever else because we can't. Maybe if she was a normal child, but she's not. She's *not*, and I *can't*."

My fingers grip the seat cushion, and my eyes water from the dust, but I hold my breath, listening with all my might.

"I'll help you find her. It'll be okay."

"You don't know that! There's always someone staring at her. Always someone teasing. What if they go too far? What if—" Mom's voice rises and I shrink with every word, my hoodie bunching against my face.

"We'll find her," Koschei's affirms, and they drive in silence for a while.

"I shouldn't have left." Mom flips the blinker and we whoosh into a different lane.

After a few minutes, Koschei asks, "Marlene, is it so bad if people tease her? So what if she has to look people in the face and say, 'Yes, I'm disfigured. Get over it.'"

"Kelsi!" She gasps.

"There are worse things than being scarred. She's able-bodied and could live a full life if you didn't . . ." He trails off.

"If I didn't what?" Mom's tone is empty. Dead. A corpse talking. The car roars as she accelerates onto the freeway.

The hoodie brushes against my face again, tickling my nose. My lungs burn.

"Marlene, I know you mean well, but you're coddling her too much. You're teaching her that she has something to hide. She's so full of shame, she can hardly function."

"How many kids do *you* have?"

"None. You know that."

"And you're the expert." She snaps.

"In this, yes. Yes, I am."

Unable to hold my breath anymore, I pinch my nose, my eyes watering.

"Maybe we need a break."

"Aw, come on, Marlene. Don't say that. You've been alone for so long. We both have."

"I have Sophie."

And that's when my traitorous nose decides to sneeze. Super loud.

The tires screech, and I'm plastered to the back of Koschei's seat as the car decelerates in a heart-stopping lurch.

"What the—!" Koschei cries out.

I survive the stop, but it doesn't matter because the car pulls over.

Mom's going to kill me.

KAMAITACHI

Mythology is rich with vibrant small creatures. Some are beloved across the globe like the talking creatures of Narnia, or the many-tailed kitsune foxes, tricksters inviting curiosity more than fear. Others such as kamaitachi sickle weasels are the bane of feudal warriors in Japan and should be given more space. Revered for their amazing speed, the kamaitachi uses glamour to appear as dust devils. With fur resembling a hedgehog and ultra-sharp scythe-like claws, they attack in threes.

The only way to heal a kamaitachi wound is to burn a calendar and press the charred remains against the wound. Where the ashes touch, magic reverses time and damage to make limbs whole again.

But the best defense against the kamaitachi is to be aware of your surroundings: look up and listen. Put away distractions and electronic devices and take note of details in nature. If grass rustles where there is no wind, or a cool breeze fans your ankles while the rest of the air is still, step away! A kamaitachi may be on your heels. Open your eyes and ears. Don't let attention to a virtual world rob you of experience and safety in the real one.

FIFTEEN

Japanese Gardens Should Come with Swords

Well, the good news is that I'm still breathing. The bad news is that I had to do all the chores in the whole house plus all of Witch Barrett's chores.

For *three days*.

I've never seen Mom so mad. She almost crashed, which scared her, which scared me. Koschei drove the rest of the way home after that because Mom needed the time to explain exactly how *not* happy with me she was.

I suppose the other good news is that Mom didn't go out with Koschei that night. But I don't feel as happy about that as I thought I would. The stupid demon is probably sending guilt-trip vibes with his special powers.

Along with doing all the chores, I didn't get to go anywhere. Not even to fairyland with Autumn.

School. Home. School. Home.

The end.

I think if it wasn't my birthday week, I might have been grounded forever. Moral of the story: don't hide in the car unless you enjoy punishment and want to make your mom really, really, really mad.

After my grounding is over, Mom, Autumn, and I spend our first exploring day at the Japanese Gardens. Mom says if we have time, we might stop by the zoo, but we'll see. (When grown-ups say, "We'll see," it usually means "Not a chance," but you never know.)

Mom likes the stone garden, which is a bunch of rocks in the middle of some finer gravel that's been raked into patterns. But to me, it's just rocks. *My* favorite part is the strolling pond garden, specifically the crooked wooden bridges of awesomeness.

The gardens are really beautiful, kind of spectacular actually, but the space between my shoulder blades keeps tingling. It might be because I had to leave my book in the car in case of rain, but I keep looking over my shoulder at the tiny stone temples because I can't help feeling someone is watching us. It's like the barrier between the monster world and the human world is really thin here, and creatures could cross over anytime they want.

I lift my movie-star glasses to see if anything else pops into view, but it all looks about the same.

The wooden planks under our feet thunk like coffin lids as we cross over ponds and streams. Lily pads and ducks drift beneath us. After our third lap across the crooked bridges, Mom pulls out a book and sits on a bench. "You've got until I finish this chapter. Then we'll go."

"Come on!" Autumn skips ahead and we wander under overhangs of brilliant red leaves and sweeping willow trees.

I follow her off the bridges and around the corner to a larger pond, and we watch the koi slip in and out of view, phantoms surfacing to reality before slipping back into darkness.

"Have you seen anything?" I squint at a shimmery silver and orange koi which circles lazily near the shore. Maybe it's not a phantom at all, but some sort of water dragon waiting to eat kids who get too close.

"Not yet." Autumn scans the trees. "It feels like there's something here, but I don't see anything other than rocks that we could use. I suppose we could use a rock, but how would you know which is magical? There's a rock. Over there's a rock. Here's another rock. They're all so, so rock-ish."

A breeze flutters the leaves on the trees, and the sun peeks from behind clouds.

Suddenly, something flashes below a willow tree hanging over the path. I gasp, "What's that?"

"Where? What did you see?"

It shines again and Autumn darts forward, but I grab her hand to stop her. Something about this feels too easy. Like bait for a trap.

We inch closer, but don't trespass under the shadow of the hanging branches.

"This doesn't feel right." My brain flips through dozens of possible monsters, but I can't see anyone around, monster or not. "Can you tell what it is?"

"I think there's something shiny, there by the twig." She points. "I could get it for you. If you're scared, I mean. Not that you should be embarrassed or anything. Sometimes shadows scare me too, but not in the daytime under a tree."

"It's not the shadows. It's something else. Let me think."

We squat down and stare hard at the pavement where the darkness meets the light. I catch my breath as two teensy-tiny spiders flail delicate arms and disappear under the cover of the shade. The sun fades behind a cloud for a few seconds before shining again. In the tangled shadows of the willow, a web pattern crisscrosses there and is gone so fast, most people wouldn't see it. But I did.

Pulling Autumn back a step, I whisper. "It's a spiderweb."

"On the ground? Those spiders were too little for—"

"No." I pull her back another step and study the trunk. "The whole tree is a spiderweb. There's a jorōgumo in there, a demon spider-woman. They can disguise themselves as anything, lure people into their web, and kill them! Sometimes they even pull people into the water to drown them."

We both eye the water suspiciously.

"I don't see her." Autumn ducks to peer under the low-hanging branches.

"I think the shiny thing is bait. She knows we want it, so she's using it to get to us." I think for a minute and then whisper directly in Autumn's ear so the jorōgumo can't hear. Beside us, the vines sway in the breeze and the tree creeks ominously.

"You think that will work?" She eyes the tree. "What if it gets us anyway?"

"Then we scream like crazy and hope someone hears us before she bites us."

Three minutes later we're back at the edge of the shadow, each of us holding the biggest stick we can find. If the webs can't hang onto us, she can't catch us, right? I hope I'm right.

We glance at each other and my heart's pounding so hard, it might smash its way out of my chest and flop onto the ground.

Maybe this isn't a good idea. Maybe it's too dangerous and I should just leave things the way they are. Is it really worth putting Autumn in danger to find a cure?

Mom's voice echoes in my head:

Maybe if she was a normal child, but she's not.

If it weren't for the hemangioma.

Those dreams can't happen.

It was the first time I'd heard her say the words, but I'd felt them every time we walked past a group of kids playing together. Mom might not know exactly what's wrong with me, but she knows it's bad. Bad enough to make her cry.

No. I can't let it go. Even without Koschei, I'm losing her. I won't let this cure go without a fight!

Reaching forward with the stick, I slide the branches to the side, careful not to let them touch me. Autumn moves in behind me, her stick by my shoulder, parting the leaves like curtains made of tentacles. A spiderweb tickles my cheek and I rub it away, fast as I can. A vine slides along my stick and starts to fall over it, toward my face, but I roll the stick and flick the branch off.

We move slowly, careful not to bonk into too many vines at once and set them swinging. At last we reach the center of the shade and I stoop to pick up the shiny thing.

Autumn makes an *Ooooh!* sound and I do a little victory dance. A real crystal glitters in my hand. Its broken chain dangling, the two-inch long, teardrop-shaped pendant shimmers, reflecting both light and darkness. The princess said I'd know it when I saw it, and boy was she ever right!

Dropping the stick in my excitement, I hug Autumn and cry. "This is it! We found the first ingredient!"

Something in the back of my head screams that I forgot something important. Then I remember: the crystal was bait. And we . . . We're standing right in the middle of a trap!

Wind rattles the trees and branches moan, low and angry.

A whole clump of vines reaches right for us and I tackle Autumn out of the way, both of us sprawling on the pavement as we scramble for our sticks. Slithering along the ground, a webbed tentacle reaches for Autumn, but I swipe it aside.

The shadow of the tree morphs into a giant spider-body, the branches moving like arms, wicked fingers strumming the webbed lines.

"Go!" I yell, batting another whip of green before it can catch us.

She lurches forward, but skids to a stop, swinging her stick in front of her face before a vine can touch her. With every step, the webs whip more violently from jorōgumo's anger.

We fight our way through, back to back, each of us batting furiously at the constant assault. Every time I swing one vine out of the way, another slips in—one almost whipping me right across the face. I can almost hear jorōgumo cackling as she plucks webbed strings of her giant wooden puppet.

Swish, step. Our breaths come faster, each of us working as hard as we can. And then it happens. A tangle of vines loops over Autumn's head.

She spins, gasping, her eyes wide with panic as a spidery noose wraps around her neck.

"No!" I whack the webbed line so hard it snaps off, but I keep going, spinning my stick in a full circle.

The vines explode outward, and we tumble through the last

curtain of green and onto the pavement outside the shadow of the tree.

Scattered willow branches lie on the ground all around us, like gasping fish snatched out of water. The last vine clings around Autumn's neck, and I jerk it free, flinging it to the depths of the shadows.

"That was close!" she gasps, her eyes bright with excitement. "I thought it had me for sure!"

"It did!" I'm so full of relief, my laugh blubbers out all watery and my whole body's wobbly. "Are you okay?"

"Yeah. Do you have it?"

For a horrible moment, I think I might have dropped it, but the pendant dangles from my hand, the chain wrapped between my fingers and the stick. "Got it."

She hands me my movie-star glasses, which have a big scratch on one side, and I slip them back on. With the scratch, the world has a kind of funny diagonal slash of brightness.

The clouds block out the sun, darker this time, and the breeze morphs into a frigid gale. Leaves roll out from under the tree, and the shadows seem to reach to pull us back under.

"She's coming after us!" Autumn cries, and we run.

The faster we go, the more leaves tumble around our feet, as if the wind is attached to our heels.

"Autumn," I gasp. "It's not her this time. It's sickle weasels. Kamaitachi are invisible, but can cut the legs right out from under people."

"Cut our legs off?" She squeaks and runs faster.

Every leaf and twig that hits my bare calves sends a zing of fear through me.

I grip my crystal harder and zigzag, trying to throw the

kamaitachi off our trail, but the whirlwind blows against my ankles even more. If they weren't invisible we could dodge them, or fight back, but invisible like this, all we can do is retreat.

We cut across a corner between some fiery-red bushes and I slam into Autumn, both of us toppling onto a bed of ornate flowers.

"Hey! Stay on the path!" An old man in a green jumpsuit scolds, waving his clippers at us.

"Sorry!" I scramble after Autumn and we don't stop to breathe till we find Mom.

Tucking her book into her purse, she checks the bench and stands. "Are you ready to go?" She plucks a leaf out of Autumn's hair. "I think we better save the zoo for a different day. Is there anything else you want to see here?"

"No!" We shout in unison. Both of us breathing hard, we hold hands and hurry along behind her.

Finally, we jump into the car and slam the doors, watching as the wind and leaves flail uselessly against the glass.

"That was epic." Autumn claps her hands and grins in triumph. "That strangle-tangle willow was out to get us with its creepy kraken-fingers!"

"More like Cthu-leaves." I laugh. Autumn kind of mushes all the monsters together, but as long as we escaped the jorōgumo, who cares what she calls it?

Even with wrinkled clothes, mud on her knees, and a smudge of dirt on her cheek, Autumn is prettier than any flower I've seen all day—and a monster-fighting ninja besides.

I stare at her legs and point at the trickle of blood running down her ankle. "Is that deep?"

She blinks. "I didn't even feel it. Look at yours!"

I cross my foot over my knee and wonder at the fresh set of paper cuts, patterned together like a claw had swiped for my leg. If we had been one second slower, I'd be running on stumps for the rest of my life.

The car thrums to life and Mom pulls out of the parking lot. "Don't you think the garden was fantastic? I hear it's breathtaking in the spring too. We could go back—"

"No thanks!" I cut in, and Autumn and I share a smile.

One brush with those monsters is enough.

THE SAD TALE OF MEDUSA

Born as the only mortal of three Gorgon sisters, Medusa was a beautiful maiden who vowed to live as a priestess of Athena, the Goddess of Wisdom. But when Medusa caught Poseidon's attention, Athena was enraged. She transformed Medusa into a hideous creature with snakes for hair and cursed her so she could never look upon a man again without turning him to stone. Medusa wandered far and wide, alone in this serpentine form. Some say the many snakes of Africa fell from her head as she traveled across the continent.

Eventually, Perseus cut off her head. In the moment of her death, two sons burst forth from her body: Chrysaor, a giant with a golden sword, and Pegasus, the beautiful winged horse. Thus were both giants and flying horses born of a wretched and lonely creature.

SIXTEEN

Zoos Are for the Birds

Mom won't let me bring a pocket knife to the zoo. I tried to explain that I might need to fight off a wild creature, but she laughed. Laughed! That just goes to show she's never had to fight off a jorōgumo with a stick. Seriously, an ancient demon versus a stick? We're lucky to be alive.

I walk with Autumn, my *Big Book of Monsters* snug in my backpack beside a sprig of sage and a twig from a hawthorne tree, as we pass the zoo's gift shop ahead of Mom. A stick and a tiny branch don't seem like much, but since Mom is being completely unreasonable about the knife, it's the best I've got.

Autumn skips along the path and then pauses to watch a shaggy white mountain goat scamper over giant boulders. Mom and I watch too, but my internal heebie-jeebie alarm keeps going off, sending prickles down my neck, and I glance around to see if any monsters are sneaking up on us. None of the people passing seem to be hiding a cyclops eye, or extra arms or legs, but you can never be too careful. A low buzz of voices and an occasional slappity-squeak of stroller wheels make it hard to listen for any monster noises, but I keep my eyes peeled as the crowd slips past us under the watchful gaze of the giant totem pole guarding the path.

Carved with wide grimaces, toothed and beaked animal faces stand one atop the other all the way up to a huge eagle with wings spread at the top. Probably it was a normal thunderbird who got tired of throwing lightning bolts and decided to sit up there and rest, but then got stuck and couldn't leave.

A shadow swoops from the trees and alights on the tip of the totem's outstretched wings, then caws and flaps before settling down to watch all of us below. I try to tell myself it's just a crow, but it cocks its head and stares at me until I know the Crow God sees through my human disguise.

I stare back, wave a finger, and whisper, "No tricks, Chulyen." I've got enough trouble without a Native American trickster god running amok.

We wander over wooden bridges sheltered by wide canopies of trees past the black bear and bobcat enclosures, where they snooze on logs and watch us with half-closed eyes.

As we round the corner to the elk meadow, we pass a woman with metallic sunglasses and a mass of dreadlocks spilling over her shoulders and down her back. Green ribbons weave through her serpentine locks and match the long green nails—more like talons really, clutching her tiny gold purse. Who knew Medusa liked the zoo? Just in case she decides to double back and turn us into statues, I keep an eye on her till she's out of sight.

I'm watching Medusa so hard I almost bump into the elk standing on the side of the path.

Elk?

My head whips around and I jerk Autumn's hand to a stop, but instead of an elk, there's only a man in a worn cowboy hat with feathers tucked into the band on both sides. I'm positive I saw an elk, or something like it. Peering closer, I study the man by the path, searching for any sign of transformation.

His dusky-tan face is lined with about a million wrinkles, kind of like the inside of a walnut. Wisps of gray hair escape from his long braid and frame his face in soft glow. A thick, beaded string with a clasp hangs around his neck like a tie, and a leather pouch dangles dead center on his chest. He shuffles on scuffed boots and winks at me when he sees me looking.

"Caw, caw, caw!" Chulyen soars overhead and lands in a tree behind the old man, who nods like he understands every word the black bird says.

"Sophie, where should we go next?" Mom calls from the corner, a zoo map open in her hands.

I step away from the man, once, twice, then turn around and walk faster. I know I've seen him before and I try to remember, but it slides out of my head like pudding dumped down a drain. I'll have to check later.

Autumn hops from foot to foot in an excited little fairy dance. "Let's see the elephants!"

Overhead, the zoo train chugs along on high trestles, the wooden cross pieces shaking leaves, pollen, and pine needles loose to fall around us like fairy dust. I scan the debris for anything magical, but nothing really shines out.

We pass a pride of lions who must've gotten a petrifying

look from Medusa because they're frozen solid, more bronze than stone. A couple lionesses stand nearby with cubs locked forever in a playful tumble while the lion's fanged mouth sits wide open in a silent roar. Little kids climb over the statues and poke at their eyes and faces.

Autumn runs up to stroke the lion's mane and touch his sharp teeth, but I stay with Mom. I can't help thinking those poor lions are still in there, wishing they could move again.

Beguiled by a magical smell, Mom buys each of us an elephant ear scone to munch on while we walk the paths over to the elephant yard. Coated with cinnamon and sugar, the scones drip honey and melt in our mouths.

Everything would have been perfect if it weren't for Chulyen. Perching on the rail beside us, that old trickster preens, his feathers shining metallic blue in the sunlight. When I try to walk past, he caws and clicks his beak, sidling down the rail.

"Looks like somebody wants our scones." Mom tears a little piece and tosses it onto the path behind us. Chulyen swoops down with practiced grace and snatches it before the dozen or so finches who land after him can touch it.

I rip off another piece and toss it farther back. "There. Now leave us alone."

"One time," Autumn says, "I saw this show where a crow was raised by people, and it could do all sorts of things like open pop bottles and cupboards, anything that had food inside. I think he even rode on cars and liked to steal things from people. He could do all sorts of tricks."

I nod solemnly. That sounds exactly like the sort of thing Chulyen would do.

Autumn licks her fingers clean and watches a baby elephant

swim in a gigantic pool while the big elephants toss water over their backs with their trunks.

We make it to the Birds of Prey outdoor show just as two women walk out on stage in a green polo shirts and khaki pants. We settle onto the grass near the back to watch. The cool grass is soft and inviting, and the ground slopes down in front of us to the stage at the bottom so everyone has a perfect view.

The speakers crackle from the stage, "For the safety of both you and our birds, please stay seated while the birds are in flight."

One by one, the trainers call out birds which swoop down over our heads and eat treats from their hands. An owl launches from a perch on one side of the audience to a separate perch on the other side, its wide face pivoting as its huge eyes look this way and that.

"Aren't they amazing?" Mom asks.

"Oh, they are. His feathers are so fluffy, I just want to touch him and run my fingers all over him. I bet he'd be the softest, most silkiest thing I ever touched. Don't you think?" Autumn wiggles her fingers in the air as if she were already stroking his feathers.

I study the huge gloves the trainers wear and shake my head. "It would probably bite your fingers off."

"Birds don't bite fairies." She sniffs. "Everyone knows that."

She might be right, but regular monsters would probably be fair game for those crushing beaks. I slip my crystal out of my pocket and let it slide over my fingers. Flip, flip, flip, it catches the sunlight and feels warm in my hand while hawks and toucans fly over our heads.

"Through rescue efforts like those at the zoo here," the

zookeeper says, "the great California condor has made a come-back from the brink of extinction. Not one condor was left in the wild in 1987, but today we have a growing population. Watch out for that wingspan! Condors have a ten-foot spread from wing tip to wing tip."

The crowd gasps when a massive black bird with a naked pink head launches itself from a cage behind us high on a platform. It swoops close to the ground, skimming over people's heads as it flies right for us.

Autumn squeals and I duck, my heart pattering away at the awesome sight. When it flies right over us, I feel the wind from its wings as it blots out the sky for that one instant.

A smaller black shadow darts in front of me and hits my hand, and I scramble back, swallowing a shriek. I shake my stinging fingers and spy Chulyen flapping away to the top of a nearby pole—my crystal in his beak. I want to be on my feet instantly, but the audience still isn't allowed to stand. So I watch in frustration as the trickster plays with my crystal way up there. My gut churns like a bag of marbles dumped in a washing machine.

Autumn and Mom watch the condor hop around on stage, but I couldn't care less. My future, my life, dangles from Chulyen's beak, and he knows it. His *caw, caw, caw* almost drowns out the zookeeper, who calls another great bird over the crowd to perch on her thick leather glove.

I crawl behind Mom and Autumn, keeping low. As soon as I clear the grass, I'm on my feet and running to the base of the pole. There's nothing to climb on, no way up, and he just sits there, watching me! His head cocks to one side, then the other,

like he's trying to decide which eyeball is best for watching me suffer.

"Give it back." I don't yell, because a god can hear really well, but I try to put all the force I have into the words. If ever there was a time to have some monster power work, this was it. With one last look around, I take my sunglasses off and slip them into my pocket so I can look that old tricky crow right in the eye. I try again, lowering my voice and speaking with as much power as I can. "Give it back, now. Please."

"He doesn't give things back."

I jump, startled, and stare at the old Native American man with the feathered cowboy hat who sits on a bench a few paces away.

"Old crow, he doesn't give things back, unless you make a good trade." He rummages in a pocket and draws out a small bag, half full of popcorn. His liquid eyes peer at the crow and he lifts the bag in salute. "These are better. Come try a few, my friend."

The man scatters a handful on the ground and small birds pounce on the pieces.

Above us, Chulyen complains with loud caws, but the birds ignore him and start taking off with the offering.

"Look away," the man tells me. "As long as you're watching, he'll hang onto his prize only because you want it."

Forcing myself to watch the end of the bird show, I listen as hard as I can. Is Chulyen still there? Did he fly to some other place with my crystal? Just when I think I can't stand it one second more, I hear a flutter of black wings by my feet and the trickster drops my crystal to gobble the popcorn.

I start to rise to grab it back, but the man tsks. "Wait." And

he throws another handful of popcorn farther away. When the other birds go for the new feed, Chulyen hops in the midst of them, flapping and cawing to protect his catch.

"Now get it."

I snatch my crystal up and clutch it to my heart, relief so thick I feel tears trying to leak out my eyeballs.

"That necklace is special to you, eh?" he asks.

I nod and slip it into my pocket so no more crazy gods can steal it.

"Mine is special to me too." He lifts the leather pouch so I can see.

"Is it magic?" I ask.

He nods. "It is my medicine bag."

"How do you know what to put in it?"

"Many things have power, but some things call to you so strong, they make powerful medicine for you."

"They say your name?" How weird would that be if a rock started calling for me? *Hey, Sophie! Over here!* But then, the crystal kind of called to me, didn't it?

"Not in words." The man taps his heart. "They call to you in here. It could be anything. A pinecone. A bead. A carving. A stone. Each person's medicine is different."

"And it heals you?"

"It heals my heart, my spirit."

Spirits have got to be harder to heal than a monster mark, right?

"Sophie!" Mom calls. "Time to go, honey."

"Coming!" I wave goodbye and run to Mom and Autumn.

"Where're your glasses?" Autumn asks. "Is that what the crow took? I think I have another pair at home but they might be shaped like strawberries. Do you mind having fruit on your face?"

Suddenly aware of the masses of people around me, I clap my hands over my face. She's right! I don't have them on at all. I peek through my fingers toward the place where the man stood, but don't see them. I do see the man though, he's walking away with Chulyen sitting right on his shoulder! In the shadow of his cowboy hat, his head is turned like he's having a conversation with the Crow God.

A girl wrinkles her nose at me and I remember the glasses in my pocket and jam them back on. With my face safely covered, Mom takes my hand, and I can think again. What sort of man can understand crow language and can make a god of mischief give back what he'd stolen? Just before he turns the corner, he casts a shadow on the wall of a building and I see the shadow of an elk.

No. Not an elk, a caribou.

I'd spoken face to face with the Caribou Man.

On the walk back to the car, I can't decide what I should tell Autumn. I could say that the Caribou Man is so powerful he can create famines. That he's a leader for all animals and when he speaks they listen. That the tribes fear and revere him so much, they are careful to treat all their hunts with great respect so he doesn't get angry.

He has the power to speak with anyone and anything, and he chose to speak with me. Me! Without my glasses. And he didn't shudder, or look away, or stare. A warm bubble grows inside my chest till I feel a little tingly. Caribou Man spoke to *me*.

"Caw, caw!" Chulyen circles over the parking lot in a slow arc, not quite leading us, but close. Maybe he came back for one more shot at my crystal. Several more black birds fly near him and they tumble about in the air before gliding away.

Something white flutters down from where the crows used to be, and I nudge Autumn. "Look, something's falling."

We slip through a row of cars and follow the white thing until we're close enough to see it's a feather. A white *peacock* feather. Not the whole thing, just a bit of the stem and the eye.

"Wow." Autumn gasps, but I can't hardly hear her over the pounding in my ears. My heart drums a quick beat, and I know it's my heart speaking to me. This is an item of power. A gift. Healing medicine from Chulyen.

"I think he wanted to say he was sorry for taking my necklace." I cup the precious gift in my hands and wander to Mom by the Buick.

Autumn lifts a string of pink beads off her neck and shakes them high over her head for the retreating crows to see. "Come back! If you've got another feather, I'll trade you!"

MONSTER TRAPS

Monsters often use deception to lure unsuspecting people who wander too far into a false sense of security before closing the trap. Sometimes fae sing sweet melodies or dance, inviting anyone lost in the woods to join in, though once a human starts dancing, they will never be able to stop. Worse, a creature may invite a human to dinner, only for the human to discover that the invitation was for them to *become* dinner.

In one such clever ploy, a cirein-cròin disguises itself as a tiny silver fish and allows fishermen to capture it in a net. Once brought on board the boat, the cirein-cròin transforms into an enormous sea monster who eats the entire crew and sinks their ship.

Things in nature are best left alone. Take care that you don't tread living creatures beneath your feet, nor take wild things from their homes. Wild things are not meant to be tamed. And unlucky is the person who tries to take sneaky beasts like a cirein-cròin home for a pet.

SEVENTEEN

Haystack Rock Should Be Off-limits to Zombies

A re we there yet?" Autumn pulls another long licorice string from the bag and nibbles on the end. My licorice is only half gone, but my lips are busy pulling it in bit by bit like spaghetti. It's only fun if you don't use any hands. Besides, my fingers won't stop stroking the peacock feather we bound to my crystal with fine golden wire Witch Barrett gave us. She double-checked my work and even fixed the part of the chain that broke when Chulyen stole it at the zoo.

"Almost. About ten minutes." Mom coasts our Buick down the tree-lined highway on our way to Cannon Beach. For my last adventure day, I tried to get Mom to go to Salem, because I'm sure to find more witches there, or Crater Lake volcano, or the Witch's House, or the Shanghai Tunnels, but Mom said she was in the mood for a day at the beach, and she's the driver so she wins. I did win the battle for my goggles today, though. I told Mom the sand might be blowing around and this way,

I wouldn't have to worry about getting anything stuck in my eyeballs. (I think she was mostly tired of fighting.) Sadly, my monster book had to stay home. Sand, salt, and water kind of stink for keeping books nice.

We had to wait for a half-day at the end of the week since it takes over an hour and a half to drive to the coast. The orcs and goblin at school were trouble all week, as usual, but with Autumn beside me, the days passed pretty quickly.

As we pull up to the beach, dozens of kites and seagulls glide high on the wind over the sea and sand below. Mom cuts the engine, and I peer at the bright spot where the sun hides behind gauzy clouds.

"Don't forget your jacket, Sophie," Mom calls before opening the door and letting in the brisk, salty air. Together, we zip up our hoodies, grab the kites, and step outside. I keep an eye out in case anything *calls* to me. You never know, something as little as a leaf or a bit of torn cloth might be an item of power.

The waves roar, and the sea seems like a living thing that calls to me, teasing and promising wonderful things if only I'd jump in. Unfortunately, I can't fit the whole sea on my necklace, call or no call.

I show Autumn how to set the kites flying high and then tie them down to a piece of driftwood so they can't blow away. Once in a while, a break in the wind lets them fall, but mostly they soar. Mine is a red dragon with a long, spiked tail that wriggles like he's swimming through the sky. Autumn's is a butterfly that swoops and bobs, a delicate ribbon of color against gray-blue clouds.

The tide is out, which is lucky even though it seems like the walk to the water is miles away. With every step, the wet sand hugs my bare feet and each footprint fills with water when I lift off. People clamor all around the hulking mass of Haystack Rock, a mammoth formation that juts out of the water like an entire cliff decided to take a stroll but then forgot how to get back to land. Some of the people wear vests like the crossing guards at school, and they stand beside signs telling people to stay off the rocks, which are covered in living sea animals.

We wander on sandy pathways through a labyrinth of rocks and pools. Black mussel shells with blue highlights pack in tight clusters, and red, purple, and blue starfish cling to rocks both above the water and below in the tiny lagoons carved at the base of each rock. My favorite are the anemones that flutter underwater like alien flowers, their green tentacles swishing this way and that with each tiny wave. Deep-purple sea urchins bumble slowly along, their spines constantly moving in a slow-motion spiky ballet.

Autumn and I kneel down at the edge of a pool teeming with life, and I reach under the cold water, my finger barely touching the fringe of an anemone. Its little tentacles grasp for my finger, hugging me tight in a sticky embrace.

"Does it hurt? I mean, do they sting you?"

"No. It's nice, but you got to be careful. If you touch too hard, or pull away too fast, it can hurt them, especially the urchins."

"William would love this. The smells, the sounds. Someday, I'm going to bring him here so he can touch anemones, and pet starfish, and feel sand between his toes, and . . ." Autumn's voice quiets until her words fail. She swallows and clears her throat like she wants to say more but can't.

Oh, Autumn. My heart squeezes to see her in pain. I pluck a white clamshell from the sand and press it into her hand. "You could bring him a little piece of the sea with this. It's kind of like a promise until you can show him the rest."

She sucks a deep breath and closes her fingers around my gift. "A promise. Yeah. He'll like that. And it even smells like the ocean—oh! Look at the fish!"

Several silver fish dart out from beneath the rock overhang and zip around to the side where the water connects to another pool, but one lingers and circles the pool lazily. Autumn reaches for the water, but I grab her hand and hold her back. "Wait till that fish leaves." Something about it seems wrong.

A wave ripple rolls through the pool and the image of the fish distorts for just a second into something much, much larger, kind of like the fish started to expand, but then remembered it was in a tiny pool and shrunk back fast before we could see too much.

Gotcha! Probably the cirein-cròin doesn't know I saw through its disguise, but I keep quiet anyway.

I pull Autumn up and wander closer to the sign people. "Let's keep looking."

We're careful not to pass the signs, but explore beside them as we tiptoe on the sand around rock formations and pools like a game of tide pool hopscotch. Something still feels off to me, even though we've left the cirein-cròin long behind us. I look for Mom, but she's visiting with one of the sign people and seems fine. A family with little kids squeals over a starfish, and an old couple strolls through the tide pools hand in hand. Everyone is talking to someone, except for a man dressed in tan stripes who stands just outside of the rocky area, watching us all.

We round a corner and one of the rocks is long and

serpentine but rears up at the end like a chicken head—or maybe a rooster.

"What does that look like to you?" I nod toward the formation.

Pursing her lips in thought, Autumn leans closer. "Kind of like a snake, but with a weird head and maybe arms? Why? Do you think it's a monster? Should we run?"

"No, it's okay. I think it's dead, but it probably used to be a cockatrice. They turn living things to stone just by looking at them."

"Wow! Well it sure was busy around here. Look at all the rocks."

I laugh, but then I follow the direction of the cockatrice's beak. The monster died when it was looking straight at Haystack Rock. Staring hard at the enormous cliff, I glance around to the needles rising from the surf farther down the beach, then back at Haystack. "Maybe it died because it turned something too big to stone, and the change overwhelmed it. See those spires over there?"

She nods.

"Don't they kind of look like the toes of some real big feet? And the closer bumps, they could be knees."

"But if those are feet and knees, then this is a . . ." Her eyes widen at the behemoth that is Haystack Rock.

"A giant." I agree. "See that fold in the rock there? I think that could be a coat, or maybe a cloak. Like he tried to hide from the cockatrice's stare by pulling it up over his head, see?"

Autumn gasps, "Oh! I see it! Wow. So he turned to stone and has been stuck sitting here ever since. How sad. He's got all these people here, and he can never talk to anybody."

"It's probably good for the people that he can't. Giants eat people and grind their bones into bread."

"Eeew!" We laugh, but my heebie-jeebie alarms go off again, and I glance behind us.

The striped man is walking into the rocky area, weaving closer with every step.

"Let's go back to Mom."

Change is in the air, and the water rolls in a little stronger with each wave. Every step I take sinks a little more. "The tide's coming in. Go faster," I urge.

We run toward the shore and don't slow down till we pass Mom, who is still visiting with the sign people in their reflective vests. Water surges hard enough to escape the little pools and rush in a thin sheen over the top of the sand. The sign people break away and head for their different signs, each pulling them out of the rising water and carrying them to safety.

I search behind us for the man in the rocks and spy him walking slowly after the sign people. Something white and long trails from his hand, his stripes seeming more like mummy wrappings or bandages from this distance. I smack my fist against my hand. That's where I've seen him before: The Bandage Man of Cannon Beach. Supposedly, he was a local who died in a mill accident and has been doomed to haunt the road like a zombie ever since. No wonder I keep getting weird vibes. My monster senses can't relax with a zombie wandering around.

"Is that a cockatrice too?" Autumn nudges me and points.

At first, I think I see a horse statue beached on the sand with its wild mane frozen and its front hooves reaching, but then I notice the fishtail hindquarters disappearing into the sand. Not a horse, more of a hippocamp, half horse, half fish. How it came to be petrified like a tree, I have no idea. Maybe that old cocka-trice got it too.

The creature's body is partially buried where it had drifted in on the tide with tree roots jutting up around its shoulders in a halo. Bits of white speckle the tangle of roots, and I feel the pull of something special, something powerful. The thing I've been searching for is here. I take a step closer to check it out but freeze when I notice there's someone standing beside the tree.

The Bandage Man.

I almost swallow my heart.

Part of me wants to run to the car as fast as I can, but the special power rests in the tree roots only a few feet away. Besides, this is my last day! Mom won't bring me back for months. It's too far, and costs too much money in gas, blah, blah, blah. I bet if Koschei the Deathless asked her to drive she'd jump at the chance.

"What is it?" Autumn whispers.

"There's something in the roots."

"Something . . . special?" Her eyebrows raise so high, I can't even see them under her blonde bangs. At my nod, her voice gets quieter. "It's not a spider tree, is it? A geronimo?"

"Jorōgumo," I correct. "And no. No spiders." But the Bandage Man may be worse.

"Awesome. Let's go see!"

She's gone faster than I can grab, and I'm stumbling after her in case that zombie decides to have my fairy friend for a snack. A few feet from the root bundle, the sand dips sharply and water fills the gap. There's no way to reach across without falling in. Both of us peek at the tide sliding in across the sand, each wave bringing it a little closer than the last. Another few minutes and this will all be under water.

"Can you see?" Autumn prods, "Is there anything here that you need?"

Dozens of luminescent white shells speckle the roots like a whole colony of sea snails lived there once, but then abandoned ship when the tide took their mansion for a watery ride. They all seem the same, sort of white with brown stripes, except for one near the top where the hippocamp's eyes should be. I point at the spiky twisted thing with purple lines. "That one. That's the one I need."

Wet footsteps squelch closer, and I glimpse Bandage Man shambling around our side, his hollow face and dead black eyes searching the ground.

"Come on!" I lead the way around the other side, keeping the petrified sea horse between us and Bandage Man.

Mom, clueless as always, greets him like he's a normal guy and not some zombie. "Can I help you find anything? What are you looking for?"

He lifts plastic webbing that hangs from one hand. "Anything that doesn't belong."

"You collect litter?"

"Sure. Litter, towels, children, whatever is left behind." He chuckles, but the hair on my head stands straight up. He's not looking for litter, he's looking for us!

The pool of water surrounds the tree on all sides, but near the smallest point of the tail the gap is narrower, and we leap across, onto solid wood. I start to teeter up, but my balance isn't so awesome and I almost fall in.

"Let me get it." Autumn slips by me, light on her fairy feet, and practically skips up the trunk. I bite my lip as she kneels at the top, the dead roots curled around her like wooden fingers.

Beside her, Bandage Man steps around the corner and starts walking toward our only exit.

"Come on, come on!" I urge under my breath.

Her tiny fist pumps the air with a spiked, white-and-purple shell poking out of her grasp.

Ten steps away, Bandage Man closes in. No longer pretending to look for anything on the ground, he stares straight at me and licks his lips. Would he eat me right here? In front of Mom?

Before I can decide my ghastly fate, Autumn is there, tugging my arm and we leap across, racing away from the zombie. "C'mon, Mom. Let's go!"

With our hands locked, the spines of the special shell digs into my palm, but I don't mind. We found what we came for, and the fact that we did it together makes it that much better.

GREMLINS AND WAR

While fighting World War II, small monsters called gremlins made the lives of the British soldiers very difficult. These pint-sized men lived inside the Royal Air Force (RAF) planes and delighted in causing malfunctions and accidents. The RAF made posters depicting tiny men tripping up people and breaking things to remind pilots to vigilantly check each plane to guard against sabotage from invisible gremlins. Gremlins also delighted in oil spills, toppling supplies, and other mischief. At first, the RAF pilots feared the gremlins were working for the Nazis as magical saboteurs, but gremlins caused just as much trouble for the Nazis as they did for the RAF. Gremlins were equal-opportunity mischief-makers. Surprisingly, having the small creatures to blame for mistakes actually lifted morale for the fighters since they did not blame each other for serious mistakes. The RAF learned a universal truth that searching for solutions is far better than wasting time looking for someone to blame. After all, they knew who the *real* troublemakers were.

EIGHTEEN

Farmers Market

The best Saturdays are the ones that start at Beaverton Farmers Market. Some people might wake up on a Saturday and waffle about what to do, but not us. The market isn't an option, it's a tradition. We market like most people church. Mom teases that it's cheap therapy. In the time after Dad left, she didn't go places, but I was tiny then, so I don't remember ever *not* going.

Sometimes I wear my goggles, sometimes shades, and sometimes I keep my hair down for a curtain, but the vendors always seem to know who I am anyway. I don't mind that they know, because they're more family than strangers. It's *my* market. The other customers are just visitors.

Mom's on the phone talking to Autumn's mom, and I'm trying to listen in, but Autumn's mom is doing most of the talking so I mostly keep hearing "Uh-huh," and "I'm sorry to hear that." Finally she hangs up. "Autumn's little brother is having another procedure today, so it's just the two of us. Will you be alright if I stop by the library?"

"I'll be fine. But how is William? Is Autumn with him today?"

"Autumn's whole family is with him today, but never you mind. He's in good hands. Now, don't forget to grab our order from Mr. Gwydd, and don't leave this block. I'll come back as soon as I can." Mom slips me a little money and drops me off by the roadblock at the corner of Washington and 3rd.

The moment the passenger door opens, the sweet, hollow tones of a pan flute fill the air, the Peruvian music mixing with the spicy aroma of sausages, tamales, and popcorn. In the spring, giant flower bouquets and baskets fill the aisles, but this time of year, most of the leftover flowers hang high over our heads on poles like petal-filled pompoms.

The starting bell has already rung, and customers bustle from booth to booth. A trio of boys push past and almost knock me over. With green baseball hats and hoodies, they dart about like we can't see them, but their camouflage really only works in military bases. You'd think gremlins would be more careful about not standing out in a busy place, but they don't seem to care.

"Hey! Watch it!" The Waffle Man shouts when one of them darts between his table and a customer.

He's still grumbling about the unruly trio when I pass and head for the park. Usually, I start my lap through the market right away, but today, I need something a little different. I spent all night trying to *feel* if my amulet was good enough to heal me yet, but no matter what I do, it just sits there. I'm missing something, but I don't know what. I can't go anywhere else, Mom already said no to more adventures, but there must be some way to finish my cure.

I'm hoping I'll find answers in Pegasus's Pirene Fountain. Sure, people call the market fountain some other name, but they can't fool me. Why else would there always be musicians playing and people sitting around the fountain, writing poems and whatever, if it wasn't really the fountain of inspiration? I've yet to see Pegasus actually fly here, but it's easy enough to see where his hooves were. He pounded straight lines in the cement right through the middle of the splash pad so water can gush out.

Already kids are squealing and running through the fountain as it shoots out of the ground in mesmerizing patterns. I think maybe nymphs hold the controls because sometimes the geysers play tricks on people who walk through the fountain area, thinking they're safe, then bam! A geyser shoots up right under them. I know better than to trust the fountain pattern, so I left my *Big Book of Monsters* at home. Besides, I discovered years ago which vendors are monsters, so I don't need it here.

At the edge of the splash zone, I take a deep breath. Time for inspiration.

Pegasus, please. I need a cure.

The words repeat in my head as I take one step, then another—exactly what those tricky nymphs were waiting for. Jets whoosh up all around me and I close my eyes tight, letting it soak my hair and clothes.

Cure. Cure. Cure?

I wait a minute, but no new ideas spark inside my brain. Maybe only one of the streams is magical? Just to make sure, I walk slowly over each hole. The spray alternatively bubbles or shoots as it soaks me.

Three minutes later, I emerge from the fountain more drowned than anything, but I still don't know what to do.

Part of me wants to admit the fountain was a dud, but the rest of me is hoping all this water of inspiration needs time to sink in. Shoes full of water, squelching with every step, I meander past the band with their flutes and drums, and into the market again.

Water drips from everywhere: my hair, my clothes, even my nose.

"Hey, Sophie." Matthew, a regular at the market, steps aside for me, his bright eyes twinkling over his full, curly beard. Flip-flops cling to his bare feet, and tufts of coarse hair stick out from the bottom of his frayed jeans and his red flannel neckline. For a sasquatch, he's a pretty nice guy, even if he could use a bit more deodorant. Like always, he waits in line at the booth for Flock Together Organic Farm. He probably knows the nice "farmers" behind the counter are actually fauns even if all the other customers in line have no idea. Really, it's super easy for them to be organic, I mean, with a crew of half-goat men to eat all the weeds, it's easy as pie, or hay, or whatever. Organic might mean pesticide- and herbicide-free, but it sure doesn't mean magic-free.

Mama Italia hums as she passes a bag of dried pasta to a lady and waves at me.

I wave back, but keep walking, hoping the water of inspiration kicks in quick before I run out of time and have to meet Mom.

Someone knocks into me from behind and I stumble. "Sorry! Ugh, you're wet!" One of the stupid gremlin boys barely bothers to look at me before racing ahead in a game of tag.

"Is that a half-drowned rat, or our Sophie I see?" Dressed in a dapper, striped suit, the Popcorn Man stands beside his gold-trimmed popcorn wagon, eyes bright and merry. "So glum today? Not even a word of greeting? Well then, I've got just the thing." With great ceremony, he twirls his tongs in the air with a flourish and plucks a perfectly golden puff of popcorn from his treasure trove and offers it to me.

When a leprechaun offers you a piece of his treasure, it's best to say "thank you," even if you're not in the mood. You never know if it'll lose its glamour and turn back into gold later.

But before I can grab the popcorn, the gremlins are back, tearing through the aisle and knocking each other all over the place. One of them spins into me, trips, and sprawls onto the cement under the booth table beside us.

"Hey now, watch out, you bunch of ruffians!" Popcorn Man shakes a fist, but I'm not watching the gremlins. I'm watching the display table piled high with delicious gourmet sweets start to tilt ever so slightly.

The whole thing is going down!

Mrs. Courtney's tower of melt-in-your-mouth pastries teeters and she grabs for them, but she's on the wrong side to do anything but watch it fall.

I lunge for the corner of the table and grab it, holding it with all my might. "The leg!" I pant, "Fix the leg—quick!"

Popcorn Man pulls the gremlin out by his foot and adjusts the table leg. When I let go of the corner, my arms shake from the stress.

"My goodness, I thought I was going to lose it all today. Thank you!" Mrs. Courtney fusses with the display, readjusting the few sweets that tumbled out of place.

I shrug, uncomfortable with all the attention. It's one thing to have a leprechaun and a sasquatch know your name; it's another thing entirely to have a whole crowd of people staring at you. Some of them stalk after the gremlins, who race away, but most keep staring.

My hair! All that running around must've pulled it back too far. Quickly, I run my fingers through my hair, pulling the curtain back down over my face.

Gremlins make trouble and knock things down, but do people stare at them? No, they stare at me. The whole thing is rigged.

"Sophie, I've got your mother's order." The bearded dwarf across the aisle beckons to me.

The crowd parts to let me through, and I hurry to Mr. Gwydd's booth, grateful to have something to do besides stand there and wish the ground would swallow me whole.

"Quick thinking there, holding up the table like that." He rummages through a pile of bags, plucks one with *Marlene* scrawled across it, and hands it over.

I shrug. "Anyone would have done it."

"Ah, but anyone didn't. You did." He runs a long-nailed finger over one of his fairy carvings on the table. Rich wooden dragons, mermaids, centaurs, and more mundane creatures sprawl across his table, some hanging from leather ties, and others bonded with metal or jewels. His tongue slides over his bottom lip and he mumbles to himself—either thinking aloud or speaking to his miniature creations. With a nod, he plucks a necklace from a hook and turns it for me to see the carving: a wooden oval with a paw print hole cut through the center. "Every carving means something. This paw print walks her own path, fearless, but kind. Someone who steps in when others need help and follows her own destiny. I think this one is for you."

Gingerly, I accept the gift and hand him Mom's payment. "Are you sure?"

"I am. Maybe next time it'll be my table that needs saving. Tell your mother hello for me."

"I will. Thank you." The pendant seems to burn in my hand. Is this the last piece? Is it enough? My thumb rubs over the holes left by the paw print. A large one for the center pad, small holes for each toe, and tiny slits for the claws. If the water of inspiration is going to tell me anything at all, it's got to be soon, because I'm drying out fast!

The pendant slips into my pocket easy enough, but I snatch it out again in case my wet jeans ruin the wood finish. With Mom's paper bag under my arm, and my paw print in my fist, I wander toward the library.

An art exhibit lines the sidewalk, and I walk between dozens of canvas paintings.

I pause beside a large oil canvas where a Native American girl stands on a bridge between tall feathered pines, a giant moon rising behind her and reflecting off the water far below. I wonder if the Multnomah princess saw a moon like that. Full of light and magic.

Walking slower, I see another painting of a woman sitting crisscrossed beside a koi pond in the light of the full moon. And beside that, an image of moonlight rolling on the tides. Though different in style and detail, each painting has the moon in all her glory as the center. At the end of the sidewalk, a framed poster reads:

Moon goddess, the bringer of creation, birth,
change, and rebirth. Waxing, her power grows.
Full, she emerges with inner transformation.
Waning, she recedes. And new, she begins again.

Inner transformation.

I stare at the words until a lady walks up to me. "Are you okay, honey?"

"When is the full moon?" I ask.

"A week from next Friday, I believe." She tilts her head. "Just over two weeks. Why?"

"Because it's awesome." I skip to the corner, look both ways, and dash across the road to the library. A smile creeps onto my face, and I feel like giggling because I finally know what to do. I needed each of my special things for my amulet, but it wasn't complete because it's not the right time. The right time is the last piece, the final ingredient: the full moon. In two weeks, I'll have my own transformation, and then it will be goodbye, monster girl, and hello, human.

I spin and laugh. I'm light and dancing like Autumn. My days as a monster are almost over!

FAMILY TREE

Someone listening to leaves rustling in the breeze may swear they hear the tree whispering. Such experiences should not be brushed off as imagination, for they might have heard the secret speech of tree spirits, lesser goddesses known as dryads. Said to have exquisite beauty, these dryads may take on human form, or rest inside their trees. Some, known as hamadryads are bound to the lifespan of their trees: when the tree dies, so does the spirit.

One day eons ago, the god Hermes fell in love with a dryad named Penelopia on the slopes of Mount Cyllene in Arcadia, Greece. Their love was so great, she bore him a son, Pan. The bottom half of Pan's body was furred with cloven hooves like a goat, and horns sprouted from his head. Rather than being ashamed of his strange child, Hermes held him, taught him, and loved him.

Hermes knew that every child has something unique to offer the world—a role to fulfill that only they can play. Rather that squash Pan's individuality, he celebrated it, and the child grew to become the God of Nature.

NINETEEN

Line Up against the Wall

P.E. teachers like to torture students with yoga, running laps, push-ups, and that medieval horror, the rope climb. But when they're in the mood for some real, honest-to-gosh punishment, they break out the team captains. Seriously, lining up against the gym wall and waiting for team captains to call your name is worse than a firing squad.

Today we're in for some sort of special torture—Hades style—because Taggart and his orc friend, Ben, are the captains.

The athletic kids get called to center court first, then the cool kids, then the okay kids (Autumn gets in with this lot), then the captains do a kind of hold-your-nose-and-hope-the-other-guy-gets-stuck-with-the-losers thing. I adjust my sunglasses and sneak a peek at the kids on either side of me: Josh the booger-eater, Zack the spaz, and Nancy the crier. Everyone knows that Nancy will bawl her head off the minute she gets hit, and any ball coming from Josh needs to be disinfected before you touch it, but Zack's okay if you don't mind about a thousand high fives after every hit. I sigh, waiting for Taggart to make his pick.

"Zack!"

"Yes! High five. Fist bump. Lay it on me!" Zack skips and slaps his way down Taggart's team.

Ben sniffs. "Josh!"

Groaning, Taggart folds his arms. "I wanted him. Fine. I'll take Nancy. You can have . . ." He nods my way. "That."

"You're with me." Ben admits defeat.

At least Autumn and I get to be together, even if it is for a game of death by red rubber ball. I grin at her and give my amulet a pat where it bulges under my shirt.

"Ben's team, up against the wall!" Coach Sloan hollers and we scurry to the line under the basketball hoop while Taggart's team forms up at half-court.

Taggart wins the coin toss for first dibs, and we watch the half-dozen red balls as Coach bounces them to the other team. "Ready? And go!" He puffs into his whistle, and the balls fly.

The kids in the middle of our line by Ben spin and duck, lurching for the balls, but mostly missing. Coach starts blowing whistles at each kid that gets tagged by the ball. "Out! Out. You too, Nancy."

Her wail follows her all the way to the bleachers where it melts into little sobs.

Ben snags a ball that ricochets off the wall and launches it at Taggart, who evades it easily and spreads his long goblin fingers, catching the next ball. Awesome for him, but not so great for Josh, who threw it.

"You're out, Josh!" Coach whistles and Josh slinks off to the bleachers, a dejected finger already snaking up his nostril. He probably keeps a few boogers in store for disappointing moments like this.

The game goes on, with Autumn and me on the edge of the group, dodging here and there, but mostly ignored while the *real* players finish their massacre of the main group.

Autumn leaps up so fast, I think maybe her wings popped out, but a ball pings off her shin anyway and she waves goodbye before jogging away. "Bye, Sophie."

"Out! Out! Out! Out!" The carnage ends in a flurry of balls, and suddenly, it's just Taggart, Zack, Ben, and me.

"Seriously?" Taggart points at me and laughs, his hands curled around the ball. "Great team you've got there, Ben."

Swiping a ball off the floor, Ben rolls his shoulders and gets ready to throw. "Whatever. Tag, I can take you out by myself."

"You wish!" The goblin bounces from foot to foot, ready to dive out of the way.

"This one's for you, Tag!" Ben yells, but aims the ball straight for Zack—who is too busy watching Taggart to move until it's too late.

Smack! It bounces off his shoulder, and Coach whistles. "You're out!"

"That's cheating." Zack points at Ben. "You tricked me into watching the wrong thing. You said Taggart!"

"Oh waaa!" Ben waggles his head and wrinkles his nose. "Everyone knows you've got to watch the ball. You fell for that hook, line, and—"

Smack! The ball strikes Ben square in the face, and Taggart roars, "Ha! Sinker!"

"Out!" Coach blows the whistle.

My legs tense. Now it's just the two of us.

Taggart bounces the ball and catches it, chuckling softly so no one but me can hear. "Okay, monster freak. Now it's your turn."

"Come on, Sophie!" Autumn hollers from the stands. "Use your magic fingers!"

I almost look at her, but catch myself and watch Taggart instead.

He bounces the ball and paces like a griffin seeking the best place to pounce. When he grits his teeth, the ball flies almost faster than I can follow. "Magic this."

And I do.

Slick as a peanut rolling across my knuckles, I rotate to let the ball roll up my arm, across my shoulders, and into my upturned palm waiting on the other side. For one perfect moment, I feel my monster grin slide to the surface, sharp and powerful.

He blinks in shock and steps back.

"Taggart, you're out!" The whistle blares and the entire class leaps to their feet, whooping and teasing.

"Hahaha! Out by a girl! Out by *her*. Sucker!"

Both hands around his belly, Ben doubles over, laughing. "Magic this, he says. Ha!"

The class pours onto the floor to get ready for round two, and I run to meet Autumn, but someone shoves me from behind, and I barely keep from sprawling on the floor. My glasses clatter to the ground, and I whip around to grab them, but the goblin's foot finds them first.

Crunch! Splinters of shaded plastic skitter away in a poof of ruin that used to be my favorite pair.

"Oops." His goblin eyes almost glow with rage, and he stoops to pick up what's left of my lost shield. "Sorry. Didn't see them."

"Liar!" Autumn rips the crumpled frame from his outstretched hand. "You did that on purpose! Sore loser! Just because Sophie's better than you, that's no reason to wreck her stuff."

"She only wishes she was better than me." He sneers.

"What's happening here?" Coach wades through the class to where we stand and plucks the ruined frames from Autumn. "Who did this?"

Autumn glares at Taggart but waits for me to say something. Somehow, despite the giant rock in my throat, I manage to whisper, "He pushed me and smashed my glasses."

"Who smashed them?" asks Coach.

With borrowed bravery from Autumn, I point. "The rotten goblin did it."

But then everyone is snickering and Coach's concerned expression darkens. "No name-calling." Probably he knows Taggart's secret identity, but thinks it's easier to lecture me than deal with a real live goblin. "Did you do this?

"I tripped, Coach, so I'm not sure, but I might've accidentally stepped on them."

"We'll discuss it later." Coach blows a whistle and calls kids over from across the gym.

Behind him, the goblin sneers and turns back to the game, calling new names to be on his team.

• • •

At lunch, a flock of girls surround Autumn and me. I keep my hair down over the side of my face, but they talk over and around each other.

"Taggart almost passed out when you caught that ball."

"Did you see his face?"

"I thought I would die. So funny."

"Serves him right."

Heather, a girl with long curly hair and deep brown skin, taps the table. "How did you catch that ball?"

Autumn rolls her eyes. "I told you when it happened. She can do magic. Other things too, but I'm not supposed to say."

Six sets of eyes turn to me. "Why not?"

"You could tell them," Autumn nudges. "They'd understand. Especially after seeing what you can do. They might even be able to help when you have trouble with . . . things."

I know she wants to say goblins, monsters, and things, but my jaw locks up at the thought of explaining. I stare at her so hard, any normal person would crack, but she only brightens with her fairy-powered smile.

"Do you want me to tell them?" She offers.

Everyone at the table seems to hold their breath, all those eyes on me. Autumn thinks these girls should know, so maybe they'd, what? Fight off goblins? What could humans do? I glance at each face quickly. *Were* they all human? No. Not all.

"Sophie?" Autumn's featherlight touch covers my cold, sweaty hand.

I jerk a quick nod, and she squeezes my hand once before eyeing everyone at the table.

"I knew it would be okay! Okay girls, listen up." She leans forward and all the girls huddle close to catch the secrets. "You know the stories about monsters and witches and stuff? They're real. And Sophie can *see* them. Sometimes they hide by pretending to be people and sometimes, people don't even know they aren't human, but she can tell."

"She has magic hands and vision?" Heather peers at my hands as if runes might explode all over my skin. I follow her gaze. Maybe Autumn sees something I don't? What magic am I supposed to know?

Nodding solemnly, Autumn takes a swig of chocolate milk. "Exactly. When Sophie was a baby, a witch cursed her. She's not even human anymore, and that's why she's got powers. Not kidding. You should see what she does with little things. I mean, you've seen the ball thing, but she can make things come alive in her hands and crawl right over her knuckles like bugs—but less gross."

All heads turn to look at me, not in horror, but in wonder.

Autumn is probably waiting for me to show them my monster mark, but I keep staring at my sandwich instead. It's one thing to let Autumn see, but here, in the cafeteria, it's different. No, thank you.

"Anyway, we spent all last week searching for a cure everywhere—at the ocean, in the lair of a spider lady at a garden, at the top of a huge waterfall where a ghost princess lives—everywhere. Because she's got to use the cure on the full moon or else she'll stay a monster forever! Can you imagine? Staying a monster forever? She's only got eleven days to get ready."

"How do you know all this?" the freckled girl beside Heather asks.

"'Cause I'm a fairy. Sophie can see through my disguise.

She's even seen my wings. And Taggart? He's a goblin. Not kidding."

The girls gasp. "Is that true?"

I nod, and the table explodes in questions.

"Whoa! Are there more fairies?"

"Am I one?"

"Who else isn't human?"

Autumn raises a hand. "If you all swear not to tell, Sophie can tell which of you are *more* than human."

In the end, the table had one dryad, a sprite, and a siren-in-training (she even swam laps each week at the pool) but the others were sworn to secrecy.

I pull my amulet out from inside my shirt and show them each piece. The long chain, the crystal, the shell, the white peacock feather, and the wood paw print—all bound together with Witch Barrett's golden wire. Somehow it's almost a relief to show them. Like maybe if there are more people on my side, it'll be easier to break the curse.

"It's so pretty!" Heather runs a dark finger over the feather. "It looks magical to me."

The others agree, and when I slip the chain back over my head, I don't hide it.

A tentative smile steals across my lips and the other girls babble about their newfound otherness. What do dryads, nymphs, and sprites like to do? Should they eat anything different?

And that's when Principal Marsh walks up to the table, Taggart and Zack on her heels. "I understand you've been calling people names, Sophie. You know bullying isn't allowed here."

"I didn't," I stammer.

"You didn't call Taggart retarded? We don't use the R-word here." Her necklaces sway almost to her belt as she props one slimy hand on her hip. Her squid eyes bore right into me.

"Did too," Taggart insists. "Everyone heard you say I was a retarded goblin."

"I didn't!"

"Think very carefully, Sophie. Coach Fowler reports that you did use the R-word."

My voice becomes very small. "I called him a rotten goblin."

"Ha! See? She *did* call me names." Taggart points and wipes his face like he's crying even though he isn't.

No one seems to care that it's a different word, or that it's true that he's a goblin.

Principal Marsh clucks her tongue as if I've been caught stabbing someone in the eye. "Perhaps we need to go have a talk with Mrs. Joy." She reaches for my arm, but I slip off the bench and out of her grasp.

"But what about my glasses?" I stab a finger at Taggart. "He lost and I won, so he smashed my glasses."

"I told you it was an accident!" Goblin boy's lip trembles— *the faker.* "Everyone was running, and then you fell. It wasn't my fault. I swear."

"Was too!" Autumn leaps to her feet. "You did it on purpose."

Zack sidles up beside Taggart and points to me. "You just want to get him in trouble. You called him names the very first day you ever saw him."

"Enough." Principal Marsh's inky eyes dart from me to

Taggart and back. "We'll sort this out at the office. Follow me, Sophie. And bring your lunch. You won't be coming back."

The girls sit subdued while I gather my lunch and step in line behind the swamp monster. As we move away, I feel Taggart's hot goblin breath on the back of my neck. "You think you're so special? Magic this."

But I can't.

MONSTERS ON THE PROWL

The infamous manticore, a well-known hunter of humans, stalks prey in Persia, the jungles of Indonesia, Brazil, and elsewhere. Its melodious, thrumming call lures people close. If they knew the music rises from a throat bristling with three sets of shark-like teeth, they would run far and fast. With the body of a lion, the tail of a scorpion, and the head of a human, the manticore is well-suited for fooling its victims until it's too late. People wading through a bog or high brush sometimes mistake a manticore for a bearded man. Most do not survive such an encounter. If an opponent flees, the manticore's stinger can be thrown and impale the victims from afar.

With such a thing prowling through the trees, it's no wonder children are taught to be wary of any enticing song that would lure them into the jungle. Those who live to adulthood know that if something sounds too good to be true, it is wise to stop and think for a moment instead of following blindly into destruction.

TWENTY

The Secret Is Out

Secrets are kind of like holding a bag full of vampire bats: it's a whole lot easier to let them out than to stuff them back in.

Showing one friend, you might lose a bat. No big deal—unless that friend talks you into opening that bag wider for more friends to see. Pretty soon, there are more bats outside than in.

Today, I think I'm mostly holding an empty bag with all my secrets flown everywhere. I can almost feel them watching me, hanging from the ceiling and window arches in the halls. They flap their wings and watch me with beady eyes and fanged grins, waiting to suck my blood.

"Remember the Golden Rule!" Mom calls when I step out of the car. Ever since the email from Principal Marsh two days ago, Mom's brain has been stuck on repeat. *Be kind, be nice, don't hurt people's feelings, you know what it feels like so you should know better,* blah, blah, blah. The worst part is that I'm grounded from my book. Walking around without my monster book feels like I've lost an arm, or maybe an eyeball.

So fine, I'm a monster on the inside too. Whatever. At least I have a couple new friends. Heather waves to me as she walks to her desk. She sits on the opposite side of the classroom from me, but it's nice to know she's there. Her hair glitters with beads threaded onto the tips of a hundred long black braids that she flicks over her shoulder. Flowers dangle from her ears and a silver leaf necklace shines over her dark green blouse. I suppose she always has dressed a little like a dryad, but now it's even more.

The bell rings, and Mrs. Joy stands at the front of the class. "Class, pull out your journals. We'll start the day with ten minutes of creative writing."

Papers rustle and a book falls to the floor as everyone pulls their composition notebooks out. I hurry to do the same, but when I open my notebook, a big monster with dagger-like teeth and googly eyes stares back at me from the page. The whole thing is scrawled in permanent marker.

Mrs. Joy starts her rounds at the other side of the classroom. "I want to see you all writing."

I quickly flip to the next page, but a dragon-like drawing takes up that whole page too.

Flip.

A harpy with stupid sharp wings.

Flip.

A blob with a gash for a mouth.

Flip.

A big eye with tentacles for lashes staring up from the page.

Flip.

I know your secret.

Flip.

I know what you are.

The last word is scratched hard enough to tear the page, the red ink bleeding several pages deeper into the notebook.

I slam the book shut and close my eyes, my face burning so hot, it might even glow red under my curtain of hair.

Maybe I just imagined it? I peek inside the book once more, and let it fall shut again. Nope. It's there.

"Sophie, can you open your notebook?" Mrs. Joy's yellow skirt brushes my elbow.

I shake my head.

"Why not?"

I mumble. "It's full."

"Surely not." She slips it off my desk, and I wish the floor would swallow me whole. "It's okay if you can't think of anyth—" She gives a tiny gasp, which is bad.

Then snickers and giggles bubble up from several kids in the class, and that's worse.

"You're right. This isn't suitable at all. I think I have another notebook with fresh pages." A couple minutes later, she slips a bright-pink notebook with glittery flowers onto my desk. "There you go. I think this one suits you better."

I'm not so sure. The sparkles and colors might fit a fairy, but me? I try to ignore the part of me that thinks the first one suited me perfectly. Suits me right down to my monster bones.

When recess comes, Autumn, Heather, and I skip to the trees at the side of the playground with the other girls. More girls follow us, and I try to talk about "normal" stuff like games, and school and whatever, but then Heather pulls several girls forward.

"I told them you'd know what they were. Can you tell?"

The first couple are easy. I mean, anyone can tell a siren and a sphinx, but then the third girl stalks forward and I squirm. I don't want to be the one to tell a strzyga that I knew her secret—especially not in front of anyone.

"I don't know."

She narrows her eyes and picks at a black-painted nail. "What do you mean you don't know?"

I shrug.

"You knew what they were. So why not me? Just tell me."

I mumble, "A strzyga."

"I've never heard of that. What is it? Some kind of fairy? It sounds dumb. Did you just make that up?" She steps closer, but Autumn flits between us.

"Don't blame Sophie if you don't like what you are. She can't help it. You can't be something different just because you feel like it. You are what you are."

The bell rings, and I'm glad for the sunlight overhead. I don't know if I'd be brave enough to name a strzyga if it was dark. At least the sun keeps her owl wings and second set of fangs hidden. Her two hearts probably beat all the time, day or night, but the rest of it gets scarier when then sun goes down. My lips squish up, and I try to decide if she really didn't know what she was, or if it was some kind of test.

She steps into the shadow of the hallway and looks back at me, her eyes so dark they're almost black holes.

If it was a test, I seriously hope I passed.

I pat my amulet and step inside. Only nine more days. Then everything changes.

Autumn will probably still be my friend after I'm human, but fairies are nice like that.

"Class." Mrs. Joy stands at the front of the room. "To prepare for the spelling test Friday, I've cut all the spelling words apart. Pay close attention to the words today, because tomorrow you'll need to write them by heart." She shakes a glass bowl full of little papers for all to see. "When I come by, grab your word, but don't peek! When it's your turn, read the word, run up to the board, and write it out. Write it nice and big so everyone can read it. If we can get through all of them in eight minutes or less, I'll give you an extra eight minutes at recess tomorrow!"

As the bowl goes around, we grab a folded paper and lay it on our desks, front and center so no one can cheat.

A couple of boys slip between my desk and the one in front on their way to the pencil sharpener, but the first one swings his sweater as he goes and knocks my paper to the floor.

"Hey!" I start to stand, but the first boy is already bending to pick it back up.

"Whoops." He drops it onto the desk, a little more wrinkled than it was before. They sharpen their pencils and head back to their desks.

At her desk, Mrs. Joy pulls out a stopwatch and raises a hand. "Ready? And go!"

The kid at the far end of the room bolts out of his seat, writes *Environment* on the board and dashes back to his seat. Then Heather runs up and scrawls *Emotion* below the first word. On and on it goes. *Friction, Faction, Fraction, Geometry,* the first row's done and we're onto the next. They write so fast, the marker squeals, and almost bounces off the tray when they drop it. The next row finishes and kids are waiting, half out of their seats for their turn. "Five minutes left and three rows to go!" Mrs. Joy waves her stopwatch.

"Go! Go!" Zack and Ben pound the desk as Taggart runs his word to the board, *Harmony.*

Figures he'd get an easy word like that.

The next row's done and my mouth feels like I've been chewing on the dry eraser. It's just a word. I can do this. *I can do this!*

The kid in front of me bolts for the board, and I grab my paper in a sweaty fist. *I'm ready.*

Melody. He plops into his seat and I'm off, speeding to the front of the room. I can do this! Marker ready, I unfold my paper—and freeze.

I can't do this.

"Come on, Sophie!" Autumn cheers, and Heather and the girls call for me to hurry.

"Aw, man! She's gonna make us lose!" Zack whines, and others join in. "Just write the word!"

The paper shakes in my hand and my breath is thin, like sky eels sucked all the air out of the room.

I hear Mrs. Joy stop the clock and lean closer. "Sophie, do you know how to spell your word? Do you want my help?"

I shake my head. I know this word.

"Well then, best hurry!" Her cheerful tone makes it worse, because I don't want to disappoint her, or Autumn, or anyone. And if I don't write it, it will be *my* fault they all lose.

"One minute left," she warns, and I grip the pen harder.

Fine. It's not like I have any secrets left anyway.

I write fast in hard block letters, then stand there as half the class erupts in laughter that thrums inside my head with the power of a thousand manticores.

The next kid in my row wrenches the pen from my numb fingers and writes *Synonym* a half second before the last one writes *Trapezoid* and the whole class stands and cheers.

I plunk in my seat, and Mrs. Joy is at my side. "Sophie, may I see your paper, please?"

My fist opens and she plucks the wrinkled slip from my sweaty palm.

"This is not the paper I gave you." She turns on the class. "Who did this?"

This only makes the orcs and goblin laugh harder and point at me. I can't even muster the strength to pull my hair down or hide because what's the point? Everyone knows. It's written there right on the board so everyone can see.

MONSTER.

MONSTER RAMPAGES

It's a well-known fact that now and then, monsters rampage and destroy a community or even an entire city. History remembers some of the places monsters have wiped out, such as Sodom and Gomorrah, Babylon, Roanoke, and even Chernobyl, but many more were never recorded. In the western United States alone, dozens of ghost towns sit empty with no one left to tell what happened to the inhabitants.

Rather than looking for individual motivations for such devastation, it's better to think of these monsters as forces of nature. Wind isn't inherently evil, but tornadoes lay waste to everything in their way much like monsters set on a path to destroy. The bigger the monster, the stronger their glamour, and the harder to prove the cause of the destruction. Whether it's Gojira of Japan, leviathans from the Middle East, or some other enormous creature, when they attack, people must hunker down and hope the storm passes them by. Such creatures give free reign to their emotions and vent their pain and anger through unchecked devastation. When they've exhausted their fury, they wearily stand amidst ruins of civilization and remain unfulfilled, unhappy, and alone.

Remember, dear reader, the truth these creatures will never understand: emotion is a powerful force, and while it is easy to use it to destroy, it is far nobler to build. Things once said, cannot be unsaid. Whether emotion-fueled rampages strike a city of millions or a single person's heart, painful scars are left behind. And some scars are invisible to all except those who carry them.

TWENTY-ONE

The Day My Head Became a Volcano

I held a tarantula once at a pet store. It was actually kinda soft. And boa constrictor scales are awesomesauce. I don't mind spiders, or crickets, or beetles, or caterpillars, or millipedes, or even slugs—unless you step on one barefoot. Pretty much anything creepy-crawly is okay with me . . . except ants. Probably it seems silly because ants are so tiny. But that's the problem with ants: they are never, ever alone. As soon as you see one sneaky bug crawling up your pants, there's already a whole army of them pouring up your leg like a nasty upside-down waterfall of super soldiers. With ants, it's never one problem, it's a million at once and they all have pincers.

Today, everywhere I turn, the problems just keep crawling up.

Mrs. Joy keeps attendance by having us flip our card in a pocket on the wall with our name on it. My card used to be a flower, but today somebody switched it to a T. rex with extra fangs and horns. Better to be absent than to flip that card around.

Taggart laughs as I leave the card untouched.

Kids straggle into the classroom, flip their card, and go to their seats as usual, until the strzyga girl walks in and pins me with her death glare. She pushes Heather aside and marches straight to my desk.

"A demon?" she hisses under her breath. "You told everyone I was some kinda owl-demon?"

"I didn't want to tell," I start, but she leans closer, a pencil in her fist.

"I don't know what kinda psycho game you're playing at, but I know what's *really* going on. You're not special. You're not even a monster. What you are is straight-up *crazy*."

"You made me tell you." Didn't she remember that I tried not to say?

She grits her teeth at me, and I wonder if the second set of teeth is dropping down behind them. She's probably mad enough to rip my throat out right here if there weren't all these people around to see.

"You're a disease, Sophie." The pencil snaps in her hand.

As she walks to her desk, tremors start in my hands so I sit on them. I focus on my amulet, and just being close to it makes me feel better. My monster book probably would have helped, but Mom still won't let me bring it. Mrs. Joy gets up and says stuff about a talent show assembly next month and we look at books and people talk, but it's not until I take the amulet off and hold it tight with both hands that my brain starts working again. Do strzyga have some kind of telepathic powers to shut people's brains down? I'll look it up when I get home.

Yesterday my lunch money disappeared from my cubby again, so today, I slip it inside my desk with my amulet for safe-keeping. As class goes on, my brain settles down a little, and I do the schoolwork. If I get nervous, I just slip my hands inside my desk to feel my amulet again. Safe and sound. Only seven more days till the full moon. Then everything will be better. It will all be fine.

At recess, Autumn wiggles her fingers and opens them for us to see. "Yesterday, I touched three flower buds in my nana's yard, and today they opened! I think my powers are getting stronger. After school I'm going to try it on more. Maybe I can make things grow faster too!"

The dryads and nymphs nod. "I'll try it on my flowers to-night."

It would be cool hearing about their powers, except that I can't shake the heebie-jeebies. Nothing by the playground seems wrong, and not by the school either. In fact, it's too quiet. Where'd the goblin and orcs go?

I stand on tippy-toe searching the tires and jungle gym, finally spotting them by the trees on the far side of the playground. But it's not the normal group of creatures. The strzyga girl is in the middle with a few other kids. All of them huddle around, sneaking glances at me.

I know it's me they're looking at, and not the group, because when our eyes meet, the strzyga girl and Taggart grin wickedly. Whatever they're planning, it's not gonna be good.

We're barely inside the school for two minutes after recess when the fire alarm goes off.

"Line up like we practiced." Mrs. Joy herds us into orderly lines and off we go.

"Do you think it's a drill or a real fire?" Autumn asks from behind me.

I shrug. Who knows?

Twenty minutes later, they buzz us back inside. It wasn't a real fire, but it wasn't scheduled either. Principal Marsh steps into the classroom and points at Zack. "Come with me. The fire chief and your parents would like a word."

Everyone's eyes go wide and watch his walk of shame till he's out the door.

"Okay, now, back to your reading books." With a snap of her fingers, Mrs. Joy pulls everyone back. We all hurry to grab our things out of the desks and I do too, except . . .

I scooch back from my desk and peer inside. My books are there, and so are my notebooks, pencils, and lunch money, but that's it.

My amulet is gone.

I can't breathe.

The chair falls over backward as I rip book after book out of the desk and let them fall to the floor. Notebook pages flutter, pencils scatter, and my lunch money pings off the linoleum tiles, a quarter spinning like a top till it wobbles and falls flat.

Only empty space remains inside.

"Sophie? Are you alright?" Mrs. Joy asks.

I can feel my classmates' eyes boring into me. But for this one moment, I don't care. None of it matters. Not what they think of me, not what they'll say. The only thing that matters at all is that someone took my amulet.

It's irreplaceable.

Rage boils inside my head until my eyeballs almost pop. I jump to my feet, my fists and teeth clenched so hard I can barely speak. My hands shake, and I scan the classroom. One of them took it. It had to be. "Give. It. Back."

"Are you missing something? Is that what this is about?" The teacher tries to step in, but I'm too angry to back off, too furious to give way.

The strzyga girl smirks, and I shove past Mrs. Joy and run over to her.

"Do you have it?" I hiss.

She stares up at the thing on my face and blinks innocently. "Have what?"

My face burns so hot my monster mark's probably flashing red. "You *know* what! Did you take it?"

I let the barriers fall, my monster sliding ever closer to the surface, and she flinches when I lean close. "Where is it?"

"Sophie!" Mrs. Joy touches my arm, but I twist out of her grasp.

"What did you do with it!" I yell, and the strzyga girl's eyes flit to Taggart and back.

"I don't know what you—"

But I'm already storming over to the goblin who sits there with a big smile on his face like this is the best thing to happen in the history of things.

I want to claw that stupid grin right off his face, and I slap both hands on his desk. "What did you do with my amulet? *Where is it?*"

"Sophie, that's enough!" Fury laces Mrs. Joy's words, but I still struggle against her.

"You don't understand. He pulled the fire alarm so he could steal it. I need it. I *need* it!"

"Need what?" Taggart giggles. "A new brain?"

"Taggart. Enough," Mrs. Joy snaps. "Do you have something of Sophie's?"

His eyes go big and wide like a stupid baby cow, and he blinks up her. "I would never. You can search my desk even."

Liar. Seething magma pools in my gut and builds, bubbling, steaming—another second and I'll explode.

Snickers echo around the classroom, and everyone's watching the show. I don't even try to hide my mark, which pulses with every beat of my heart, the super-heated lava throbbing through my face.

"Are you sure? She seems to think you know something."

The strzyga girl fakes a sneeze behind me. "Crazy!"

Taggart bursts out laughing and so do the orcs.

But not me. I'm not laughing at all. Everything goes very still inside, the split second before the storm. If I had claws, he'd be dead. I grip the edges of his desk and heave with all my might, flipping it over into the aisle. Papers fly everywhere and his face goes white as he scrambles back, but I'm already closing in.

"Give it back!" I scream.

Something jerks me up, and I'm almost lifted off my feet.

"We're going to the office. Now." Clipped words fall from Mrs. Joy's lips, and I know she's truly angry. "I think we've all had more than enough. Taggart, follow me. The rest of you, clean up the mess."

She doesn't let go of my shirt until we're way down the hall, and even then, she grabs my arm again when I try to turn and look back at Taggart. I know he's smirking with his stupid goblin lips because I can feel it right through the back of my head.

He starts to whistle but Mrs. Joy snaps, "No whistling."

He settles into a soft hum, a mocking theme song in tune with each step.

At the office, the fire chief stands shoulder to shoulder with a man and a woman looming over Zack, who looks a lot less cocky than he did a few minutes ago.

Principal Marsh raises an eyebrow as her inky eyes squirt over to inspect us. "What's this?"

"I think the fire alarm was a ploy for these two to steal something from Sophie here," Mrs. Joy says, "but right now, she needs some time to think about her actions as well."

HABITAT

Monsters make their homes in environments that best suit their needs. Abominable snowmen love the ice and snow, the Mongolian death worm slides with no eyes or nose through the sands of the Gobi Desert, and swamp monsters thrive in the marshes of the world. In Honey Island, Louisiana, the local swamp monster is known to have three-toed, webbed feet. It lumbers along in a humanoid shape, possibly a slimy cousin to the more popular Bigfoot, which prefers dry forests. In Africa, the Mokele-mbembe swamp monster is less like a man and more like the Loch Ness Monster with a long, serpentine neck and an enormous body. Our planet boasts a wide variety of landscapes, and each one comes with monsters of every shape and size.

The most important thing to remember, for both creatures and humans, is that whatever their shape, color, height, or background, our world is wide enough to have a place for them all.

TWENTY-TWO

Cerberus Would like Me— for Dinner

It took most of the afternoon for the school counselor to speak with Taggart—who of course swears he's innocent— and Zack, and Autumn, and the strzyga girl, and everyone else who thought they knew anything. Finally, she calls me into her office and closes the door. She talks, but the sounds garble in my head. None of it makes sense. I let the words mush together like pudding sliding in one side and out the other. Gooey, muffled nothing.

Finally, she shakes her head and stands. A few minutes later, she returns with Mrs. Joy and I shrink a little, remembering her anger. I think she catches the movement because she tuts and kneels beside me. "Sophie, I didn't mean to scare you. Truth be told, I think you scared me a little today."

Her eyes are beautiful, trusting and kind. But there's a line of worry at the corners that wasn't there before. I've hurt her, and I know it.

"I'm concerned about what I've heard today. Everyone loves a little make-believe, that's what books and movies are for, but there's a difference between imagination and real life." She pauses like I'm supposed to say something, but there's nothing for me to say. She's a human. She wouldn't understand.

"I know Taggart and his friends have been hounding you. I can't prove they switched the notes, but I'm sure they did. I believe you that he took your necklace you've been wearing."

She believes me? Her image blurs and I wipe my eyes with the back of my hand.

"Oh, honey. You *know* I care about you. I need you to be completely honest with me, and I'll do my very best to understand."

I stare out the window, kind of hollow inside. What did it matter if she understood?

Leaning closer, her gentle voice mirrors her kind face. "Sophie, please. If you tell me why this amulet is so important to you, I might be able to help you get it back."

My eyes snap to hers. I'd heard Taggart's protest of innocence all the way down the office hallway. No way is he going to admit to anything. My voice croaks, sore from all the yelling earlier. "Really?"

"Truly. Help me understand."

Part of me aches to tell her, and maybe it'll be easier to do it since I've practiced with Autumn and the others, but still. She's a grown-up.

She taps a white rabbit with a clock on the counselor's desk and smiles. "I've believed as many as six impossible things before breakfast. C'mon, Sophie. Let me try to understand."

I focus on breathing. In. Out. All the fire has gone, and it's just me, empty. Lost.

"Do you believe that some people are not really human?"

The earth stops turning for a moment and everything is silent. Waiting.

I nod. Barely, but enough.

"Your friend Autumn is a fairy?" she coaxes.

Another nod.

"Heather is a dryad?"

"Yeah."

"And Taggart?" She waits, but I say nothing. "Taggart is a goblin?"

Relief washes over me in soft waves. She believes me!

"How did you find out what they are?"

"My book told me," I whisper.

"And what does your monster book tell you about yourself?" Almost like she has a strange magic of her own, I feel the pull of her questions. The string unraveling my most awful secret tugs and tugs, and my throat closes up. Can't she see I can't talk? Forget talking—I can barely breathe.

"Slow down, honey. Take a deep breath. That's it. No one's going to hurt you." Her hand rests against my cheek, the fingertips light against my monster mark, and I focus on her steady touch. "You're okay. It's all going to be okay. I like you." She waits till my eyes meet hers again and talks slowly so I can't mistake her words. "I like the real you, Sophie. Not an act, not pretend. I care about *you*. Nothing you say can change that. Now, I'm asking one more time. What do you think you are? Human? Or something else?"

"Something else." I mouth the words, but no sound comes out.

"Can you tell me what?"

My lips quiver as they come together to make the whispered sound. "Monster."

"Oh, honey." She rises up and cups my head against her shoulder, rocking me. I panic at first, but then melt into her hug. I told, and she loves me anyway. Maybe I could tell Mom. Maybe there was another way to do this.

She pulls away. "Thank you for telling me. Can you wait here?"

I nod, and that's the last person I see for a long, long time. Voices come and go outside the door, and eventually I recognize Mom and Koschei's voices in the mix of grown-up talk.

I sink lower in the seat and wish I could disappear right through the floor. Just open up a shaft and let me fall through the netherworld, straight to Cerberus. He'd probably wait with his three doggy heads, all of their tongues hanging out, trying to decide which mouth gets to eat me alive.

Finally, the door opens and Mom and Koschei stand there with Principal Marsh. Mom's face flushes white then pink, her lips mashed in a line like she doesn't know what to say. We all look at each other for a moment and then Koschei steps back with a hand to the side, offering me a path through. "C'mon, kiddo. We're taking you home."

The hallway is empty and Koschei's work boots squeak like dying rubber ducks all the way down the hall, but none of us talk. Maybe monsters aren't allowed to be in the school at all. Maybe I'll never have to come back. I could wait for Autumn in her fairyland everyday till she gets home from school. Pretty sure they won't kick *her* out.

Everybody loves fairies.

ZOMBIE OUTBREAKS

Throughout history, zombies have been known to pop up in different parts of the world.

Ancient Greece may have been the first nation to deal with zombies. Archeologists found many burial sites with heavy rocks piled on the dead to make it impossible for them to rise.

In the Bible, zombies make a brief appearance when Ezekiel had a vision where he raised bones from the dead, which initially had no breath in them.

African slaves in Haiti dreamt of death as a means to escape their horrible plight, but they feared to take that escape because they claimed such a death would transform them into a *zombi*, forced to roam the plantations forever, not alive, but not dead, never free to return to their homeland.

Modern movies would have people believe that zombies can multiply at astounding rates, start a viral outbreak, and take over the world, but such is not the case. It takes great suffering to change a person into a zombie—a wretched state in which death is not a release, but living is impossible.

Should a person caught in the transformation from human to zombie wish to reverse the change, the greatest elixir is gratitude—for family, for friends, for health, and for life. Once a seed of gratitude takes root in the zombie-infected heart, the sorrows fade, and the human is reborn.

TWENTY-THREE

Five Days to Go

Well, it's been two days since I got suspended from school and I'm still breathing, so that's good. But I still don't have my amulet back, and my chances of getting it back are probably a big fat zero. In five days, the full moon is gonna come and go, and I'll still be the same because nothing can fix this.

Mom went on a crazy cooking binge and made pie, cookies, rolls, tapioca pudding, and homemade chicken noodle soup. She smiles at me over the counter loaded with food like it's the most normal thing in the world. In fact, once she got over the shell-shocked zombie look that first day, she's been smiling at me nonstop, which is almost as creepy.

I eat as much as I can, but there's only the two of us and she's made enough for the whole neighborhood. Everything is wonderful except the brussels sprouts. (Everybody knows brussels sprouts are actually just mutant cabbage babies. Gross.)

Mom moves robotically from one recipe to the next, cook-ing, cleaning, watching me, and smiling. It's so weird, I almost wonder if a wraith has jumped in and slurped out her brain, leaving only this forced cheerful thing that pretends to be my normal mom. I don't think it's true, but just to be sure I wrap my silver necklace around her wrist. Wraiths totally hate silver.

Her fork scratches against the plate, and I think she's mostly pushing the green stuff around. I bet she doesn't like it any bet-ter than I do. She sighs. "Sophie, are you happy here? Did I do the right thing moving here?"

I choke on the mutant cabbage and cough, my hand catch-ing most of it before it flies across the table. "It's fine. Same as anywhere, except Autumn is here, so that's better."

"At your old school, you never had an episode like you did the other day. Is it because I'm working? Was it something I did?"

"No, Mom."

"Is it because of your dad being, well, gone?" Her question is soft, like she's afraid of the answer. I know how much those words cost her. She never talks about him. Never ever.

"No. You didn't do anything." I set the fork down and push the plate away. "It's me. It's my fault."

"Sophie."

Tired of it all, I stand up. "I'm not hungry."

She sighs as I retreat to my room, but what else is there to say? I pause just long enough to swipe my monster book off the shelf and sneak it onto my bed.

The pages greet me like old friends. Harpies, Bandage Man, Kabandhas, Nāga, jorōgumo, gremlins, Caribou Man, and Koschei the Deathless.

His skin hangs from his bones, the mutilated bits dripping off his face, and his clawed hand grips the horse's mane. Whirlwinds surround him, and he clasps a maiden in his other arm, ready to carry her away.

I try to feel the same worry about him that I should, but it's too much work to try. He's been here every day after work, talking to Mom, making her smile, pretending everything's normal. Maybe he only used to carry women away, but now he's retired from all that. Could a demon get tired of stealing people? If anyone asked me that a month ago, I'd say, *no way!* But now, I'm not so sure. Either he really is trying to be a better creature than he was made to be, or he's the best faker in the whole world.

Rain splashes against the window, and I watch the streaks squiggle down the pane. One thing about Portland is that it rains a lot. Like, a really lot. Rain is the reason our slugs are big enough to carry off small puppies. I'm not sure how giant wood ants relate to rain, but I'm blaming those on the rain too. The green everywhere is thanks to rain, but really, I'd trade a brown crusty plant here and there for more sunny days.

Hugging the book to my chest, I flop on my back. From here, I can see the tiny dragon and unicorn figurines on my shelves. I have the occasional mermaid too, but other so-called mythical creatures are hard to find at the dollar store.

Rumbling shakes the house and I don't have to look to know that Koschei is here again. Mom says he's taken her for a ride on the Harley, and that it was like riding a growling rocket through the streets. The front door opens and Mom's voice carries down the hallway. "Hey, Kelsi. Done already?"

There's a smack which sounds suspiciously like kissy noises

but I try to ignore it. "Things went a little better than planned so I thought I'd come hang out with my best girls."

That was girls with an "S." Two of us. Maybe he'll take us both away someday and we'll never have to worry about school and goblins ever again.

Chairs scrape and dishes clink as Mom sets a plate for him.

"Sophie's principal called today and said she's recommending I place Sophie in counseling. Really, it was more of a put-her-in-counseling-or-I'll-call-social-services kind of a thing."

"Counseling's not so bad. I've done it. I think most of us that survive being wounded go through it."

"But it's not her fault. They're bullying her, that's all. I've been looking at schools over in Gresham. It's not too far from work, and we could still see you, but we could try a different school and—"

"You know what I think of running from her problems. She needs to talk it out and figure out what's real and what's not."

"But the kids are teasing her, *stealing* from her! That boy was given the same suspension as Sophie, but they'll return to school at the same time. How can she go back there?"

"If it makes you feel better, I could go with her for a day," he offers. "That'd give them somebody else to talk about and take some pressure off her."

"But what about when you're not there? What about when she's alone?" She sighs. "No. I've put things off long enough. We need to move forward with the surgery. If the mark was gone, she could be normal and none of this would be a problem."

I suck a breath and hug the book so hard the corners dig into my skin. In five days, I would have been normal. But

Taggart took that all away. Stupid goblin, and stupid strzyga for helping him.

"If it's not her hemangioma, it would be something else. Cutting off the blood tumor won't change the fact that she can't stand on her own two feet."

Mom sniffles, which makes me feel like dirt—*again*.

"Aw, Marlene, c'mere. It's not so bad. Tell you what. Let's ask Mrs. Barrett to watch Sophie for the afternoon, and I'll take you to the show. How long have you been stuck inside with the rain? Two days? Three? Time for a night off."

She's quiet for a long time, and I listen hard, my heart beating in time with the tick of the clock.

Her voice is low and full of pain. "The school counselor said that if nothing changes, Sophie would never be normal. That she'd never fit in."

It's the same thing I've always thought, but it stuns me to hear Mom say it out loud.

"Maybe so. But you know what? Normal is overrated."

Mom laughs, and I wonder again if having a demon around would be such a bad thing. We already have one monster in the house.

She muses, "Maybe you're right. But you know what?"

"What?" His chuckle is muffled a bit, like maybe his face is squished against her hair.

"I'm glad you're here."

I let that sink in, and nod.

Me too.

THE WORTH OF A SOUL

Did Pinocchio have a soul when he was a wooden boy? Some say he gained a soul when he transformed into a real boy. Likewise, did Frankenstein's monster have a soul when it was created by the doctor? Perhaps he grew one as he learned more about what it was to be—or not be—human. This question of souls is hotly debated among cryptozoologists who relish the study of monsters. A soul is the essence of a living being— the special part that lives on after death. Some say that only humans have souls, but most would extend that same gift to beloved pets. So where is the line between humans and soulless abominations? I suspect monsters themselves are not sure of the answer, for they seem to fear death more than anything. Perhaps the empti- ness caused by living without a soul is the reason why demons are so fixated on making deals to steal them from humans. A word to the wise, if you are reading this, you have a soul of infinite worth. Do not trade it away for anything.

TWENTY-FOUR

Shattered

Sophie!" Autumn's hug almost strangles me to death. "You're here! I've totally missed you. It's been days and days, but you're here so everything's cool now, right?"

I nod and let the fairy-powered sunshine seep inside me. Fairy friends make everything better.

"We won't be too long. It's just dinner and a movie, so three hours maybe?" Kostchei hesitates, one hand on the door-knob.

"Oh, don't worry 'bout a thing, dearie. Out with you. Our Sophie will be fine." With a flutter of apron, Witch Barrett shoos him out the door and grins at us both. "Now then, what say ye to a fresh batch of cookies?"

"Yes! Oh, please? Please?"

She hums in approval. "Thought so. Now off ye go. I don't need any lasses underfoot while I work."

"Oh! I wanted to show you something!" Autumn tugs me

208

out the door and we're off through the tunnel into fairyland again. "It's a surprise! I mean, not to me. I've seen it. But it was a surprise when I first saw it a couple days ago. And now it's a surprise for you!"

"What is it?" I stand up and brush the dirt from my knees.

"Over here! Come on!" She dashes ahead and I hurry after, both of us bopping the ferns on the head as we pass. Our steps slow when we reach the castle and she twirls around and reaches for my face. "Close your eyes. No peeking!"

"What—?"

"No peeking!"

"Fine." I scrunch my eyes up tight.

Something rustles in the trees and bonks against the shed, then drops to the ground.

"Okay! You can look! Ta-da!"

A rope swing hangs from a branch way up above the castle and spins slowly in place with a board tied to the end.

"You got a swing?"

"Yes!" Her fists pump, and she does a little jig. "Isn't it so amazing? I was looking at the tree and I saw the rope, and I thought it was a snake, but it wasn't."

We take turns pushing each other and spinning round and round on the swing till we're sick, our hair flying like we're sprites riding the wind.

After my third turn, I slide off the swing and flop on the grass. Hopefully there're no slugs, but I'm too dizzy to check. I watch the trees spin and spin till the world finally stops moving.

"So, what are you going to do?" Legs straddling the rope seat, Autumn drifts lazily with the breeze, her golden hair lifting softly as if curled by invisible hands.

"About what?"

A couple of birds dart over our clearing and startle a squirrel who scolds from a pine tree on the other side. It might be Bob, but I can't tell from this far away.

"The full moon is in just a few days, right? Can you make another amulet?"

"No." I sit up and scooch back out of her way. "I think making the magic was a one-time thing. It's gone, Autumn. I don't know what to do."

"So, you're giving up?" She frowns. "I thought you had to change back into a human. Do you want to be a monster forever?"

"No. Of course not."

"Well then, we'll try again. We've got a few days."

I try to smile, but I'm not feeling it. Snatching a stone off the ground, I toss it up and catch it with the back of my hand, flipping it end over end from my palm to the back of my fingers. Make a new amulet? I might as well grow a new leg. "I don't know."

She squats in front of me, her sparkly blouse sending sunbeams in every direction. "Last time we started with a crystal, right? My nana has crystals on the shades and in the windows. You could use one of those. Especially if you give it back when you're done. Do you think the magic would make the crystal disappear when the cure was done?"

"I don't know." The first crystal had called to me, had made us fight for it. It seems like cheating to grab just any old crystal.

"Let's have some cookies and ask Nana."

When I don't jump right up, she tugs my arm. "Come on! It's better than nothing!"

Near the back door, we hear voices and Autumn puts her hand out to stop me. Listening.

" . . . Without a donor, what can we do?"

Like watercolors washed away in a storm, the laughter dies in Autumn's voice. "They're talking serious stuff. Better to go around to the front door, I think."

We slip inside and settle around the steaming plate of cookies on the coffee table. The first bite is heaven—if heaven was filled with gooey, chocolatey, taste-bud-exploding perfection. I moan, "Oh, wow."

Autumn's eyes flutter with happiness. "I think I died. It's so good. I'm dead now. Bury me." She grabs another cookie and rolls under the table.

Smirking, I nudge her farther under with my foot. "Haha! More for me."

"Wait! I'm alive! It's a miracle." She claws her way out the other side of the table and raises both hands triumphantly. "Ta-da!"

"So now you're a zombie-fairy?" I giggle.

"Probably." She stuffs another cookie in her mouth.

Grown-up voices drift in from the kitchen. "—it just keeps getting worse. He's fading right in front of my eyes, and there's nothing I can do to stop it."

We stare at each other across the table in silence, and flashes of grief flit across Autumn's face as she fights to stay in control.

Finally, I whisper. "Should we sneak back out?"

A blonde strand winds around her finger as she chews on the end. "Yeah. But first, we need to get you that crystal."

Alarm quivers down my spine. "But we didn't ask. What if she gets mad?"

"Shh. I'll tell her it was my idea if she even notices. Nana won't mind. Besides, you can bring it back when you're done—if there's anything left of it." She stands and studies the many crystal pendants hanging from lamps, curtains, and window frames. "Wouldn't it be amazing if it turned into a glowing ball that floated straight inside you? I bet that would cure you. But then you couldn't give it back."

Grasshoppers hop around inside my chest, and I can't decide if it's a *good* nervous thing, or maybe a prickly scared nervous thing. "Autumn, wait. Maybe we shouldn't—"

"Oh!" She gasps. "That one! See it?"

I follow her pointing finger to a teardrop-shaped crystal hanging from a gold thread high up near the top of the window frame. It's easy to believe it's magic with the way it throws rainbows on the curtains around it. Maybe making a new amulet isn't such a crazy idea after all.

Light as a soap bubble, Autumn hops up onto the chair and steps from the seat cushion to the arm of the chair.

Hands clasped in front of my chest, I hold my breath. The crystal is so high! Can she even reach it?

One hand on the back of the chair, she shifts her weight so only one foot is on the chair, the other rests gingerly on the windowsill. She shoots me a wicked grin and touches the window with one hand for balance, her other hand reaching high overhead. Her middle finger brushes the bottom of the crystal and it sways a little, splashing rainbows across the room in a jumbled dance.

"Almost," she whispers, and darts up one more time,

stretching for all she's worth. Rainbows disappear as her hand clamps down over the crystal, and she sways. "Got it!"

Except we both realize at the same time that there's no way to get it down, not without breaking the thread or something.

"Autumn! What on earth?" Her mom stands in the doorway, her hands on her hips.

"Mom!" Startled, Autumn twists, and teeters on the edge of the chair arm, her foot slipping right off the windowsill.

I see what will happen a split second before disaster strikes. But no matter how fast I rush forward, I'm not fast enough, and she falls. Not onto the chair, but onto the tiny table where Witch Barrett's special cups rest on their delicate saucers.

With a horrible crash, Autumn tumbles to the floor, along with the whole table and the tiny Goddesses of Ireland. One saucer bounces and rolls, another skids across the floor. The first cup bounces off Autumn's hand and ends up upside down, but the second cup falls farther than the rest and we watch it as if in slow motion.

It spins in the air, arcing, falling.

"No!" I shout.

Autumn's mom dives for the cup, her knees skidding on the carpet, but she's not fast enough either.

It bounces once on the floor before hitting the fireplace and shattering into a million pieces.

"Oh, oh, oh!" Autumn picks up the saucers and remaining cup, and places them gently on the table beside the cookies.

Her mom's hands hover over the broken pieces as if she's trying to force them together again with mind powers.

Like a plug pulled out of a tub, my insides swirl around, and my knees go weak. The special cup with Ériu and her pretty toga on the seashore is scattered across the hearthstone in pieces.

The room is silent as if the whole world holds its breath.

A hoarse cry trembles on Witch Barrett's lips, and she sags against the doorframe.

Autumn's mom leaps to her feet, her hands outstretched to catch her mother if she falls. "It's okay, it's okay. Maybe we can fix it." Gently, Christa coaxes Witch Barrett to the couch and helps her sit. But as soon as she's settled, the stillness of the moment is over. Eyes bright with tears, Christa turns and pins my cowering friend with a glare. "What. Were. You. Thinking?"

"I'm so sorry!" The wail bursts out of Autumn's throat, and I wonder if it's the sound of her heart breaking. "I didn't mean to!"

"Why would you climb up there? You know Nana keeps delicate things here—especially on that table. She brought those cups from Ireland. From Ireland! It was all she had left of her mother."

"I know." Hiccups rack Autumn's small body, and I want to run to her, to shield her from the pain.

"Autumn. Why? *Why* would you climb up there?"

"I had to!" Arms open and pleading, she looks at her nana with her heart in her eyes. "Nana, I'm so sorry. I was trying to get a crystal because a goblin stole the other one Sophie had, and it's almost the full moon."

"What?" Christa shakes her head.

"Don't you see? Her cure! We already had all the pieces for the spell to work, but he stole her amulet and now she can't change back."

"I'm so sorry." Words tumble from my lips, a jumbled

mumble of regret as I watch Witch Barrett blink back tears. "We didn't mean to."

Red flushes up Christa's cheeks and Autumn rushes on, desperate to make her understand. "She just needed the crystal, that's all. She was even gonna give it back, I swear! She needs to break the curse."

"What curse?"

"The curse that turned Sophie into a monster!"

That terrible glare turns to me, and I shrink as her words shake with rage. "What nonsense have you been telling my daughter?"

"It's the truth, Mom! I swear."

But she ignores Autumn's pleas and steps closer to me. "It's enough that I've got one child fighting for his life. This is the *real* world. Not some stupid fantasy. You can't imagine things away just because you want to."

"Christa." Witch Barrett reaches for her hand, but she jerks it away.

"No! Making her believe in monsters and goblins and heaven knows what else? It's shameful." She points at me. "You should be ashamed!"

I am. Oh, how I am. I back toward the door, too scared to speak or explain.

"It's not her fault!" Autumn screams. "Leave her alone!"

Rounding on her daughter, Christa shouts back. "What does any of this crazy have to do with you? Why were *you* the one getting it down if *she* is the one who wants it?"

On her feet now, Autumn fists her hands, the flush in her cheeks rising to match her mother's. "Because I'm a fairy! And she's my friend!"

Christa rocks back as if struck. One heartbeat passes, then two, then ten.

"Autumn. I want you to go get in the car."

"But, Mom!"

"No buts. I don't think this is a healthy relationship for you to have." She turns to Witch Barrett who sits with her hands resting open and empty on her lap, tears cascading silently down her cheeks. "Mother, if that girl's going to be here, I'll find somewhere else for Autumn to go. I can't deal with this, Mom. I just can't."

"But she's my friend!" Autumn rushes past her mother and wraps her arms around me. "Mom, please!"

"Listen very carefully." Christa leans closer to me, her voice low. "None of it is real. None of it."

She points at Autumn. "You are not a fairy."

"Mom!"

"And you—" She looks at me like I'm filth she's just scraped off her shoe. "You stay away from her."

I suppose after that, she left, and Autumn left, and Witch Barrett sat, and I stood, and I kept trying to wake from the nightmare but I couldn't because it was real. I'd lost my best friend. And it was real.

With shaking fingers, I touch my monster mark, the soft, warm skin bulging around my eye, the mark that separates me from everyone else.

I tell myself it isn't real, but I'm lying.

The pulse quickens inside it, a tiny heartbeat throbbing, pushing to break free. My fingers curl against my face, my nails biting into the delicate flesh. If it isn't real, maybe I don't need a cure, maybe I can just tear it off on the count of three.

One.

Two.

But I don't count to three, because I know it's real, and I'm scared.

And that's real too.

THE BIG BOOK OF MONSTERS
RIDDLES AND ANSWERS

While most monsters are content to eat people first and ask questions later, some prefer to engage the minds of their victims. For such creatures, the pleasure comes from watching doomed humans struggle to answer riddles. Troll bridges bar the way across rivers and chasms unless a traveler answers three questions, each one harder than the last.

In Egypt, the Sphinx has a woman's head, a winged lion's body, and a serpent's tail. She guards the entrance to the city of Thebes and only lets those who answer her riddle correctly pass through. The Sphinx happily devours anyone who answers wrong. Running is impossible, for with a flap of her wings, the Sphinx catches fleeing cowards before their second step.

While the lazy and foolish may be content to coast through their lives without effort, wise people spend their lives seeking knowledge from good books and excellent teachers. They ask difficult questions, seek answers, and are not afraid to face hard truths. Follow their example and you will be one of the few who may stand a chance at surviving an encounter with a monster of riddles.

TWENTY-FIVE

Monster Exposed

With Mom gone to work, and Autumn grounded from me for life, there isn't much left to do other than hang out with Bob. My back against the house, I sit with my legs straight out in front of me. Bob sits on my shoe as my peanut flips end over end across my knuckles. Autumn would have clapped for my magic hands, but Bob's version is scolding chitters if I don't finish the trick fast enough. His beady eyes follow the prize from one side to the next and back again. With a smooth roll, the peanut soars from one hand to the other then disappears inside my palm. With a flourish, I bring my hands together and make two fists, holding them out for Bob to see.

His tail flicks and he dashes forward in quick spurts and stops. Nose twitching, he sniffs one fist, then the other.

"No cheating," I warn.

At last, he stands on his hind legs and places both tiny hands on my left fist.

"Give the man a prize," I whisper and open my fingers revealing the peanut inside.

Quick as a baby Sphinx, he snatches it and races to the top of the rail to pry open his treasure.

Rising, I dust off my pants and retreat inside.

Mom made it super clear that I better have the laundry folded and done before she picks me up for my appointment today. Folding laundry is a lot like trying to put braces on a shark. There's always another tooth just waiting to pop out and mess things up again. Just wearing clothes makes more laundry. It's never done, and it *can't* be done unless you're willing to stand there and fold clothes naked.

Pretty soon our piles are sorted, Mom's and mine, with a stack of towels beside them. I'm matching the last sock when the front door opens.

"Sophie?"

"Over here." I drop the pair of socks into my basket and roll my neck back and forth. I don't want to do this. I just want today to be over with.

"You ready to go?"

No. But when has that ever mattered? "I guess."

After a way too short car ride, we pull into the parking lot at the hospital. You'd think a vampire lair with bloodsuckers posing as phlebotomists in the basement would have big stone bricks and towers, or maybe a moat, but they've hidden all the haunted-looking bits behind one-way mirror-windows and an office-style building. Those windows probably keep out enough sunlight that vampires can walk around 24/7.

Bright colors are splashed across the walls of the waiting room, and children's toys made of wire and wooden doggles make-believe that this is a happy place. But I'm not fooled. This is a holding pen for vampire dinners. Fish dart in and out of fake coral in a watery game of tag—except for the one bobbing upside down at the top corner behind the bubbler. I can't decide if the other fish picking at it are trying to wake it up or eat it.

When Dr. S finally meets us in the examination room, there's a different lady with him. She's short with thick black hair that hangs in a ponytail down her back. With a wide, bright smile, she grips my hand and gives it a good, solid shake. "Sophie, I'm Dr. Escabar."

Dr. S pipes up, "When I heard she was visiting from the children's hospital, I asked her to stop by and meet you."

"Thank you for taking the time," Mom says.

"No problem. Now, Sophie, you mind if I touch your face?"

I shrug and spin a coin on my knuckles. When had that ever stopped a doctor before?

She pokes and prods, feeling the sides and shape of my monster blob with gentle fingers. After a minute, she nods. "You say you want to take it off this summer? I don't see any issue with that at all."

"Actually," Mom says, raising her finger, "we'd like it off as soon as possible. Can we do it right away?"

Right away? My quarter falls to the floor, and I stare at Mom. "What?"

The doctors share a look, and Mom retrieves my coin off the floor and hands it to me.

"She's lived with this just fine for over ten years. Why the rush?" Dr. S asks.

"Because, she's not doing so fine right now. There're bullies and . . ." Her eyes dart to me and away. "Other things."

"Ah." Dr. Escabar taps her cheek for a moment. "Perhaps there are some X-rays we can look at down the hall. Sophie, would you mind staying here? We won't be long."

I flop onto the examination table and snatch a book out of the kid's basket at the foot of the table. "Fine."

When Mom returns with Dr. Escabar, I sit up. "Where's Dr. S?"

"He had to go to the next appointment." She slides closer on one of those rolling doctor stools and peers up at me with interest. "Sophie, do you mind having your birthmark?"

What kind of a question is that? I've wished it gone my whole life, but what if they can't get the monster part out? How do you cut out what you are? I settle on a shrug. "I've always had it."

"Yes, but do you understand that your birthmark does not define you? Every one of us has something unique that no one else has." She rolls up her sleeve to show a dark, almost black inch-long oval that stands out against her light brown skin. "I have a birthmark."

She crooks her thumb at Mom. "Even she has one."

My head whips around so fast I almost break my neck. Mom has a mark?

Mom rolls her head to the side and points to the white streak that always colors the side of her temple.

The doctor continues, "That's called a Mallen streak. She was born without melatonin in that area of her scalp which makes the mark in her hair white for everyone to see."

I stare at Mom like I've never seen her before. "I thought you dyed your hair that way."

"Nope. It's natural."

"We are all different. Each one of us with our own little fluctuation that differs us from the norm. It's part of being *human*." She stresses the last word, and I fight the urge to squirm.

When I say nothing, she shoots a glance at Mom and clears her throat. "It won't change who you are. If you have this or not, a mark doesn't make you different inside. You'll still be the same person you always were. Understand?"

All this careful talk makes me look at her hard. Does she know? Maybe. But either way, what she's saying is pretty clear. Cutting my monster mark off doesn't change the inside. It'd be like a shape-shifter putting on a new face. A shifter can have all the shapes it wants, but changing the outside—pretending to be human—won't change the fact that it's still a monster. The hidden part inside is just as important as the outside. "Okay."

"If you understand, and this is still what you want, we can schedule you about two weeks out."

"Wonderful!" Mom gushes, but I can't follow. Two weeks? The doctor just got through telling me that it wouldn't change anything. I am what I am. If I had my amulet, maybe it would be different. I could change the inside and then the outside would go away, but if the inside is still the same, then what's the point?

I realize that the doctor is watching me really close, like I'm a really interesting bug. "You don't look excited."

"Of course she is." Mom snorts. "This is what we've always wanted. It will change everything."

Dr. Escabar gently lays both hands on my knees and waits till I look up at her. "Sophie. Do you want this?"

My eyes stray to Mom, who waits on the edge of her seat, an encouraging smile smeared across her face.

"Sophie, look at me."

Dr. Escabar's deep brown eyes drag me back to her. "If you don't want to talk, you can just nod. Do you want to have surgery right now?"

Needles. Knives cutting. And none of it changing anything. I shake my head.

"Sophie!" I cringe at Mom's cry, and the doctor gives my knees a little squeeze before turning to Mom.

"I think you have some more talking to do so you're both on the same page."

Well, I may as well have killed the cat. Not that we had a cat, but Mom gripped the steering wheel so tight I wouldn't be surprised if she left finger dents. Not a word on the way out the door. Not a word when we pull up to our driveway. Not a word when she stalks into the house ahead of me.

Stepping through the door, my heebie-jeebies go off so hard I half expect a guillotine to slide down the doorframe and slice off my heels.

Mom stands in the kitchen, facing away from me with the lights off. "You know we've waited for this surgery for years. You know it, and I know it. This is what all the doctor appointments have been for. So why did you say you didn't want surgery?"

"I don't know," I mumble.

"Are you scared of the surgery itself? Are you against all surgery, or just this one?"

Am I scared of all surgery? If I had a broken arm with bone sticking out I'd want it fixed, right? So maybe not all surgery. "Mostly this one."

She whirls. "But why, Sophie? Why? Your whole life people have made fun of you, hurt you, shunned you. You can't do dance, or swimming, or, or—what about your magic tricks? You're talented, and you could be so pretty."

Gosh, it hurts. A spiky ball grows in my throat and hangs there, spines tearing at the soft insides.

"Explain it to me." Even though I can't see her face, I can feel her stare burrowing into me. "Why would you want to stay like this? Do you like being teased?"

"No." My voice croaks around the spikes.

"Do you want to have this thing on your face forever?"

"No." Of course not. That's not it.

She drops to a knee beside me and turns my shoulders so I have to face her. "So then *why?* Help me understand."

Her desperation scares me, and my voice rises to meet hers. "Because it wouldn't change anything!"

Letting go, she steps away. "It won't change anything because you think people still won't like you? It won't change anything because you think you'll still be an outcast?" She stills and something changes in her voice. "Or it won't change anything because you think you'll still be a monster?"

A gasp so strong rips from my throat that I clap both hands over my face. Oh, she knows. *She knows!* I step closer, trying to see her eyes in the gloom, but I can't see and it's dark and cold and shadowed and I don't know! My body shudders with a sob. "Mom?"

"That's it, isn't it? It's like what they said at your school." She talks so quiet I can barely hear her, even though I'm right here, reaching for her. "You're afraid the surgery won't change the supposed fact that you're a monster, so what's the point of doing it?"

Shivers run up and down my body and I hug myself tight,

trying to hold all my broken pieces inside. In the dark, Mom's cold and hard and she *knows*. It's everything I've ever feared. She knows and now she doesn't want me anymore.

"I can't believe this. I can't!" A deep growl rumbles in her throat and grows into a strangled cry. Her hands curl like claws against her forehead.

My palms cover my ears and I crouch, shaking.

Rushing from the room, she leaves me. She's gone. I knew it. I knew she wouldn't want me if she knew. But now she does know and there's no way to take it back.

Something hits the wall in my room and the light flips on. I squint at the brightness.

She's standing there, her chest heaving, her eyes wild.

I broke my mom.

But that's not even the scary part.

She's clutching my book.

"It's this, isn't it? *This* is why you think you're a monster."

"My book!"

"No! It's not your book. This is not who you are! Sophie listen to me. It's all pretend. It's fake. It's a lie! My daughter is not a monster."

Her daughter isn't, but *I* am. And now she knows it. If I could give her that perfect baby back, I would. I'd go back and stop that witch from ever casting the spell. She deserves a daughter who's normal and pretty and human. Not this. Not me.

I whimper, "I'm sorry. I don't want to be one. I didn't mean to."

"Sorry?" She shakes her head. "You don't understand. How do I make you understand?"

But then she raises my book up for me to see and opens it,

the pages flutter apart, and I see Koschei the Deathless riding his stallion through the whirlwind. A fist on either side of the spine, she grips the cover and twists, the muscles in her arms flexing as she spits the words, "This. Is. Not. Real!"

The sound. Crackling and tearing paper. Oh, the sound! It paralyzes me.

The sundered halves fall apart in slow motion, and my soul breaks in two.

First Dad, then Autumn, then Mom.

I have no one. I can't. It hurts so much. No one wants me.

A wounded animal cry fills the room, and I cover my ears to make it stop—except it's *me* making the sound.

Mom staggers back and makes a small "Oh!" but it's too late.

I'm alone, and it's broken.

I'm broken.

And I'm running out the door.

And I'm gone.

BEWARE THE MONSTERS

Monsters lurk in deep water,

    in dark caverns,

    behind mirrors,

    and on mountaintops.

They crawl under beds,

    in attics,

    through pipes,

    and in closets.

They watch you,

    hunt you,

    control you,

    devour you.

They curse you,

    pretend to be you,

And when the monster is already inside you,

A part of you . . .

    It breaks you.

TWENTY-SIX

Runaway

I run blind through the dark neighborhood with only the stars to witness my flight. Even then, I'm not hidden from monsters. Some of them, like the Greek sea monster, Cetus, hide in the stars. Even now I see him standing sentry in the night, watching me through bright pinholes in the sky. I know he's got a whale's tail, claws on his fins, and a serpentine neck with razor teeth hidden somewhere up there in the blackness. Daughters of kings were sacrificed to his glory, heroes feared him, and sailors bore witness to his majesty. I know all this because my book tells me so.

The same book that taught me about witches and water sprites, Sphinxes and cyclops, hydras and harpies, djinn and demons.

How am I supposed to know if someone is hiding a changeling or a banshee inside without my book? I wouldn't know until it's too late. How can I protect my mom if I don't even know what to protect her from?

My lungs pinch, remembering she doesn't want my protection. She wants her daughter.

I trip on a curb at the end of the street and bash my knees against twigs and blackberry vines. The skin rips open, and it stings, but I don't stop.

I can't.

Mom's voice calls from somewhere far away, but it's not *me* she wants. It's the girl she used to have before the witch cursed her baby.

That's the girl she wants.

That's the girl she needs.

That's the girl I can never be.

Under the pitch shadow of the trees, I slow and search the forest for a way in. I'm already way past Witch Barrett's house, but maybe I can still find a path back to Autumn's fairyland. It's secret, so maybe Christa won't know about it. And I can live there and hide.

Hide from the goblins, from Mom, from the whole world.

If I burrow deep enough into the forest, maybe I can even hide from me.

I push a bramble aside and try to slip through, but the thorns are thick and I can't make headway in the dark. They prick my fingers and I hiss, backing out to try again in a different place.

I'm desperate to get under cover. The old me would have hidden behind my book and waited for the scary things to pass by, but that was before Mom knew what I was.

I feel so exposed, like walking naked through brambles.

I lived my whole life with monsters. I knew them for what

they were, and that knowledge kept me safe. Even now, I remember most of it. But what if I forget? I can't remember everything. Already the details seem fuzzy and they slip from me like a receding tide. With my book, the world made sense. I was invisible, and that made me invincible.

The world is a dragon; my book a shield.

And now it's gone.

I try again and again to get through the bramble wall and into the forest, but the thorns push back, a force field of tiny wicked razors.

A stone wall blocks my way and I step into the street to slip around it and the house it encircles. Maybe the forest on the other side will have a way through. It was never this hard to get through the forest before. It's almost like someone doesn't want me to find the way. A pair of stone gargoyles stand guard at the edge of their driveway, but I don't worry too much. Probably they would only eat me if I trespassed *inside* the fence.

A frown pushes another thought through my mind. What if the blackberry brambles are guarding fairyland, and that's why I can't get inside? Maybe monsters aren't allowed in unless they have a fairy friend with them. Since Autumn's not allowed to be my friend anymore, maybe I won't ever find a way in.

With one eye on the nearest gargoyle, I lean against the stone wall and breathe. Why does everything have to be so hard? In the lamplight, blood shines on my arms from dozens of scratches. The message is clear: the forest doesn't want me either.

I slide down the wall till I'm sitting on the curb, the frigid concrete biting through my jeans and, bit by bit, stealing my warmth. Goosebumps rise on my arms and a shiver ripples out from there, jittering through my whole body.

Hugging my knees, I try to think. *Where can I hide?*

Crickets sing in the forest and something, bats probably, swoops through the leaves overhead. In the dark, the forest seems less a landscape and more a living thing.

My stomach growls.

Red and blue lights flash in the next neighborhood over, probably by my house. The police are out to catch me, the monster that broke my mother's heart. My eyes search all around for a cubby or a hole, anything to hide inside until it all goes away, but there's nothing.

My forehead drops to my knees and I'm curled into a ball, wishing to be invisible.

A cat cries, then shrieks, two of them fighting in the dark.

Misty rain sprinkles my hair, and I raise my face to the indifferent sky, letting my head fall back against the wall.

I shudder, and my teeth begin to chatter. I can't stay here. But there's nowhere for me to go. Mom knows what I am, and she took my book from me. I can't hide anymore.

A pair of moths flutter around the streetlight, their crazy flight becoming more chaotic as the rain comes faster. They can't hide from it, can't wish the rain away. It just is.

Hugging my knees tighter, I try to hold onto what little warmth I have.

I can't wish the truth away. I am what I am. All the hiding was just pretend, a lie. A role I played so Mom would still love me. No matter how much I want it to be different, I can't hide anymore. There's nothing to hide behind, and nowhere to go.

My stomach gurgles again, stronger this time. When did I eat last? Breakfast, I think. I would've eaten more if I'd known it was my last meal.

The cold seeps through my shirt, which clings to my shoulders as raindrops slip down my back. I know, monster or not, I can't survive alone.

Maybe if I beg her, Mom will let me live there anyway, but I won't lie or hide anymore. What's the point? I was the best hider in the world, and it didn't do any good. My secrets spilled everywhere, and everyone knows.

She might not want me. But I can't stay here.

I've got to go back. I'll tell her that I'll do my best. That I won't hide anymore. I won't lie. I'll be the best-behaved monster the world has ever seen. It can't ever be the same, but if I let her see the real me, maybe she can learn to be okay with that—or at least tolerate it.

I didn't get to choose how she found out, but I can choose to be honest with her now. My shoulders square up and I straighten my spine, determination sparking though my veins. Yes, I'm a monster, but I can own that. No more hiding. No more lying. She's done her best to raise me as her daughter. The rest isn't her fault. I can give her this much.

Time to go home.

Decision made, I push off the curb and stand just as a pair of headlights turn the corner, sweep the wall, and stop on me.

LOVE AND HATE

It is said that the hearts of men are stirred up in anger by Ares, the God of War. When Ares was a baby, giants kidnapped him and stuffed him into a jar until Hermes rescued him. But Ares's own parents did not want him. He was disliked and ridiculed, and the anger he carried grew into rage. Ares loved war, used boars and vultures as symbols, and wore those symbols during the Trojan War. But then Ares fell in love with Aphrodite, the Goddess of Love, and had eight children with her. Two of these, Phobos (fear) and Daiemos (panic) rode with him to war, but another son was Eros, more commonly known as Cupid, and a daughter named Harmonia, the Goddess of Harmony.

How is it possible for a god known for his hatred, rage, violence, and destruction to give rise to Cupid and the Goddess of Harmony? The answer is found by looking at the type of person he sought to make his wife. The most hated god of all longed for the one thing he never had: Love. Specifically, Aphrodite, the Goddess of Love. It makes one wonder, if he had found love and acceptance in his childhood, then perhaps he could have become Ares the God of Empathy instead.

TWENTY-SEVEN

Monsters of War

The beams shine like twin suns in the night, blinding in their intensity. It's all black silhouettes except for the headlights, and I take a step to run away before I remember I'm not hiding anymore. Not from anyone ever again. Squinting at the light, I raise a hand to shade my eyes.

A car door opens.

"Sophie?" Koschei calls. "Oh, honey, where have you been? Your mom's worried sick."

Footsteps rush toward me and his shadow blocks the light, distorting so he looms ten feet tall in the mist. He kneels in front of me and gingerly touches my arms and face. "Are you okay? Are you hurt? You're bleeding."

"I'm okay." A shiver racks my body, and Koschei pulls his hoodie off, wrapping the warm material around my shoulders.

"Let's get you in the car."

I let him guide me, a hand on my back until he opens the

235

passenger door, and I get in. With the heater on full blast, the tremors fade and I'm enveloped in warmth. Koschei pulls out his cell phone, dials, and waits.

"Marlene? Yes! Yes, I have her. What? No. She's fine. A little wet, but fine. I swear. Everything's going to be okay." His voice cracks, "Aw, honey. Please don't cry. Remember what we talked about? I'll have her home soon. I promise. Safe and sound." He pulls out of the neighborhood, gets on the freeway, and we head into the night.

Mom crying? I don't know what to think.

Thumb tapping to the beat of some old rock and roll song, Koschei passes me a stick of jerky. "It's teriyaki."

My stomach lurches, growling so hard it seems to be trying to claw its way straight to the food without waiting for my mouth to eat it. Drool pools on my tongue as I pull the package open and take the first bite. "Thanks."

"Sophie, it occurs to me that I'm long overdue on taking you on a date."

I almost choke on jerky. "Date?"

"Sure. You and your mom are a package deal. I can't have one without the other."

I'm not sure what to think about that. He could whisk Mom away whenever he wants. And me? It's hard to believe that anything I want could matter that much.

We pull into the parking lot of his shop right under the "Kelsi's" sign, and he jumps out and opens the door. "Come on, let's get you cleaned up. Then we can go on our date."

Who knew mechanics kept baby wipes in their bathrooms? After wiping the blood off, my scratches don't look near as bad. Regardless, I use three Scooby-Doo Band-Aids because, well,

Scooby-Doo. There aren't any kid-sized dry clothes at the shop, but Koschei passes me one of his extra sweatshirts which drapes to my knees and off the tips of my hands like floppy tentacles. A fleece jacket on top of that is the last ingredient to make a toasty Sophie stew. I gotta admit, it's awful nice to be warm.

In the office, Koschei turns his back to me and takes his T-shirt off, but before the dry shirt goes on, I read the tattoo across his shoulders: *Greater love hath no man.*

Can a demon even have a tattoo talking about love and man? I turn away and pretend I don't notice while we bundle into the car. Lights and tunnels fly by and the hum of the motor lulls me into a sleepy peace. I don't even notice the rain has stopped until we pull into a parking spot by the river. Some kind of festival is going on with Christmas lights and music and dancing and something delicious that teases my nose with savory spice.

He walks around and opens my door. "M'lady."

My hand in the crook of his arm, he buys two churros from the end booth, but then leads me away from the celebration. Water laps quietly against the wall beside us, long drips of light floating like oil spills glowing on the surface. Our feet slap softly against damp cement as we pass beneath dripping tree branches and disappear into the night. In the river, a huge ship sleeps docked, an arch of white Christmas lights twinkling from bow to stern. Finally Koschei leads us to a covered bench with a view of the river and sits down. I settle in beside him, munching on my churro.

"Do you know my mother had a birthmark?" Koschei touches the back of his hand between his thumb and pointer finger. "Right here. A wine stain. But not me. I was born without a scratch. Not a freckle, not a mole. Nada. I was perfect."

Like I was! I watch with wide eyes. Did I misjudge him? Maybe he's not a demon, only cursed like me.

"I grew up on a farm, worked hard, played hard, loved my family and my country. In fact, I loved my country enough to join the army and go overseas to protect it. One day, my convoy stopped to help some kids who were having trouble herding sheep off the road. A couple of these kids were like, five years old. And there was an older kid with them. I thought he was their protector."

A couple strolls by, hand in hand, the man speaking softly to the woman. We watch them pass, but I'm listening so hard to Koschei that I almost forget to breathe.

"I remember a bell jingling on this sheep's collar, and the littlest boy had his fingers entwined in the thick wool as he scolded it, trying to get the beast to move. But when we got near, there was this flash of light that hit me like a train. I remember pressure, just huge pressure on my chest like there was a leviathan crouching on my lungs, and it burned. The burning hurt more later than anything, but that blast knocked me hard enough that I was in and out, so I didn't feel it all at once."

The words stop, and he stares at the ship for a long while, like maybe he forgot I was there.

A tugboat pushes a barge down the river, the light rippling in dips and troughs in its wake. In the dark, the impossible seems possible, with war and monsters transforming demons into men.

He takes a shuddering breath and shakes his head to clear the memories of bodies, sheep, and burns.

"Anyway, the explosion was one thing. Living with it was another. Do you know I had some friends I've known my whole life who couldn't look at me after?"

I shake my head. Koschei lost friends? Who knew he ever had any?

"Yeah, at first, it really bothered me. I felt like a freak and was embarrassed. Sometimes I'd wear stuff to try and hide, but then, I realized that the people who really mattered to me, the people who really cared about me, they didn't care what I looked like. They liked me for who I was on the inside."

His gaze rests on me, and even in the moonlight, I can see the bumps and creases that mar his once perfect face. "That's when I decided to *own* my scars. All of us carry monster marks, Sophie. It's just that some of us carry them on the outside."

The churro squeaks down the wrong windpipe, and I choke, coughing while he pats my back. When my fit abates, he brushes my hair away from my monster mark, with a gentle finger and doesn't flinch or look away. "Do you think Autumn cares what marks you have on your face?"

"No." She barely seemed to notice it.

"What about Mrs. Barrett or your teacher, Mrs. Joy?"

I hesitate a little, because I'm not sure Witch Barrett would want to see me, but that's because of broken china, not because of my monster mark. But Mrs. Joy likes me, I'm pretty sure. "No."

"Do you think I care if you have a birthmark?"

A slow smile slips across my face. Compared to Koschei's face, my mark is nothing. "No."

"Then believe me when I say that it's the same for your mom."

"She wants it off."

"Because she thinks it will make life easier on you, yes. But not because she thinks it will change who you are inside. Sophie, she loves you. The inside you. The real you."

I frown at this. If she liked the real me, then why'd she yell?

"Do you think I'm a monster?" he asks.

"Maybe," I admit.

He nods. "Fair enough. What about the people who did this to me? Do you think they're monsters?"

Anyone who could hurt people *that* bad has got to be a monster. "Yeah. They were."

"Were they? Because they looked like kids to me. Normal little kids. I don't think they were monsters. For a while I thought maybe the people that strapped the bomb on that older kid were monsters, and maybe they were. But now I think maybe war itself is a monster."

I try to imagine a monster as big as a whole war and I can't. Maybe Ares, but even he isn't really a whole war.

"But you've got to think about who is making the war, which goes back to people. Normal people who make bad choices."

The last bite of churro gone, I crinkle up the napkin.

"I read your book, Sophie. When I took your mom to lunch a few days ago, I saw all those monsters in there."

The monster book was *mine*. He had no right to go snooping around in there. I bristle at the invasion but can't work up the energy to protest. I'm just too tired.

"If I had a monster book," he continues, "it would be a lot smaller. I think it's the choices we make that make people monstrous or not. It's a choice, not a curse, not what you or I look like."

Everything he's saying is sort of like trying to drink a tidal wave with a straw. I can't quite catch it all, can't quite understand.

He sighs. "You know, I've seen you help your mom around the house even when she doesn't ask. I know you try to protect her. You're kind to small animals—and you're smart! It takes some serious brains to read a book that big." He lowers his head and looks straight in my eyes. "This is the point, Sophie. You are not a monster to me. You are perfect just the way you are. Mark or no mark, it doesn't matter. You're still you, and that's beautiful."

We sit for a while, his strong arm around my shoulders, and watch the boats and tugs slip by on the river, their ghostly silhouettes reflected on the water. When the misty rain starts up again, he leads me to the car by the hand and kneels beside me. "Are you ready to go home?"

A drop of rain trickles down my neck and I nod. I'm cold, and confused, and spent, but mostly tired. So very tired. He gives me a hug and holds me tight, his strong arms radiating comfort as he whispers into my hair.

"I'm glad you're safe, hon. Your mom loves you, truly. And so do I. You might as well get used to that because I'm here for the long haul. I'm not one to leave a man behind. I'll always come for you, and I'll always try to keep you safe."

I dreamed of lights flashing by like fireflies and a journey where Koschei the Deathless rode with me on a white steed made of whirlwinds to a far-off land. As we rode, his skeletal visage faded, the missing parts filling in, until he was just a man, not a demon.

My head on his shoulder, he lifted me gently, and carried me home.

VENOM

One of the difficulties in studying monsters is that some creatures are so venomous that it is nearly impossible to observe them at all, even from a distance, without dying. Created when a cockerel hatches a toad or serpent egg, a basilisk is considered the king of all cobras. Near the ancient city of Cyrene, an infant basilisk measured barely a foot long, and yet was so toxic that it left a streak of poison everywhere it went. Some basilisks retain more of the rooster look from their cockerel parent, but more often, they appear as impossibly large serpents, almost dragon-like with their green and gold shimmering hide. A glare from a basilisk can turn any living creature to stone, but its real weapon is its intelligence. The creatures are patient and sly—positioning themselves in places where a man might look into their eyes by accident. Like most creatures of darkness, the most dangerous place to encounter a basilisk is in its lair.

Tread carefully when confronting such beings with poison in their souls, who seek after the dark, for they can drag you down and lead you to destruction. If they seek your pardon, offer forgiveness freely, if only to prevent the poison of resentment from taking hold inside your soul. Unlike a true friend who would brush aside your faults and see you for the person you hope to become, poisonous creatures will always seek to turn your heart into stone.

TWENTY-EIGHT

The Goblin's Lair

I wake to bacon, eggs, blueberries, and hugs. Snuggled under plush blankets on the couch, I watch cartoons, eat popcorn, and talk about anything and nothing with Mom. We pretend everything is normal, and she holds me carefully—not too hard, not too soft—a glass doll perched on a shelf ledge. It takes a while, but my wooden body relaxes against her side till we fit like silly putty squished together. Every so often, she pats my back for a while and I pat her knee. It's a secret code that needs no words.

Are you still there? Pat, pat.

Yes, I'm here. Pat, pat.

I love you. Pat, pat.

Love you back. Pat, pat.

After lunch, a lady comes to visit. Her slip-on shoes thud softly in the corner, and she pads across the floor to the couch where she sets down a big orange bag and settles with her feet crisscrossed.

Curled up next to Mom, I watch her warily from the safety of my blanket.

"Hi, Sophie, I'm Ms. Cloe." She smiles, her tight black curls bobbing against her rich brown skin. "Your momma invited me over to play some games."

When I don't say anything, she leans over the coffee table and lays out a board game with bright squares around the outside, a spinner in the middle with numbers around it like a clock. Then she pulls out a big present wrapped in yellow stars and makes it dance a little before passing it to me. "Sophie, you get to reveal the grand prize!"

I probably should have been excited to open the present, but this is all so weird. I keep sneaking glances at them both. But when I tear the paper a little, the word *magic* peers back at me. Magic? Grabbing a fistful of wrapping paper, I tear the sheet free and stare at the Magician's Apprentice Ultimate Magic Kit. Complete with top hat, wand, and over fifty different magic tricks!

"Oh, wow." I breathe. It's *the* kit. *My* kit! The one I've been wishing for forever! Weird or not, I'm gonna win this game.

Ms. Cloe sets three different pegs on the board in the first square and asks, "Marlene? Do you want to start?"

"I'd love to." Mom reaches forward and spins the dial which ticks fast then slows and stops on number three. She moves a game piece forward three spaces.

Pulling a card from the deck, Ms. Cloe reads, "Okay, here's your question. What is your favorite food?"

I almost blurt out, "Sushi!" But I bite my tongue and half

a second later, Mom says, "Sushi—the kind with seaweed all wrapped up. Not sashimi or that nasty kind of sushi that's just a chunk of fish sitting on rice. I like the real wrapped up sushi rolls."

"Thank you for sharing!" Ms. Cloe nods and spins the dial. "Alrighty, my turn." It lands on a two and she moves her marker two places before drawing a card and reading. "What is an activity you like to do?" She taps her chin. "Hmm, I like to go on walks with my dog—I have a chi-weeny named Leeloo. We set out really early in the morning when the sun is just starting to rise. I like how the neighborhood is quiet then, as if it's only the two of us in all the world."

"Nice," says Mom. "Thank you for sharing."

They both look at me, and part of me wants to hide under the blanket. This smells like a trick. But with the Magician's Apprentice Ultimate Magic Kit sitting right there, I grab my big-girl pants and give the dial a spin.

The plastic dial whirrs around and stops on six. Ms. Cloe draws a card. "What makes you sad?"

What kinda stupid question is that? "Stuff."

"Beep! Short answers don't count. Did you notice your mom and I both gave longer answers? Try again," Ms. Cloe says.

"Take a minute and think." Mom pats my back. "If you don't tell the truth, you can't move forward."

Dang it! The truth? I twist the edge of the blanket and gaze at the Ultimate Magic Kit for a little extra bravery. "It makes me sad when people make fun of me."

"Go on," Ms. Cloe urges. "Why do you think they do that?"

"Because. I'm—" I squirm in my seat. "Different."

I'm scared she's gonna ask for more, but she just smiles and says, "Thank you for sharing."

Mom's question is "Who is your most favorite person?"

"Oh, that's easy!" She wraps her arms around me and squeezes. "Sophie is! I love this girl right here more than anything in the whole world."

"Is there anything that could ever change that?" Ms. Cloe asks.

"Nothing." Mom catches my chin and looks me straight in the eye. "I will love you, Sophie, forever, and ever, and ever."

A bubbly kind of warmth squiggles around inside my chest and a smile keeps trying to sneak out, but I smoosh it back and press my head against Mom's shoulder.

The dial whirls as Ms. Cloe takes her turn.

We go round and round. Sometimes the questions are silly, and sometimes not. Somehow, I tell them about my amulet, and all the hard work I did with Autumn, and how it was stolen, and then Autumn was stolen too. Well, grounded anyway, but it's the same thing for me.

Ms. Cloe scores an eight, and she taps each square as she passes me. The tap, tap, tap of her peg on the cardboard makes my hands sweat. Did she just win my magic kit? Finally, she stops three squares from the end and reads her card. "What does it mean to be human?"

"Oh, that's a hard one." Mom pats my back, but I frown. How hard can it be for a normal human to say what it means to be themselves?

"Well, let's see," Ms. Cloe says. "A human needs courage to do what's right, even when it's hard. Wisdom to know what's right and wrong. Justice is important, but only if it comes with mercy. And most of all, humans need love. We care for those we love, and hurt when they hurt, and are happy when they're happy. It's that togetherness that makes us all human."

But what if monsters feel the same things? Then what? Does that make them a human-monster sandwich?

I spin a seven and bonk Ms. Cloe's peg on the head as my marker jumps past hers and onto the last square. Only one question left, and the magic kit is *mine!*

"Sophie, what makes you happy?"

Gosh, after all the other stuff, this one is so easy I almost bounce right out of my seat. "Being with Mom and Autumn, and doing magic tricks, and I think maybe being with Koschei too."

"Koschei?" Ms. Cloe's eyes flick to Mom.

"She means Kelsi, I think."

My brain chews on that for a minute. Do I mean Koschei? Or is it really Kelsi? Who is he really?

"Looks like Sophie beat us all fair and square!" Ms. Cloe claps her hands.

"Yes!" I almost tackle the box and drag it down to the floor to open it, but then I notice Mom watching me. "You can't peek. A magician can't reveal her secrets."

She laughs. "Put it in your room, then, Little Miss Magician."

Magician sounds so much nicer than monster. I scooch the word *monster* over inside me to make room.

Cloe leaves, but not before promising to be back again soon—and I don't mind nearly as much as I thought I might. Besides, if there's any chance of getting more magic kits from her, I'm in!

Later, I wear my shades and Mom walks with me around the neighborhood. Our hands swing back and forth, swish, swish, in time with our steps. "What'd you think of Ms. Cloe?"

"She's nice," I admit. It'll take weeks to master all the tricks inside that box.

We stop in front of a house with more weeds than grass, and Mom faces the door. "You said it was Taggart who took your amulet?"

"Yes." All the squishy, nice feelings poof away in an instant. "Why?"

"Because we're going to ask for it back." And she steps over tufts of grass jutting up between paverstones like green porcupines and leads the way to the door.

"Wait!" I hiss and dig my heels in. Taggart lives here? Nobody just walks right up to a goblin's lair! I jerk my hand, but her fingers hold me fast. "Mom! No, wait!"

"Don't be scared, honey. Remember what Ms. Cloe said? Sometimes we need to have courage. It doesn't hurt to try."

It might if we get eaten. I glance at the crushed pop cans which hang on a dead bush beside the porch like Christmas ornaments. What if a whole pack of goblins live inside? Taggart might be hiding a whole army of the long-fingered nasties!

Mom rings the doorbell and hugs me to her side so we're facing the door together while we wait.

Music blares inside somewhere, and the flickering light of a TV glows blue inside the front room window. For just a moment, I think maybe we lucked out and he's not home. Or better yet, maybe this isn't even his house!

But then the door opens and Taggart stands there, shirt

untucked and hair messed up. His gaze meets mine and he narrows his eyes. "Why are *you* here?"

"Hello—Taggart, is it? Nice to meet you. Sophie says you may have something that belongs to her." Mom nudges me forward.

"Mom!" Pushing me into a goblin lair? My heck, next she'll be tossing me down a basilisk's throat. And why's she being so nice anyway? He's a *goblin* for heaven's sake.

"Ask, honey."

"Ask me what?" Taggart eases back and closes the door a little.

I clear my throat. "I want my amulet back."

"I don't have a stupid millet." Rage simmers in his eyes as he glares at me, hatred rolling off him in waves. I've seen him mad before, but not like this. He despises me for coming here, to his lair, and it's so strong I take a step back. Why would he care? If anything, he should be strongest here in his own kingdom.

Mom squeezes my shoulder and whispers in my ear, "Courage."

Right. He can hate me, but Mom doesn't. And this time, I'm not running away. I stare right back at him. "Not millet. Amulet. You took my necklace from my desk."

"Prove it." He sneers, but a door slams inside the house and Taggart flinches, his face paling instantly. "Just go. Please. Go and I'll give it to you. I swear."

"Who's at the door?" A young guy comes up behind Taggart, grabs the doorframe, and jerks it open wide. He's handsome, with strong arms and clean-cut dark hair, though the frayed edges of his flannel shirt hang over worn jeans. But when he looks me over, I can't help but see something serpentine behind those black eyes, something dangerous. "What do you want? Did he do something again? Taggart, I swear if you—"

"No!" Mom interrupts, "There's no trouble. My daughter knows your brother from school, and we just stopped by to pick up something. Nothing to worry about."

"Huh." The serpent shoves Taggart out of the doorway. "You heard her. Get it, bro. Don't want to keep your lady-friend waiting."

Taggart's chest rises and falls quickly, like he's been running for hours, but he doesn't complain. With one last panicked glance at the three of us, he sprints into the house.

"Kids, right?" The serpent crooks a grin at Mom and shrugs. "You sure he didn't get in trouble again? 'Cause if he did, Dad'll kick his—"

"He's just getting something for me. No big deal," I blurt, and Mom pats my back. I don't even know why I said it, only that here, in this place that should be Taggart's sanctuary, he seems helpless and alone. I know what that feels like, and I don't wish it on anyone. Not even Taggart.

Taggart runs back to the door, a big wad of paper clutched in his hand. "Here. Take it."

I almost object, because I'm here for my amulet, not for a wad of paper, but as soon as it rests in my hand, the extra weight proves that there's more there than what I can see.

"That's it?" Taggart's brother stares at the paper, his lip curling. "You came all this way for that?"

"Yes. It's special to me. Thanks, Taggart." I back away from the door, and Mom melts back with me.

The serpent snorts, "Whatever," and slips into the shadows of the house, but Taggart stays at the door, watching.

"Thank you." Mom waves when we step onto the sidewalk. "I hope to see you again sometime soon, Taggart. It's been nice meeting you."

Slowly, he lifts a hand, like he wants to wave goodbye, but forgot how.

I've got the weirdest feeling that he'd rather come with us than stay here.

TALISMANS

In many cultures, there are stories of talismans that ward off evil and give aid. They may be rings, necklaces, or some other jewelry. Sometimes they are carved or tattooed into the skin. Talismans can be made of scrolls, carvings, or stones. The key to a talisman isn't what it's made of: it's the intent with which the item was created. These objects are collected and imbued with the belief and faith of the owner to the point that they become magic in their own right. Unlike a hex bag or some sort of cursed item, talismans do no harm to others if they are accidentally or intentionally left behind. In fact, some people create talismans specifically as gifts to bring positive energy and luck to those who need it most.

Where a talisman fails, service can often succeed. Should you see someone in need, look for ways to lift their load. Clean, carry, spend time, and listen. Often small kindnesses can heal invisible wounds better than any spell.

TWENTY-NINE

One Day before the Full Moon

Mercy.

That's what Mom called the things we said at Taggart's house. In that place, he seemed less like a goblin, and more like a scared kid. Maybe he's just tired of living with his own monsters, so it leaks out at school and splats on other kids.

Mom says she's proud of me. That I've got loads of courage for facing Taggart. I've heard of courageous lions and heroes. But whoever heard of a courageous monster?

I wish I had my book, so I could look it up, but it's in pieces and probably thrown away. There might be a monster who was brave in there somewhere, but I can't think of it.

My amulet really was inside the wad of paper—though the peacock feather is a little munched, like it had a really bad hair day. It's not missing any pieces though, so I think it will still work.

I should be planning, because tomorrow is the full moon, but I keep getting distracted by Mom. She hugs me, tells me she loves me, asks me what I'm thinking, and tells me I'm beautiful. I think maybe something is wrong with her eyes. It's weird, really. Ever since she ripped my book in half, she's been hovering around me like a dryad guarding her tree, always there in the corner of my eye.

Mom says I need courage again to fix things with Autumn's family, and that cookies will help. So, we make a bunch. At first, it's my job to roll the dough and put it on the baking sheets, but I eat half the cookie balls so Mom takes over. One cookie for the oven and one for me seems pretty fair, but Mom wants the cookies to actually get cooked. So, whatever.

An hour later, I hold the plate of cookies tight and stare at Witch Barrett's house. She called my mom and invited me over. Which is great, except I keep remembering how her wrinkled face crumpled when her tea set shattered. It's my fault the cup broke, so I'm the one who broke her.

Truth is, I've been stalling. I wrote a note. Then added stickers to the note. Then drew a picture of the Irish goddess by the sea. That was kinda hard. I remembered the toga she wore, and the rocks and stuff, but without the picture to copy from, I'm sure I missed something.

The sidewalk to her house seems like it's a million miles long, but suddenly I'm at the door and I knock the gentlest knock that ever there was. Part of me hopes she won't hear so I can leave the plate and run home, but that doesn't seem very wise or courageous.

Footsteps creak inside the house, and the front door swings

open wide. My Autumn smiles the biggest smile I've ever seen right there in front of me.

"You brought cookies!" She whoops, and the sound makes me feel instantly better. Sort of like her voice tosses invisible Band-Aids all over my heart. A week ago, I would have looked to see if that was a fairy thing, but for now, I'm just happy it's a friend thing.

She pulls me inside, grabs the cookies and sets them on the coffee table, then wraps both arms around me and squeezes tight. "I missed you."

It takes a couple tries because my stupid lip keeps trembling, but I finally hug her back and whisper, "I missed you, too."

"What's this?" Witch Barrett steps out of the kitchen and wipes her floured hands on her apron. "No need for tears, dearies. Everything's alright now."

I stare at her and my tongue glues itself to the roof of my mouth, but I've come all this way. I've got to say something! What would Mom tell me?

Courage and wisdom and stuff.

I pull away from Autumn.

Courage.

"I'm sorry about your teacup. I brought you a picture of the goddess so you can remember her, and your mom."

"Ach, child. I accept the apology. 'Tis brave of you to give it. Accidents happen, but sometimes we all need reminders that things—even old and precious things—aren't as important as the people we love. And, dear Sophie, I do love you."

My traitorous lip trembles all over the place, and I hold my card out for her to take, but she brushes it aside and pulls me tight for a long hug. Her soft kisses peck the top of my head.

"There, there. We had a lot of hurt the last day you came here, and I'm sorry you caught the brunt of it. I was wrong to let that happen. Forgive me?"

I nod, my face enveloped in the ruffles of her apron.

A buzzer sounds from the kitchen and she lets me go. "You girls visit, I've got rolls to look after."

"Nana says you got your amulet back. Is that true? I hope so. The full moon is tomorrow night, and we did all that work. Mom says it's make-believe, but I think it can't hurt to try, right? I mean, even if I'm not a fairy, I want to finish what we started. Besides," Autumn says, her voice dropping into a whisper, "it might still be real!"

Not a fairy? I frown. Does she think that she's not one because someone told her to think that, or does she just know inside that she's something else? I reach inside to see if the monster part of me is somehow different than it was—but I feel the same. I want to be different, free from any monster stain inside or out. Koschei and Mom may say that my monster mark doesn't matter, but it's hard to believe that when it's made me different my whole life. I admit, "I still want to try."

"Of course! We need a plan for your amulet! What do you need for it to work?"

"I need to go someplace where the moon can reach me. You know, without trees and stuff in the way."

"So maybe somewhere high up? Like on a hill? But with no trees. We can figure it out, I'm sure of it. Do you need anything else?"

Anything besides a magic amulet loaded with powerful talismans? I don't know. For the millionth time, I wish for my book.

If I had it, I could check. "I can't remember anything else. I think all I have to do is stand in the moonlight with my amulet."

"That's it? Are you sure? I was expecting something more . . . more magical. I think you need words." She gasps. "Oh, like Pinocchio. His dad wished on a star, but you need the moon. Maybe you need to hold your amulet and say what you wish for in the light of the moon, and then it will come true!"

Actually saying it out loud? I'd feel silly for sure. Someone might hear me. I purse my lips. "I don't know."

"What's the worst that can happen? We try and you stay the same? Unless there really is a spell, and we do it wrong and both turn into frogs. That would stink."

I glance at the frog prince statue. "I'm pretty sure my amulet won't turn us into frogs. Besides, the prince was cured at the end of his story, not changed into something worse."

She snatches a cookie from the plate and stuffs it into her mouth. "That's good, 'cause I don't think I'd make a good frog. Eating flies all the time? Bleh. Maybe we could be the kind of frog that eats cookies instead."

"There's no such thing." I sit beside her on the couch and run my fingers over the doily on the couch arm.

"Says who? Look at this." She yanks a purple backpack from under the couch, unzips it, and pulls a black hardback book from inside. "You know how you showed me your monster book? I made one too!"

Made one? But how can anyone make up a book about monsters? My book is filled with facts and true stories. It says so right inside the front cover.

Autumn grins and opens the black book. Inside, bright drawings of fairies and dragons cover the page with little notes scrawled beside each picture. Reverently, she turns the page and a gingerbread house sits on a seashore, a witch in an apron and a goddess in a toga stand hand in hand beside a sidewalk made of gumdrops.

"Do you like it?" She turns another few pages and images of mermaids and flying sea creatures I've never heard of flip past. "At first, I tried to draw what I remembered from your book, but then I thought up more things that were so cool I just had to draw them too!"

"You made up new monsters?" There're already so many kinds—why would anyone want more?

"Uh huh, and fairies and stuff I'm still thinking up names for. Like these flying dinosaurs with spines shaped like chairs so we can ride whenever we want. I call them seat-a-soaruses. Okay that's silly, but I'm working on it." She points to a pair of flying girls with golden bands connecting their hearts. "What would you call magic people who are together in their hearts even when they can't see each other? I was thinking maybe fly-hearts or heart sisters."

"Heart sisters?" I can't help but notice that one of the girls has shoulder-length dark-brown hair like me, and the other has long blonde pigtails like Autumn.

"Well, what else would you call us?" She laughs. "I've got loads more to show you."

"But you can't just make up monsters." It'd be like making up animals in a zoo. Who does that?

"Silly, how do you think we got monster stories in the first place?"

The phone rings in the kitchen and Witch Barrett answers,

her mumbled *hello* barely audible. Something clatters to the floor and Autumn and I both stare at the empty doorway.

"He what? Is he okay?" Witch Barrett asks.

Autumn runs for the kitchen, her book of made-up monsters forgotten. "Nana?"

"But he's responding to the new medication now? Praise be," Witch Barrett sniffles, and I follow Autumn to the kitchen where she throws her small arms around Witch Barrett's hips and hugs her fast.

"What is it, Nana? Is he gonna be okay?"

With a wrinkled hand on Autumn's head, Witch Barrett nods as she listens. "We'll just have to pray harder then. Okay, we'll come see you both tomorrow. Be strong, Christa. Our brave Will is a fierce little soul. He'll not give up the fight."

She hangs up and strokes Autumn's tresses. "Your brother had a bit of a scare, but they've got him on a new medication."

"Is he better? Please say he's better. I've been praying awful hard."

"I know, lass. We all have. But, perhaps this new treatment will buy him the time he needs. Have faith, love. The good Lord has our William well in hand."

"William is getting worse?" I remember his gasp of delight when I did my magic trick with his stuffed puppy. It seems so unfair that little kids can be so sick.

"He's in a coma," Autumn whispers. "That's where they sleep and don't wake up for days and days." She fidgets with the hem of her shirt and pulls it down hard, her little fists clenched. "I just want him back. Why is that hard? They're doctors. They should fix him." Unshed tears brim along her lashes, and she draws a shuddering breath before burying her face in her nana's hip again, her arms squeezing tight.

"Is he ever gonna wake up? What'll happen?" Surely a witch could look in a crystal ball or something and peek at the future. If I had a crystal ball, I sure would.

Witch Barrett pats Autumn's back. "Ach, I wish I knew. When you were here last, my Christa thought she was losing her boy. Have you ever been so scared and angry that it's hard to breath? That's what she's feeling right now. She's terrified."

Images of running scared and alone on a dark night flicker inside my head. It's hard to imagine a grown-up being scared like that. "Is he gonna die?"

"Not today. But Heaven knows, every day with that boy is a gift."

I wonder what's worse, to be born sick or to be born a monster. And if a sick kid is a gift, would a monster kid be a curse? Mom doesn't seem to think so right now, but maybe she's just confused. Autumn's mom was really angry when we broke the tea set—maybe almost as angry as my mom was when she ripped my monster book in half. Maybe that's what love does.

It makes you crazy.

HUNTERS, STUDENTS, AND SURVIVAL

Cryptozoologists are sometimes called monster hunters, but I prefer to think of them as monster students. Admittedly, some do study monsters only for the thrill of the hunt—big-game hunters in pursuit of the greatest prize ever known to man. Others, myself included, simply want to learn the ways of these mysterious creatures. The last type of monster student cares not at all for trophies nor scientific learning, but rather learns out of necessity. These poor souls have had a glimpse into the world of magic and know there are no superheroes coming to save them. They know that when deadly foes gather against them, the only way to survive is to rise up and save themselves.

THIRTY

Full Moon Night

My first day back at school isn't as awful as I thought it would be. Mrs. Joy claps her hands when she sees me and gives me a hug. "Oh, Sophie! We're so glad to see you back. I've missed you!"

The strzyga girl doesn't look at me, which is fine, and neither does Taggart, but the way he avoids my gaze, it feels more like *he's* the one hiding from *me*. Everyone else keeps sneaking peeks, like they're not sure if I'm gonna explode again or not.

At lunch, Autumn and Heather help me think of good places where the moon might be really bright tonight. The bridges over the river would be the best spot ever, so high and pretty, and no trees in the way—except it's a freeway, so cars. Probably better to not try a place where I might die. Parks are cool, and the zoo is up high, but Mom wouldn't let me go there after dark. Parking lots have loads of empty space where the moon could reach me, but those tall lights shine so bright they

263

might get in the way of real moonlight. We try to talk quietly so no one can hear, but it's hard because the kids at the next table keep blabbing on about some show they saw last week.

Autumn watches the other kids for a minute, then grabs my arm. "The hospital!"

"What?" Heather and I stare as Autumn bounces in her seat with excitement.

"Nana said we'd go to the hospital tonight, and it's on a hill! It's up high, there're no trees in the way of the windows. It's perfect!"

Never have I ever put the words *perfect* and *hospital* in the same sentence. Too many vampires and who knows what else creeping around in there. I squirm. "I don't know."

"Think about it. There's even a tram that flies over the whole city and climbs up to the hospital. It's high, way above the trees and we could see for miles! Can you imagine what the moon would look like from up there? Now all we gotta do is get your mom and Nana to let you come with us. Nana totally will, I'm sure of it." She takes a bite of her sandwich and nods to herself.

"Did you see the way the monster exploded?" A kid at the next table stands, his arms spread wide for maximum size. "When the hunter stabbed it, ectoplasm splattered everywhere!"

"Gross!" squeals a girl.

A blond boy waves a burrito at the first kid. "It wasn't ectoplasm. That's from ghosts. This was some kinda tar. Monsters have black stuff instead of blood. Everyone knows that. Didn't you watch last season? Monster hunting would be so awesome."

"Tar stuff? How do you know for sure? Have you ever cut open a monster to find out?"

"No, doofus, next time I see a monster I'll let you know."

The boys jostle each other, teasing and bragging about what they'd do, given the chance to be hunters.

Have I ever seen my blood? Sure. I've skinned my knees lots of times. So that black blood thing can't be right, can it? I don't mean to stare, but I kind of zone out, thinking. On the wall behind their table, yellow and red stars decorate a bulletin board of posters chock-full of student council ads begging students to vote because *Billy's the Best! Vote Max for Maximum Awesomeness!* A bright pink *Hanna the Happy Choice* poster almost blocks the assembly notice which reads *Got talent? Share it with us!* I suppose monster hunting could be a talent—a gross one, but still.

"What are you looking at, freak?" The strzyga girl blocks my view of the poster, a food tray in her hands.

"Come on, Sophie." Heather tugs my arm. "They're just stupid."

A ripple of snickers breaks out, and I gather my lunch. The faster we can scram out of here, the better.

"Wasn't she the girl who wigged out last week?"

"Yeah, wonder what color *her* blood is?"

We run outside, but it doesn't take back what they said. If there are TV shows about monster hunters, and if they know I am one, then maybe someday one of them will come after me. Not just to bother or tease me, but to hunt me. Before, I worried that Mom wouldn't want me if she found out about my secret, but maybe there's more to worry about.

"Don't stress." Autumn slips her arm through mine. "After tonight, it won't matter what they say because you'll be cured, and whatever you are now won't matter. Those guys can all go soak their heads."

"In a toilet." Heather grins and pokes my arm. "Tag! You're it!"

Turns out, I'm faster than Heather, but slower than Autumn, and when little kids join in to play tag, they don't care what my face looks like, or what color my blood is. They only want to play.

After school, it's late afternoon before Witch Barrett convinces Mom to come with us to see William at the hospital—on the tram!

"Now you'll know what it's like to fly!" Autumn flaps her hands a couple times and pretends to lift off. "The tram is always my favorite way to visit!"

Later, tickets in hand, we stand on a cement platform which has two huge rectangle holes cut into it on one side with a fence all the way around it so no one can fall in the holes. Curved white poles stick out of the sides of the rectangle, pointing up toward the hill like giant chopsticks waiting for a sushi roll to slide between them. A wire stretches way overhead and goes up and up till it disappears over a white tower into the distance. Trams hang like silver bullets dangling from the wire, one of them rising up and away from us, and the other dropping closer. When it gets close enough to almost touch the white poles, the tram slows to a crawl, as if reluctant to be caught.

Finally, the doors slide open, people pour out, and we walk inside. Autumn and I skip to the front window and she spreads her arms wide. "You ready? Just wait! It's not scary, but we are going really high up."

The door closes and I hold tight to a rail with one hand, my other resting on the lump under my shirt where my amulet hides. I know it can't fall through the window, but it feels better to touch it, just to be sure.

Our tram wobbles a little but is mostly smooth as we rise away from the platform, up and up, past the white tower on the mountain and then higher, way up to another platform with giant white chopsticks at the base of a big building on the mountainside.

Autumn points to trees and houses far below. "Look! A kid riding a bike—and a dog! Nana, come see!"

Witch Barrett waves from the center of the tram where she visits with Mom. "I can see well enough from here."

From this high up, it could be an ant on a bike and we wouldn't know the difference. I lean closer to the window and peer out. "It's more like a really slow roller coaster than flying, I think."

She snorts. "Use your imagination!"

I flap my hands a couple times to make her happy, and she grins, flapping her fingers right back.

Whispering so only I can hear, she leans closer. "Now imagine it's nighttime. And the moon is rising right over those trees. It's a totally clear shot for the moonlight, don't you think?"

"Maybe." I peer up at the overhead lights. "But at night, the lights might get in the way."

"Not if you're flat against the window. The lights would be behind you."

It might be a good backup plan, but I'd feel better about a place where the moon was the only light. Somehow, I know I'll only get one shot at this. Either the magic works, and I'm cured tonight, or I'll stay this way forever.

The tram docks with no trouble and we walk through the

hospital grounds past statues of fish splashing out of the wall and a crazy goat balancing a rabbit on its head. An elevator ride later, Witch Barrett checks us past the nurses' station.

We walk into William's room with the droid bodyguards— except this time, he's got even more tubes in him and his eyes are closed. Lines drape from the beeping machines and cling like webbing to his arms and chest. A tiny tube disappears into his nose, and white tape straps a blob of plastic to his mouth with a bigger, clear tube flowing out over his chin, like a pale serpent burrowing inside his small body.

Autumn's dad turns from the window, his weary face lighting up at the sight of her. He rounds the foot of the bed and drops to one knee, arms open.

"Daddy!" whispers Autumn as she throws herself into his giant embrace, blonde strands of hair catching on his mustache.

Christa stretches from her chair and smiles weakly at Witch Barrett. "Mom? You're here. His color is better today, don't you think?"

Will doesn't look like he's got any color to me. His skin is smooth like a porcelain doll, and just as fragile.

Autumn switches from hugging her dad to Christa, and I lace my fingers through Mom's.

If there is a fight going on here between droids and humans, William is losing. Little pads with wires stick out of his chest, and both arms are wrapped in tape, IV tubes, bandages, and a blood pressure cuff that hums as it fills with air and squeezes his scrawny arm. With dark circles under his eyes and his bald head, he seems more cyborg than kid.

Reaching up on tippy-toes, Autumn kisses William on the cheek and curls her fingers around his. "Hi, William. I brought my friend Sophie to see you. Remember the magic tricks she showed you? She'll show you more when you wake up." She lets her forehead rest against his for a moment. "Get better fast, 'kay?"

Mom pulls a tin box from her purse and hands it to Autumn's dad. "Some treats to keep you going."

"Thank you." He pops the lid and smiles at the gooey-delicious chocolate chip cookies inside. "Did you make these?"

"Sophie did." Mom's gentle hand pushes me in front.

He taps the tin and holds a cookie up for us all to see. "Genius idea, Miss Sophie. Sometimes when the world looks the bleakest, things like this make all the difference."

"That's right." Christa stands, and I flinch. She was plenty clear with how she felt about me last time we spoke. Not only did I not listen or stay away from Autumn, I followed her all the way here where her other child slept. "Sophie, I'm sorry I yelled at you. I don't expect you to understand."

I'm not convinced she actually likes me, but at least she's not trying to kick me out of the room. I shrug. "It's okay. I get sad and scared too sometimes."

She laughs softly. "Maybe you do understand then."

While the grown-ups talk, Autumn and I find the bathroom, but there're no windows in there. The waiting room has large windows and bright colors. I think they work extra hard to make this a nice place since the little rooms are not the nicest for the people who have to live there.

Autumn presses her hand against the glass, both of us watching the sky fade to orange and purple as the sun starts its slide over the horizon. She sighs. "It's pretty here. Before Mom started letting me stay with Nana, I'd stay here when Mom and

Dad needed to talk with doctors. I like watching birds and trees. Sometimes, there are superheroes here too."

Fairies and monsters are one thing, but superheroes? I roll my eyes. "Oh, come on. You can't fool me."

"No, really, guys in superhero outfits hang from ropes outside while they wash the windows. They're pretty nice—they wave at us and stuff. William used to get so excited when they did his window. I knocked on the glass so they'd see us, and then they'd pretend to fly or climb like Spider-Man while they washed."

"Do they come every day?" Maybe getting to see superheroes flying in the windows would make it worth it to stay in the hospital once in a while. My doctor sure never said anything about it.

"Nah, only once in a while. But I'm pretty sure I saw the moon almost every night. It rises right over those trees after dark. Do you think you could make your wish right here?"

We both look up at the lights overhead. It's still too bright, but outside, parking lot lights already flicker on as evening gloom swallows the last of the day. Seems no matter where we go, there's always something in the way. "I don't know. Let's see where else we can find."

We check the stairwells and hallways like ninjas slipping from doorway to doorway. Stopped at a drinking fountain, we jump and almost run when a nurse pushes a cart loaded with glass tubes full of blood right past us.

She slows and smiles a toothy smile. "Are you lost? Do you need help?"

"No, thank you." Autumn wipes drops of water from her lips. "We just needed a drink before going back to my brother's room."

"See?" I whisper when she rolls away down the hall. "That's why vampires love places like this. That was probably their snack cart. Let's get out of here." The image of the nurse keeps changing in my head, flickering between vampire and human. A couple weeks ago, I could tell—I always *knew* which people were monsters and which weren't, but now . . . I can't decide. How do normal people live like this—never knowing who people really are?

We find a bunch of really well-lit areas and a broom closet, but no dark rooms with windows. Wandering back to the first waiting room, we stop by the windows again, but the sky has gone dark and city lights twinkle far below.

Autumn cups her hands beside her eyes and leans against the glass to block the light. "Maybe if you held up a blanket like a superhero cape! It could block the light from the rooms inside and only let the moon touch you."

"That might work, but we don't have a blanket." I check the waiting room, but other than a few small pillows, books, and toys there's nothing else helpful—except a dark corner of the room where the overhead light has burned out. "We could try there where it's not so bright, but it's still so light in here. Do you think we could borrow a blanket from your brother's room?"

"Why not? Let's go ask. This is it, Sophie. I can feel it. This *will* work." Autumn squeezes my hand. "Are you ready to be cured?"

Gosh, ready for what I've wished for my whole life? "You better believe it!"

QUALITIES OF HEROES

To defeat a monster, a hero must have strength, determination, and courage. Imagine a knight facing a dragon, yet lacking the strength to draw a sword, or a fellowship on a quest to save the world but then turns back and gives up the moment things get hard. Both would be foolish.

The quality heroes need most is courage. That is not to say that heroes are never afraid, in fact a total lack of fear points more toward insanity than bravery. Courage doesn't apply when things are easy. No one ever courageously took a nap in a hammock. Courage surfaces when a hero experiences real fear and hardship yet has the moral fortitude to complete the quest. With courage, a hero may face his fear and fight anyway. That, dear reader, is the only way to win.

THIRTY-ONE

Miracle, Interrupted

The nurses' station seems more busy than normal, with several doctors deep in conversation, a few nurses gather around them, listening. They don't notice us walk past and into William's room, but we freeze when we hear the parents talking on the other side of the cloth curtain.

"So, Kelsi brought her home?" Christa asks.

"Yes," Mom breathes. "I can't tell you how frightened I was, but he called as soon as he found her. She was asleep in his arms when he carried her in."

"It's those brawny arms of his," Witch Barrett adds. "Any lass with sense would do well to swoon with a man like that around. Do take note, dear Marlene. Sophie had the right of it."

Autumn crosses her eyes at me and pretends to faint, her mouth shut tight to keep the giggles in.

I stick my tongue out at her and ease to the side of the curtain to peek around it.

"Mrs. Barrett, you're such a tease. Seriously, though, he's been such a good thing for both me and Sophie."

"Did you see him today?" Autumn's dad asks.

"No, he's taking care of a special project for me, but we'll see him tomorrow."

Apparently tired of waiting, Autumn pushes me into the room and asks, "Can we have snacks? Is the cafeteria open?"

"There you are! Where did you two get off to?" Christa stands beside William's bed, her hand stroking his bald head.

Witch Barrett sits in the chair beside my mom, and Autumn's dad leans against the windowsill, the outside world dark behind him.

"We were looking around." Autumn squeezes my hand and we share a smile. "Can we talk to William while you guys get snacks? I bet you haven't had a break in forever."

Christa worries at William's blanket, pulling it up a little and tucking it around his ribs even though he hasn't moved since the last time she did it. "I should probably stay . . ."

"The girls are right, honey." Autumn's dad stretches and takes Christa by the hand. "The girls will be with him, and the nurses are right outside the door. He won't be alone."

"Should I stay?" Mom hesitates, but I shake my head. I'm not sure what Autumn has in mind, but the wheels are turning inside her head so fast, I can almost hear it. Best play along.

"You should go too, Mom. We'll be fine. Promise."

"Here." Christa passes Autumn her cell phone. "If anything happens, call your dad right away."

Reluctantly, the grown-ups lead Christa out and gently close the door.

Autumn grins like a sphinx with an especially tricky question up her sleeve.

After a quick glance around the room, I fold my arms. "I don't see any extra blankets in here. So, what are you smiling about?"

"Check this out." She reaches up above William's headboard and flips a switch.

The whole room goes dark except for a moonbeam which falls across the floor, silhouetting the droid machines beside the bed. Without the inside lights on, the window becomes a portal for the night sky to flow inside this very room.

"Wow! We don't even need a blanket in here. It's perfect!" I walk to the window and reach out for the night. The stars are so bright, it's almost a surprise when my fingers meet glass instead of sky. The moon is still rising, not quite clear of the trees.

"Say the words," she urges from the gloom near the head of the bed. "This is your chance."

I want to, but the moon isn't high enough yet, and a spell like this will take all the magic we can get. "Let's wait, just another few minutes. The moon needs to be higher."

"Okay, but we can't wait too long, or they'll be back." She starts humming a lullaby to her brother.

Other than her quiet song, the rest of the world seems to hold its breath, waiting for the magic moment when I can say the words for the spell.

The moon inches up, clearing the trees bit by bit, and I start to tremble. It's excitement and hope, I tell myself, but I know it's more than that.

It's fear.

I have been *this* my whole life. What will I be like once I'm cured? Will my friends recognize me without my monster mark? Will Mom know who I am? I can't help but wonder . . .

Will it hurt?

I've never questioned my desire to be normal, to be human. Having a monster mark means I'm alone. It means I can't go out and do things other kids do. I bite my lip. Well, I *can* do things, but we don't because it's harder to hide in a store or swimming pool. People stare.

I've always hated the staring. Tiny kids aren't afraid to point and ask what the thing on my face is, but that's not as hard as older kids who make fun of me. Not everyone does. Sometimes people try so hard *not* to stare, they pretend I'm invisible and don't see me at all. People don't know how to act around me. It would be so much simpler for everybody if my mark was gone.

Am I doing this for them? Or is it for me?

Things would be easier for Mom if I wasn't different. She wouldn't have to worry or change things for me if I was normal. *She would love me more if*—but even as I think the words, I know it's a lie. She loves me now, and she'll always love me no matter what I am. Monster, girl, normal, different, she wants *me*. Just me. Sophie.

Autumn stops humming mid-verse. "Is the moon high enough yet?"

"Almost." The great pale sphere seems to hesitate, resting on the tips of the trees, lingering there, gathering courage for her flight across the heavens.

No matter how many times the sun pushes the moon right out of the sky, burning her soft night away with the day, the moon still rises. She comes again, and again. She changes all the time, but she's still the moon. Sometimes her courage wanes and she's just a slip of herself, but then she gets brave again and shines for the whole world to see.

I push my nerves aside and take a breath. I don't need to be afraid of change. I can be brave too.

The peak of one last tree clings to the edge of the moon as if pleading with her to stay.

Almost time.

I pull my amulet out from under my shirt and cup it in both hands. The words I've longed to say teeter on the tip of my tongue, ready to spill out and make me whole.

"I wish—"

The door to the room opens, and Autumn's dad pushes the cloth curtain aside. "Why are the lights out?"

I clasp both hands over my necklace to hide it and blink as he flips on a night-light.

"It's nighttime, Dad. William is sleeping." Autumn hums another few notes as if to prove that all we were doing is helping him sleep, then passes him Christa's cell phone. "Did you eat already? Where's our snacks?"

"Mom's bringing them up. The doctor called and said he needs to meet with us."

Autumn and I glance at each other, then at the window. Grown-up meetings can take ages. Have I lost my chance forever?

A few minutes later, Mom and the others file in along with a doctor in a long white coat, his stethoscope draped around his neck and tablet in hand. He glances around the room. "Is it okay to discuss your son's condition in front of everyone? Or would you prefer they step out?"

Mom stands and sidesteps toward the door. "I'll just find the ladies' room."

I start to stand to follow, but Autumn laces her fingers through mine and squeezes with the strength of a griffin. Her meaning is clear: Don't go.

Christa's voice is brittle, her body rigid beside her husband. "Please continue."

"Excellent. We've been discussing Will's case. As you know, we've had him on an aggressive bone marrow stimulant program for months with cyclosporine and prednisone."

Witch Barrett leans close to me and mutters, "They've pumped over a hundred different medications through that boy."

"Exactly." The doctor adjusts his glasses and peers over the screen on his tablet. "Everything we can do to restore him, we've done."

"Wait. Are you giving up?" Autumn demands.

"Giving up? No. Of course not. He's stabilizing. We'll bring him out of the coma tomorrow and start preparations for the next phase. We found a match—a bone marrow donor who matches all five points."

A strangled cry bursts from Christa, and she claps her hand over her mouth, burying her face in her husband's shirt.

Stroking his wife's back, Autumn's dad blinks back tears. "A match. You've found a donor? When will this happen?"

"Within the next two weeks. The donor is willing to come in as soon as we're ready. We need to suppress his immune system for the next ten days, so visitors will be extremely limited from here on out. We'll monitor his counts closely and watch for signs of rejection. We can go over more of that later, but if all goes well, he'll soon be on his way to recovery."

"Praise be," whispers Witch Barrett.

"The next few days will be crucial. We'll get Will's levels where we need them to be, and we'll make sure everything is in place for the procedure." He ducks his head a little to see Christa's face better. "This is a good thing. This is what we've been hoping for. It's an excellent match."

Wiping her eyes, Christa smiles and gives a watery laugh. "I know. I've been praying so hard. What do we need to do?"

Seeing her vulnerable like this, it's hard to remember her as the same person who yelled at me a few days ago. I slide a glance at Autumn who watches the conversation with wide eyes.

"I've got some forms for you to sign . . ." He turns his tablet aside and pats his coat with his free hand. "I seem to have left the forms in my office. Do you care to come with me? Or I could bring them right back."

"We'll come." Autumn's dad pulls Christa after the doctor as he exits the room. Witch Barrett and Mom meet up just outside the doorway, and we watch Autumn's parents until they disappear around a corner.

"It's a miracle." Mom hugs Witch Barrett for a long time.

I stand inside the door of the room, unsure of what to do. Clear of the trees, the moon hangs in the center of the window, beckoning to me. Another few minutes and my chance at a cure will be gone.

Autumn follows my gaze and leans close before pushing me gently back into the room to shut the door. "Go for it. I'll stall them."

"Ma'am, I'm sorry, but visiting hours are over." Someone—probably a nurse—explains from outside the door.

Mom laughs softly. "Sorry, we got carried away there. Where's Sophie?"

"I know!" Autumn volunteers. "She ran to the bathroom while you and Nana were hugging. I'll show you."

If anyone can lead Witch Barrett and Mom on a goose chase, it's Autumn.

With a deep breath for courage, I hold my amulet carefully, flip off the light switch, and walk into the moonlight.

THE LOST PRINCE

And when the prince saw it was the witch he had treated with such cold indifference, he wept. "Please, have mercy. I beg you. Let me live."

"What would you do with mercy?" the witch asked.

"I would build a kingdom revered by all for its beauty and strength. And all who lived therein would bless your name for your power, great lady."

"What good is a kingdom if the people are lost? What good is strength without compassion? How useless wisdom without kindness?" The witch spread her gnarled fingers and a whirlwind grew within.

The powerful curse swept over the prince who cried as his body twisted and shrank. "Mercy! Pity! My kingdom, I am lost!"

"When someone offers you, the lowliest of creatures, pity, mercy, kindness, and love, you will know wisdom, justice, and strength. The lost will be found. The hated, loved. The monstrous, made human."

With a swirl of wind, the witch was gone, and on the log where she had stood sat a frog.

THIRTY-TWO

The Wish

Alone in William's hospital room, the flashing lights on the droids seem wary, little beacons to ward off any danger for their charge. A soft and steady blip on a screen records his heartbeat, another his oxygen, and another his IV. I don't know if he can hear me, but even if he can, I don't mind. Somehow, I know he wouldn't mind me saying my deepest wish here.

I grab the chain from my amulet and pull it off, weighing the magic in my hand. I try to remember all the ways I've ever heard of cursed people transforming into humans again. The frog was kissed. The beast, loved. The beauty, awakened. Pinocchio's wish granted. But the littlest mermaid was forgotten and transformed into sea foam, forever lost to the man she loved.

Magic doesn't always work like we want it to.

The moon seems to hover right outside the window. So

close, I could talk to her like a friend and she would understand. I'm sure she knows why I'm here and is waiting for me to start the spell. All I need is the right words.

Ms. Cloe says humans have courage, wisdom, justice, mercy, and love.

Courage means doing the right thing even if it's hard. Am I courageous? My mom thinks so. Autumn thinks so. I think so too. It was way easier when I hid all the time and let my mom face all the hard things, but now I have to face them myself. So, yes, I have courage.

It took wisdom to know how to make my amulet, so maybe I'm a little bit wise.

Ms. Cloe says justice and mercy are linked, and I'm trying to be fair and kind to everyone—even when they were mean to me.

I hold my strange and wonderful amulet up to the window and twirl it in the moonlight before checking the next thing on my list. Time seems to press against me with each passing second. Every tick of the clock a reminder: the moon waits for no one.

Ms. Cloe says humans have love. This is one that I'm sure I've got right. I've loved my mom with all my heart for my entire life. I would do anything for her, *be* anything to make her happy. And Autumn. Who knew I could find my very own heart sister? And Mrs. Joy, and—I sigh as I admit it to myself—a little part of me even loves Koschei.

That was the list. Right? I have the items of power, and I have all the qualities. So, I must be ready to be human—aren't I?

I press one hand against the cold glass and hold the amulet up so it hangs in the center of the moon. My heart races as I try to brace for whatever change may come. Will my mark just disappear? Or will it rip flesh off my face like when a werewolf transforms? A shudder wiggles up my spine. I hope it won't be like that.

"Courage," I whisper. Wisdom, justice, mercy, and love. I look the moon straight in her beautiful, pale face, and hope she sees those things in me, but something niggles in the back of my mind.

Koschei says it's not what we look like, but what we do—our own choices—that makes us a monster or not. Am I making the right choice? Will this choice make me more human? I think so. I hope so. If it all comes down to choices, I can choose to be human, make my choice so powerful that it sticks and makes the magic real.

Steady beeping pulses from the droid behind me, each blip a witness to William's determined heart.

I borrow some of his strength and try to order the words inside my head, so I don't mess up.

I wish my monster mark would disappear. No. It's more than that. I don't want to fix only the outside, I want to be better all the way through.

I wish the witch had never cursed me. That's not right either. We wouldn't have moved here if I had always been normal, so that means I'd never have met Autumn, or Witch Barrett, or Koschei. I don't want to change my friends. I want to be here, where we are.

I wish to be cured, to be human—yes, but more than that—I wish to never be a monster again.

Beep, beep. Beep, beep. William's heart beats with mine, and I'm glad I'm not alone.

I turn to smile at his small body bathed in the soft glow of the moonbeam, and everything stills.

It's not what you look like that makes you human, it's what you do.

I have a cure.

I've got it right here in my hand, and I'm going to use it . . . on *me*? Me, who can walk, and talk, and play with my friends. Me, who is alive without machines or medicines or donors. Me, who can feel my mom's arms around me and hug her right back. Me, who's going to grow up. Me, who can go home.

The hand holding my amulet trembles, and I blink really hard. This has been my dream for so long. I will *never* get this chance again. Can I really give it up?

He'll probably be okay. He's got a donor now, so he'll make it. Probably. Maybe.

But he's so small and pale. Fragile.

If I use this cure and walk out of this room healed with perfect skin, my monster soul erased and my humanity made whole—can I live with knowing I could have saved him?

No.

My heart rips in two. I can't use the cure on me, not when he needs it so desperately.

It wouldn't be human.

Cupped in my hands, I hold my beautiful amulet in the moonlight, gazing at it one last time. A teardrop splashes on the crystal and another soaks into the feather. I touch each in turn, the paw print, the crystal, the feather, the shell. I *found* them—fought for each one of them. But maybe they were never meant for me.

I slip the amulet inside Will's hand and help his fingers close around it. Just to be sure, I tie the string to his wrist so it can't fall off. Caught in his tiny fist, the crystal seems to glow, and I know it's time to make my wish.

My hand on his chest, I wipe the tears from my eyes. With all the magic my necklace can give and all the power inside me—all of me, monster or not—I make my choice and lift my face to the moon.

"Heal him. Make him better so he can come home and play and grow up. This is my wish. My gift to give."

A shiver courses through me, from the top of my head down through the tips of my toes. With the power of my choice, it makes it all real. I *feel* the magic leave me and, with my love, pour into William. Moonlight fills my vision and for a moment, light is all I see. It washes through my mind, cleansing away the fear and worry.

There's a shift inside me. Something cracks, breaks, and re-aligns inside my soul. I gasp at the warmth in my heart and hold onto Will's bed for support. Did the moon heal me anyway— even though I wanted the cure for William? The moon wouldn't play such a cruel trick, would she? No. Her peaceful radiance soothes my fears and I know—*I know*—everything will be okay.

With the moon sliding up toward the top of the window, I ease around the bed and walk to the door. My fingers on the handle, I look back. Glowing in the moonlight as if resting on a cloud instead of a bed, William sleeps, his monitors beeping steadily with each beat of his strong heart.

"Sleep well, William," I whisper. "I hope you get better real soon."

Emerging from the room, I close the door quietly be-hind me and walk to the waiting room. Moments later, Mom,

Autumn, and Mrs. Barrett hurry around the corner. "Sophie! We lost you. Where have you been?" Mom reaches for me and hurries to my side. "Are you okay? Have you been crying?"

"I'm fine, Mom. I'm fine." I smile. "Sorry I worried you. I wanted to say goodbye to William."

"It *is* hard to leave the wee one there alone," Mrs. Barrett agrees. "I hardly can pull myself away sometimes."

Autumn slips her arm through mine as we walk toward the elevator, and she pulls me close to whisper. "Did it work? Did you say the words?"

"Yeah, I think it did."

"But you still have the mark." She watches me carefully, as if she expects me to be surprised that it didn't disappear.

I touch my face, feel the warmth of my hemangioma, and squeeze her hand. "It's okay. I didn't wish to be cured."

"What!" She bites her lip when Mom and Mrs. Barrett glance at her, then whispers. "But you had the cure right there. Why didn't you do it?"

"Because William needed it more."

Autumn's lip trembles, then she hugs me so tight I can barely breathe. My throat aches, but I hug her back and whisper into her hair. "I had to give it to him. I just knew—if I used the cure on myself, I *would* be a monster."

A choked cry hiccups from her lips, and her small body shudders. "Thank you!"

And I know more than ever that I did the right thing. The human thing.

And that's when I know.

The wish worked on both of us.

THE BIG BOOK OF MONSTERS
WITH EYES WIDE OPEN

Now you know what is hidden, the real things that go bump in the night. As promised, I shared everything I know of this strange and terrible world of monsters, holding nothing back. But with knowledge comes responsibility. The next time you see an innocent about to step off the path in the forest, pull them back. Do not be overwhelmed by the terror and misery of fools who ignore your warnings, they aren't worth your tears. Watch for glamour's shimmer from the corner of your eye, and trust no one with sharp, hungry smiles.

Protect those you can, and make peace with those you can't. But the world need not seem bleak, for light shines through darkness and hope tempers despair. May your travels bring more brownies than basilisks, more dryads than demons. Our world is a wonderful, magical place, and now that you know the hidden secrets, there is so much more for you to see.

THIRTY-THREE

The Best Kind of Magic

With the open pages of my magician's apprentice book pressed against my chest, I stand at my bedroom window, watching Mom and Kelsi mark the lines of her soon-to-be herb garden in our backyard. Mom says he's building it because he likes to keep busy, which makes sense since he's already fixed or replaced everything in the house that could possibly need fixing.

The sight of the two of them holding hands gives me warm fuzzies, and I close my magic book and slip it onto the shelf next to *The Big Book of Monsters*. Out of habit, I run my finger down the spine over the familiar bump-bump of the embossed parts. It's been two months since it was torn in half, and almost that long since Kelsi showed up the day after the full moon with the newly repaired book in his hands. Mom had asked him to fix it as a special project, and I was grateful, but nice as it was to have my old book back, it ended up on the shelf before the afternoon was over. I suppose I didn't really need it anymore.

"So?" Autumn asks from her perch on my bed where she sketches her latest magical creature creation. "Are you ready? Any more last-minute practicing?"

"No," I snatch my top hat from the shelf and sink onto the bed beside her. "I think I've got it."

The doorbell rings, and we race each other to the door. Autumn beats me and yanks the door wide for the pizza delivery guy.

"Hi, I've got a Hawaiian, a supreme, and a pepperoni." He opens a flap and slides the boxes free, releasing mouthwatering whiffs of fresh-baked pizza. Whenever we get pizza, Mom always orders way too much because leftovers are Kelsi's favorite.

"Perfect! I'll get your mom." Autumn dashes away, leaving the door open.

"Cool hat," the guy says, holding the boxes out for me to take.

"Thanks." But when I lift the warm boxes, my gaze catches on the dark purple wine stain that covers most of his right hand, disappears up his sleeve, and peeks out the top of his shirt collar where it reaches the base of his ear before fading into normal skin tone.

He catches me looking and winks. "I see you've got one too. Nice birthmark."

"Thanks. Yours is pretty cool too."

My hemangioma has deflated a lot in the last couple months—so much that Dr. Escabar thinks it'll be mostly an empty sack by next summer. Probably that's when I'll trade the soft blobby tissue for a scar. Surgery won't get all of it, just the biggest parts, but that's okay because I don't mind it so much anymore.

"Coming! I'm coming." Mom bustles in and rummages through her purse before passing him some money. "Here you go. Thank you."

"No problem. Have a good night." He waves as he steps off the porch step, and I carry dinner to the table as Mom closes the door.

"Is Mrs. Barrett coming?" Kelsi pulls out a chair for me and then for Mom as we settle around the table set for four.

"No, she wanted to visit with William before the show." Mom serves a slice for Autumn and me, long strings of cheese stretching until we break them off with our fingers. "She'll meet us there."

"Can we go see him yet?" I ask.

"Not yet, but soon. Another month or so, and we will." Mom smiles. "His immune system is still recovering after the transplant, but he's getting better. Sometimes miracles take a little time."

I smile, remembering my own miracle. "Some miracles are worth waiting for. It's part of the magic."

"Speaking of that, Mrs. Barrett says he's excited to see you again. Did you do a trick for him? Something about a Lego?"

"Yeah." I wipe a string of cheese off my chin. "He thought it was magic."

"I saw it." Autumn raises a finger. "She made the Lego disappear and reappear by his stuffed dog. He loved it."

"Doesn't surprise me, honey. You are the best kind of magic."

Our pizza is the perfect melt of cheesy deliciousness, and Autumn and I inhale our pieces almost as fast as Kelsi.

Something clatters outside the window and we look up to see Bob hanging onto the feeder, his whiskers buried in bird-seed as he munches away, his arms hugging the perch for all he's worth. When a bird flies by and scolds him, he loses his grip and falls. Twenty seconds later, he's in position to leap onto the feeder again.

"His disfigurement doesn't seem to slow him down much." Kelsi nods at the missing ear.

"Nah. Bob's a busy guy. Nothing stops him from doing what he wants."

Halfway through her pizza slice, Mom passes me a napkin. "Anything else you need before you get ready?"

"Hmm." I try to think: I've got my hat, my wand, scarves, rings, and cards. Mrs. Barrett sewed a sequined red vest to go with my black pants. I don't have a cape or anything yet, but that can wait till next year's school talent show. "I think I've got everything I need."

"Do you? I think you're still missing something." Mom grins conspiratorially at Kelsi, who hands me a present.

"Hey, it's not my birthday." I try to give him a dirty look but fail when my smile gets in the way.

"Open it!" Autumn bounces.

I rip it open and catch my breath. Inside is a real magician's hat—not a pop-up kid's toy like mine, but a satin-lined classic black top hat with a shiny red bow nestled inside. I breathe, "Oh, wow."

"And the bow is for your hair, so it doesn't get messed up when you do your magic tricks!"

Autumn pulls the bow out and wiggles it so the light catches the sequins and tosses glittery sparkles across the room. "Let's do your hair."

"Okay."

After Mom works it over, pulling my hair up and away from my face in a nice French braid, Autumn secures the end with the bow, which matches my vest perfectly.

"Now put the hat on." Autumn presses the velvet black hat into my hands.

I set it on my head at a slight angle and glance in the hall mirror. Awesomeness with just a little bit of attitude.

Perfect.

"I'll go start the car." Kelsi grabs his jacket and heads for the garage while I grab my bag of supplies.

"Are we ready?" Mom touches my cheek. "Is this where I say break a leg? Or is there something else magicians are supposed to say?"

"Good luck works just fine," I laugh as Autumn slides up beside me, a big grin on her face and her hands hidden behind her—though the corners of whatever she's holding poke out.

"I made you something." She whips a glittery poster out from behind her back and holds it up for me to read.

Sophie the Magnificent

The poster shines with glitter lettering and curled ribbons glued around the edges. She wiggles it back and forth. "It was my mom's idea. We've got a stand and everything already in the car. Now you'll have a hat *and* a sign. It's like you're the most official magician ever! Do you like it?"

"I love it." And I do. I'm not sure about the magnificent part, but it has a nice ring to it.

She slips her arm through mine and squeezes in that special way BFFs do. "You're gonna do great. I just know it."

All at once, I have to blink quick to keep tears back because I'm so thankful for my friends and my family. They've been there for everything, and when I'm up on that stage, their faces will be the ones I'll look for. They love me, and I love them. No matter what happens in the show tonight, I'm happy right now, and that's pretty darn awesome.

We start to walk to the car, but I'm not quite ready to let go of this moment. "Hey, Mom? Can you take a picture?"

"Sure, angel." She pulls her cell phone out and fiddles with the screen while Autumn and I wrap an arm around each other's waists and lean our heads together.

"Okay, you ready?"

We grin at each other. "Ready."

She holds up the phone. "Smile, Sophie!"

And I do.

Acknowledgments

Heartfelt thanks to everyone who helped bring this story to life:

To my brilliant agent, Stacey Glick, for believing in Sophie's story.

To Lisa Mangum for being the best, kindest, most sneaky, awesome editor and friend ever, and to the staff at Shadow Mountain who fell in love with my story and made it real—Chris Schoebinger, Heidi Taylor Gordon, Richard Erickson, and Malina Grigg.

To my husband, Mike, and our beautiful children, Deanna, Thomas, Matthew, Mary, and especially little William, who waited up each night for a new chapter to be read before bedtime.

To my wonderful parents, Brian and Sue Foster, who read everything I ever wrote, and cheered for every draft.

To John Roscher for being the best host ever, to Nicki Stanton for lighting a fire under us all, and to Marcy Curr for letting me hole up in her basement and hide from farming, and for feeding me so I could finish this book.

To J. Scott Savage (aka Uncle Jeff), who took me under his wing, patiently answered all my newbie questions, and guided me as the best mentor ever. I will always be grateful.

To my beta readers, whose suggestions made this book so much better (I'm looking at you, Courtney), and to the many writer friends who have inspired and taught me so much over the last decade.

To my teachers who made me believe I could write, and praised me even when my epic novel was a single page long—including pictures.

And to the hydra lady, who made fun of my hemangioma when I was little. It broke my mom's heart, but it left me the seeds that grew into this story.

Author's Note

Sophie's story is dear to my heart because I know how it feels to be bullied because I looked different from everyone else. When I was a child, I had a hemangioma on my forehead that stuck out so far my bangs couldn't cover it, no matter how hard my mother tried. Because the tumor was made up of blood vessels, I could feel my heart beating inside it when I was playing hard or really upset.

The incident at the grocery store where the hydra lady says, "Hey, look, kids! That girl doesn't need a Halloween costume. She's already got one!" is an exact quote of what a woman once said to my mother and me. Another woman told a classroom full of kids that I had the mark of the devil. Kids asked if it was a goose bump, or hamburger, or if my brains had leaked out. My dad had to chase away some bullies who had followed me home, called me names, and pushed me into the street. Sometimes, after a bad day of bullying, I wished I could just rip the mark off my face and be like everyone else—but it was a part of me, and wishing didn't change that.

My parents decided to take an active role in educating the people around me so they would know what a hemangioma was and understand that it wasn't icky, or gross, or contagious. Whenever we moved to a new place, my dad would go with me to the elementary school and talk to the kids about my mark and let them ask questions. After those talks, kids befriended me and noticed when bullies came around. Like Autumn, my school friends would speak up when they saw someone being mean to me, and sometimes they would stand between me and the bullies until they left me alone.

I didn't let the bullies stop me from doing what I wanted to do. I climbed trees, went swimming, wrote poetry, brought my tarantula and snakes to show-and-tell, and played in the tide pools.

This is my message to anyone who experiences bullying: Don't let the bullies define you! I've been there, I know it hurts to be teased, but don't let it stop you from doing what you want. Find something you enjoy—a hobby, talent, or challenge—and practice that skill. Know that someone out there, maybe even someone in your same school, needs a friend as much as you do. Be that friend. Stand up for each other. And know that you are not alone.

You can always find me at WendySwore.com, and I would love to hear your stories and what you thought of the book.